Jeffrey
Thomas
THE RETURN OF ENOCH COFFIN

Jeffrey Thomas

THE RETURN OF ENOCH COFFIN

WEIRD HOUSE

ISBN: 978-1-937128-61-6

"The Lunar Gate" is original to this collection
© 2025 by Jeffrey Thomas
All other stories previously published as detailed on page 243

Cover Artwork © 2025 by Frank Walls

Interior design by César Puch

Editor, Curtis M. Lawson

Editor and Publisher, Joe Morey

Weird House Press
Central Point, OR 97502
www.weirdhousepress.com

Table of Contents

Introduction

There is a terrible omission from this book.

That is, a group of six stories written by the late W. H. Pugmire (May 3, 1951-March 26, 2019). The stories in question were titled *Ye Unkempt Thing*, *Beneath Arkham*, *They Smell of Thunder*, *Mystic Articulation*, *Ecstasy in Aberration*, and *Unto the Child of Woman*. These were Wilum Hopfrog Pugmire's contributions to our joint short story collection called *Encounters With Enoch Coffin*, published in 2013 by Dark Regions Press. Let me tell you how that collaboration came to be, and how I approached my own contributions to it.

The most important thing to know straight off is that the character of Enoch Coffin began as Wilum's creation, though Enoch had yet to be fleshed out, shall we say, like the faceless creature in my story herein, *Matter of Truth and Death*.

Wilum had the idea that he wanted to write a series of stories about a New England artist, loosely inspired by Lovecraft's Richard Upton Pickman. For this project, Wilum—who was not himself an artist—hoped to collaborate with a writer who *was* also an artist, to bring that perspective to the character. To that end, he first approached our mutual friend Stanley C. Sargent (who sadly preceded Wilum's death by one year). For whatever reason, Stan declined the project, and so Wilum next approached me, knowing that I was also an illustrator ... who had, in fact, illustrated a number of Wilum's stories for various small press publications. It was actually through illustrating one of his stories that we first became acquainted, in the early 90s. (I went on to publish Wilum's first American collection *Tales of Sesqua Valley*, a chapbook consisting of ten stories, through my imprint Necropolitan Press in 1997.) Though I'm not really one to collaborate—even with my brother Scott Thomas, a brilliant author of weird fiction in his own right—as a great admirer of Wilum's work I jumped at the chance, daunting as the prospect initially was of finding a method with which to approach this collaboration.

The most daunting part was that, though Wilum humbly dismissed himself as a mere "Lovecraft fanboy," he was in truth a singularly original and distinctive author, with a lush poetic voice. From the start I decided not to emulate his voice so much as complement it; a tricky balance, but I was by then familiar enough with his style that I felt I was able to pull it off. However, that still didn't sort out how we were going to split our writerly duties in the course of things. He suggested I begin a story and then turn it over to him, and so I started writing *Matter of Truth and Death*. Soon, though—and this was really the only way to do it—he suggested we both write our own separate stories about the good Mr. Coffin, and we'd read each other's work along the way ... playing off the events and such of each other's tales. For instance, Wilum's answer to my story about Enoch's father, *Fearless Symmetry*, was answered by his story about Enoch's mother, *Unto the Child of Woman*. This back-and-forth approach turned out to work beautifully, and as I have said in a number of interviews it was probably the most fun I have ever experienced writing a single book.

Wilum's Enoch stories tended to take place in Lovecraft's fictitious locations, such as Arkham, Dunwich, and Innsmouth ... and in his own invented, unearthly setting of the Sesqua Valley in the Pacific Northwest. Alternately, my own approach then was to set my stories in real-life New England locations: Boston, Salem, and so on. To further my personal formula, I decided that each of my own stories would take its spark of inspiration from one of Lovecraft's inventions: say, the "colour" from *The Colour Out of Space*, or (of course) the ghouls from *Pickman's Model*.

Also, each of my stories would revolve around a different approach to creating artwork: sculpture, oil painting, pen and ink, etc. (Our multi-talented Mr. Coffin is not only versatile in the visual arts, as you will find, but in the mystical arts as well.)

Early on I asked Wilum to give me some prompts for what Enoch was like. Whereabouts should he live? (Again taking a cue from Pickman, Wilum said Boston's North End, so I ended up finding an appropriately inspiring house on Charter Street, opposite the Copp's Hill Burying Ground, via Google Earth's street view.) What did he wear, what did he look like? (A youngish Tom Berenger, was how Wilum envisioned him.) I'm straight but Wilum was gay, so I asked him if Enoch should be gay as well. Wilum suggested Enoch didn't care about such limitations, only sensuality in any form, so we ran with that.

The book was enthusiastically received in our little circle of weird fiction aficionados, and so inevitably Wilum and I discussed whether to attempt a follow-up. It was Wilum, I believe, who suggested we should next do a novel about Enoch … but that brought us back to the quandary of how to go about the process. As before, Wilum suggested I start things out and we'd roll from there, taking turns at writing chapters for an alternating effect, much as we had done with the collection. However, after I had only managed to squeeze out about a chapter and a half, and with very little sense of a plot by which to continue, Wilum and I both conceded that we just weren't feeling it. Enoch, it seemed, had been lightning in a bottle. In 2017, in an email to Wilum I wrote: *"The bad news is, I really doubt I can do this Enoch Coffin novel. I had a nice start to it written, and I even read our book again in its entirety for inspiration (taking tons of notes along the way), but my drive kind of fizzled out. It isn't that I don't LOVE our character, and collaborating with you, but I'm just not productive at all these days."* This was true, and it wasn't until a few years later that I found my way back to writing novel-length fiction after a long time away. Similarly, Wilum's response was: *"Actually, this isn't bad news in a way—because I was DREADING having to try and work on a novel. I don't think I have it in me. Writing is not coming easily—mostly because I just can't get interested in working on anything."* Ah, the stubborn muse … such a bitch! Of course, Wilum was also dealing with health issues to which he would succumb only two years later, at the age I am at the time of this writing.

We did, however, manage to meet in person for the first and only time (we lived on opposite sides of the country, Wilum in Seattle whereas I'm the actual New Englander) in 2013 at NecronomiCon in Lovecraft's own Providence, Rhode Island. Before that, our interaction had been through a rich correspondence of written letters, audio cassette recordings, and ultimately email for over two decades. Our last conversation, while Wilum was in hospice care, was over the phone … and his last words to me were "I love you." I am forever grateful that at the last I was able to tell my friend how much he had meant to me.

But I guess I'm getting off topic. Let me circle back to what this book—without Wilum's contributions—actually consists of.

Small presses are notoriously hard to sustain, and as I write this Dark Regions Press (which had a good run) is sadly no more, the result being that *Encounters With Enoch Coffin* has gone out of print. Maybe you've read that book already, and have acquired this book for its new material. If not, and you're interested in reading Wilum's own half-dozen stories about Enoch Coffin, I hope you can still find a remaining new or used copy somewhere online. Several other of Wilum's collections are also now out of print, sorry to say, but I urge you to check out his titles at, for instance, Hippocampus Press.

I don't own the rights to Wilum's work, but I was unwilling to at least let my own Enoch Coffin stories go out of print. Therefore, I proposed to Weird House Press that I collect my half-dozen tales, and two other pieces (not in the original collection) in which Enoch appears as a side character. The first of these two, *The Brothel in the North End*, was a contribution to the publication *Forbidden Futures*, wherein writers are invited to pen a story based on their choice of artwork by the talented Mike Dubisch.

I chose an image of ghouls, for which I decided to resurrect my old pal Enoch. For the second piece in question, author Cody Goodfellow (who had invited me to contribute to *Forbidden Futures*) asked me to participate in a round robin story for a special booklet for the 2019 H. P. Lovecraft Film Festival® & Cthulhucon, called *The Challenge From Beyond*, the other participants being S. P. Miskowski, Scott R. Jones, Christine Morgan, Jessica McHugh, and Orrin Grey. For my portion, which gets the round robin started, as a tribute to Wilum I again brought back Enoch, who is "mourning the recent death of a dear friend, a writer." I feel the piece, which I here give the title *The Mummified Hand*, works fine as its own little tale, but I liked how the other authors ran with the story, each bringing some new aspect or development (as one would hope!), and I especially appreciated how Orrin Grey gathered up the threads at the end and even returned the action to Enoch, bringing the story neatly full circle—and in the process, being the third author to have written of Enoch Coffin.

So now … coming full circle to that novel Wilum and I had planned to write, and for which I wrote a chapter and a half (plus some notes) before abandoning it …

For this collection, I had initially thought to simply share that novel material as a curiosity. But then I wondered: could I revisit that concept now, to flesh this book out … and to enjoy the company of Enoch Coffin once more? And in so doing, commune in a way with the spirit of my departed fried? Might it be, then, a posthumous collaboration? Talk about a "challenge from beyond"!

Part of me worried it would be too sad or even disrespectful to write any further Enoch Coffin material without Wilum here to take part, or at least to read it. Which is why I had never before contemplated doing so; that is, until our collaborative book had officially gone out of print. It was this that ultimately inspired me to keep our character alive, and to even revisit him to see what he's been up to in the decade-plus since his original appearance.

Introduction

As I write this introduction, I actually haven't begun working on that story (which I've decided to write as a novella instead of a novel), besides the aforementioned preexistent material, which I shall incorporate. But I trust that I am going to find my way, find the right approach for this project, just as I did at the birth of our shared character.

Wish me luck as I embark on that endeavor, Wilum. I want your soul to live on in these pages, to make up in some way for the omission I mentioned at the start. You will never be omitted from the hearts of all the readers who have been fortunate enough to enjoy your singular, transporting fiction.

— Jeffrey Thomas, Massachusetts, 2024.

Matter of Truth and Death

The cry of the beast was the combined final roar of every last dinosaur at the moment of mass extinction. The forlorn moan of a pod of sperm whales dying on the floor of the ocean. The howl of a hurricane at its vertex of strength, before its long diminishment. The long, single cry of the beast was all of these sounds at once, and yet even those comparisons could not capture its haunting resonance, its unearthly essence.

He had no idea how large the creature was, but it must be colossal, and yet there was something skeletal, wasted, in its aspect. It rested on all four weirdly-bent, bony limbs, its emaciated body the same color as the rock upon which it was perched; a grayish-green, as if it were a chameleon that had changed its hue to blend in. The only other color was a white cloth or gauze wrapped around its hairless head, completely concealing its face. But as it called out, the depression of its elongated open mouth could be seen through the material that bound and blinded it.

The roughly-shaped block of green stone the beast squatted upon was the last in a string of similar blocks of varying sizes. He was not sure how many of these crude blocks there were, but all of them hung in the sky in defiance of earthly law, like fragments of an exploded moon in orbit around a globe. Yet above and below, instead of the blackness of space, there was only churning white mist. Against all this formlessness, only these hovering blocks. Maybe they were not fragments of something destroyed, however, so much as pieces yet to be assembled. Assembled into what, though?

So then, could it also be that the beast was not so much wasted away, as yet to be given its substance? Not crying out in impending death, but wailing in despair for not knowing what its final form must be?

As he gazed upon the floating chain of blocks, he noticed that there were odd symbols engraved into their surfaces, marks he had at first taken to be natural fissures. He could not decipher their meaning, but he sensed a potency in the carvings. What beings had incised these vast symbols, and how had they managed it with the rocks hanging in the void as they did? How gigantic must these entities be? Larger, perhaps, even than the wretched titan that crouched on the very last of the suspended fragments?

As if in answer to his question, he saw two immense arms emerge from the boiling, glowing mists. Two impossibly gigantic arms reaching toward the first in the string of suspended greenish blocks. His heart thudded in awe, for this being did indeed dwarf the enormous howling beast. It must be a god, with the powers of destruction and creation in those ten spread fingers.

And as he breathlessly watched, those hands took hold of the first hovering rock. They gripped it with such strength that the fingers dug deeply into the substance of the block. That substance proved malleable in the god-like entity's grasp. The two clutching hands squeezed, squeezed tighter, until the gray-green block was squashed and lost its form. Consequently, the odd glyphs carved into the surface lost their form as well.

With the symbols thus obliterated, a spell was broken and the vision faded from view, swallowed in the mists. But in the final moments before even that luminous fog lifted from his eyes and Enoch Coffin returned to himself, he realized that the two gigantic hands that had crushed the block of clay had been his own.

II

Enoch Coffin roused from the self-induced trance of his waking dream to find himself again in his artist's studio, seated at a heavy wooden work table much spattered with old paint. His hands rested on the tabletop in front of him, and in them he had crushed a large blob of oil-based greenish clay, extra pliable from the warmth of his skin. He smiled in satisfaction, and still holding the mass of clay he rose from the table and turned toward a raised cement base he had molded in the center of the attic's floor.

Upon this makeshift pedestal crouched an odd figure, as large as himself. It was a bent-backed thing, with weird crooked limbs like those of a dog—a dog with human hands and feet. But the figure was merely an outline suggested by lengths of copper wire, its curved spine a bent piece of rebar, rooted in the cement block to support the wire skeleton. The head was merely suggested by several loops of the wire, a cloth draped over it.

The artist knelt down as if genuflecting and began pressing the clay around the right foot and lower leg of the framework. With sensuous strokes his thumbs smoothed the warm clay, which had the feel of human skin. And still he was smiling. Looking up at the veiled head, Enoch said in an arch, satisfied tone, "One obstacle removed. One step closer to you. When I finally stand before you on your pedestal, I'll tear that mask from your face—and know you."

Still shaping the artificial flesh with his skillful fingers, Enoch glanced behind him at the large package of clay resting atop the table. Tomorrow he would sit and concentrate on the vision again, focus on that image of the beast perched upon the last in a whole archipelago of clay blocks. Once more his dream self would slip through the weave of the curtain that separated this world from that other, and the mere vision would be replaced with awesome reality. At least, as much of a representation of that *other* reality as his human mind could process. But he had never let his human mind limit him in the pursuit of his art.

Each hovering block was etched with a binding spell, to keep the wailing prisoner isolated. But one by one he would eliminate those obstacles that separated him from his model. And with each block he destroyed in that world, when he returned he would add another mass of clay to the barren skeleton. The beast was the feral avatar of a Faceless God—a wild aspect of that god, which the god itself had imprisoned. Yet Enoch Coffin felt like a god himself, making Adam from the "dust of the ground."

He did not believe that this entity had no face, but only a hidden face. He was determined to see it—and reproduce it.

III

With his concerns now returned to purely terrestrial matters, Enoch was prepared to leave his abode to take dinner and perhaps some carnal dessert at the apartment of a lady friend who ran a gallery on Newbury Street, and had even set upon his head his floppy-brimmed slouch hat so as to embark, when a figure stepped across the threshold of his attic studio unannounced. Enoch had witnessed—had conjured, both in his art and literally—many sinister things, and so he did not startle easily. His reaction to seeing this figure admit itself into his private sanctuary, then, was not one of fear but of anger.

"Will Ashman!" he exclaimed. "What the hell do you think you're doing, letting yourself into my home this way?"

The uninvited guest was an attractive young man with a tall, slender build, who looked as though he should move with a dancer's grace. Instead, he nearly collided with a small table by the door holding a lamp and a stack of sketchbooks. Ashman corrected himself with a little chuckle, but almost tipped back on his heels in so doing. He caught himself, staggered, and replied, "Sorry, my friend, very sorry. I did ring the bell, you know."

"The bell hasn't worked in decades."

"I knocked, too." Ashman had caught sight of a large unframed canvas leaning against a wall, and stumbled toward it to bend down and take a closer look. His expression twisted with confusion, then disgust. "It's perverse, your obsession with capturing ugliness so beautifully."

"If I didn't hear your knocks, that doesn't give you the right to let yourself in here."

Ashman straightened up again, grinning. "That will teach you not to lock your door in Boston."

"So it shall. Now if you'll excuse me, I have somewhere to be."

"Oh! So rude! But I know, shh, I know—it's I who am rude. Yes. So terrible, am I."

"So drunk, are you."

"Forgive me, Enoch," Ashman replied, with his smile now twitching almost imperceptibly. "I suppose I'm still mourning."

Enoch was mindful of a row of steel sculpting implements close by his hand, some with arrow-like tips and others with little hooks like dental probes. He had known that their exchange would soon turn to this matter, and he was wary. In a calmer tone, he said, "I'm sorry about your wife, Will."

"Sorry? Sorry, are you? What are you sorry for, exactly, Enoch?"

"I'm sorry that she killed herself, of course."

"Did you love Shoshana?"

"Will, don't talk foolishly. She was only a model to me."

"Oh! And did she know that? But of course she did. Maybe that sad knowledge prompted her decision, eh?"

Enoch lost his calm tone when he replied, "I'm sure your own difficulties had a lot more to do with her decision, Will, and your difficulties existed long before I met the two of you, so I won't have you laying Shoshana's suicide at my door."

Ashman cackled wildly, then clamped his hand over his mouth. "Sorry ... sorry ... but what an image you just put into my head! Me laying Shoshana's dead body at your doorstep. You should paint that, don't you think? Better yet, let me exhume her for you, maybe in a few years when she's more like the rest of the things you paint, and she can model for you once more!"

"You must leave this instant, Will," Enoch said in his most composed tone of voice. It was also his darkest, grimmest tone of voice.

Ashman ignored him, moving—as Enoch had feared—to the skeletal framework upon its crude pedestal. He didn't touch it, however, and didn't even remark upon it. To his layman's eyes, it was too insubstantial a form as yet to register as anything. Instead, the man went on, "As further proof of your perversity, in the painting of my dear wife I commissioned—yes, I introduced you to her myself, didn't I?—in that painting you made the beautiful Shoshana appear ugly, haunted, close to madness."

"I painted what I saw in her."

"It was a mirror she couldn't handle. Do you know she slashed your canvas to ribbons before she slashed her own flesh?"

Enoch made an involuntary sound of pain.

"Ah! But did you groan that way when you found out Shoshana was dead, or is it only your painting you mourn?" Ashman held his arms out wide. "Why not me, Enoch?"

"Why not you, what?"

"Why haven't you asked to paint me?"

"I didn't ask to paint your wife; you paid me, as you just stated."

"Why not paint me now? All right, I'll pay you, then! Paint me ... paint me as you see me, too!"

"You wouldn't like what I see."

Ashman had already begun opening the front of his shirt. A button tore free and clattered across the attic's ancient floorboards. "Why won't you paint me?" the man sobbed the words now, undoing his belt and the front of his trousers.

As Enoch watched the young man remove the remainder of his clothing, and once again spread wide his arms as if crucified to an invisible cross, the truth dawned on him at last. How could he have missed it before? Will Ashman wasn't jealous that the artist had taken his wife as a lover. He was jealous that Enoch hadn't taken *him* as his lover, instead.

At the same time he took in this truth, he took in Ashman's wasted form. Had he always been this emaciated, or was it a result of his anguish? The man standing before him, wracked with sobs, was little more than a skeleton himself. The handsome features of his face had belied his actual condition. "Hideous, aren't I?" Ashman blubbered. "Do I repulse you?"

"No," Enoch stated, and he meant his words. "I find you terribly beautiful, actually."

The nude figure dropped to his knees, and now held his arms toward the artist in supplication. "Then make me your model! Me ... make *me!*"

Enoch acted on inspiration then, upon the artist's instincts he trusted more than he trusted conscious thought. After all, though of course much purposeful decision-making was part of each artwork he produced, Enoch Coffin also believed very much in intuition, and in the providence of the "happy accident." Such gifts as seemed to be given him by unknown powers he could almost credit as his collaborators.

What Enoch did was dig his hands into the open package of clay on his work table, soften and warm a glob of it between his squeezing palms, and then approach his kneeling visitor. He reached out and smeared the greenish clay upon Will Ashman's face. Ashman closed his eyes and smiled rapturously, letting out a little sigh at the contact of the other's hands.

"My poor, poor golem," Enoch cooed, next smearing the clay down Ashman's neck, his shoulders, across his hairless chest.

"Yes," Ashman whimpered. "Yes!"

Before he had approached Ashman, and unknown to him, Enoch had pocketed one of his steel sculpting tools, one of those with a sharp little hook at its tip. With Ashman's eyes still closed and partially sealed by the sticky membrane of clay across his face, he didn't see Enoch raise this implement now and poise its tip over his forehead. Ashman gasped loudly when the tip bit into his flesh. As Enoch carved through the clay and into Ashman's flesh, he was reminded of the binding spells engraved on the archipelago of floating blocks in that other realm. The three symbols he inscribed, however, spelled out the Hebrew word *emet*, or "truth."

Ashman groaned in pleasure, not pain, as thin trickles of blood oozed from his new clay skin where it had been wounded. He lowered himself onto his back on the bare floorboards. And Enoch Coffin lowered over him, forgetting his dinner plans, forgetting his former disgust for his visitor. Happy accidents, and all that.

IV

That howl, more lonely than the bleat of a foghorn turned to a deafening volume, cut through the swirling white masses of fog that filled this world. Enoch stood upon one of the hovering blocks of stone and smiled with satisfaction at how much closer he was drawing to that beast on the final block, each time he willed himself into this realm. And each time he came here now, he felt more in control of his abilities, no longer becoming overwhelmed and forgetting himself.

He could see, this time, that the bandages that blinded and masked the semi-human crouching beast were stained through with spots of blood. Was this a new development, or had he been too distant previously to make out this detail?

No longer suffering disorientation, he was not surprised when he directed his gaze to the block upon which he stood, and soon saw two vast hands reach out to take hold of it. These were his hands, his godly appendages, and he watched them crush the malleable block between them. One more stone removed from the barrier between him and his prize. One step nearer to what lay behind that gauze, like a corpse's winding sheet hiding his model from him.

V

Much of the sculpture's body was complete now, though its copper skeleton was just barely concealed beneath its gaunt form. All that remained, really, were its shoulders and head, which was still only a series of wire hoops. Enoch felt exultant in his work; he could sense the power of the clay as he shaped it in his hands, caressed it smooth with his fingertips. It was the *blood* that had made the clay more potent. For after he had removed the bloodied material from Ashman's face and upper body, he had returned it to the batch of clay on his work table.

For several days now Enoch hadn't heard anything from Will Ashman. He was relieved, as he had feared the man would cling to him like an orphaned child after that one feverish night in this loft. On the other hand, he found it odd, and finally a bit worrisome. He hadn't wanted to acknowledge that he might have played any kind of part in the suicide of Shoshana Ashman, but if her husband were to do himself in likewise, Enoch wouldn't be able to deny his contribution. And so, reluctant as he was to do so, when he wrapped up work on the sculpture he broke down and phoned Ashman's office. His secretary, however, informed Enoch that the man had called in sick for three days straight. Enoch next called Ashman's home, but there was no answer. More reluctant than ever, nevertheless he left his house in the early evening to look in on his former patron.

VI

Enoch Coffin's house was located toward the bottom of the hill on

Charter Street in Boston's North End, three stories tall including the attic that contained his studio, fronted in weathered dark shingles that looked like bark, and wedged tightly between taller brick row houses. Directly across the street was the extreme tip of Copp's Hill Burying Ground, the resting place of Cotton Mather. Enoch enjoyed having quiet neighbors, and wished they were all dead on his side of the street as well.

He had never liked automobiles, and one of the benefits of city life was the public transportation, but as it happened the Ashmans owned a condominium in one of the brick row houses on narrow, one-way Sheafe Street, only a few blocks away. Thus, Enoch thrust his hands into the pockets of his brown suede jacket, the brim of his hat pulled low as if to shade his eyes though it was already dusk, and set forth on foot.

When Enoch arrived at the building he rang the bell, which he heard distantly inside, and when no reply came he knocked loudly. Again his efforts went unrewarded, so he tried the door and found it locked. Irritated that Ashman followed his own advice, and feeling that he had at least made an effort to look in on the man, Enoch had started to turn away when he heard the door crack open behind him. He looked back and saw Ashman's eye at the opening, glittering at him in the darkness that had filled this thin alley-like street. Ashman recognized him from his hat, if not the face it shaded, and held the door wider, gesturing for Enoch to enter. If he spoke, it was too faintly for the artist to hear.

Ashman escorted Enoch into a parlor, and right away the artist could see that his painting of Shoshana was gone from the wall where it had hung. The light in the room was low. Ashman wore a silk kimono-style robe, but its front was open and he wore nothing underneath. It was not just the shadowed lighting, Enoch was sure, that made the man's ribs stand out like rungs in a ladder, his pelvis jut as if to tear through his dry yellow skin. The man's cheeks were sunken shockingly, his sockets pools of ink, and whatever good looks he had retained mere days ago had dissipated. The Hebrew word for truth still showed on his forehead, black with crusted blood.

"Your office said you were sick," Enoch said. "Get thee to a doctor, man."

"A doctor?" When Ashman spoke, it was in a cracked wheeze. "It isn't illness at work in me, or even grief, and you know that, Enoch; I can see it in your face. It's your black magic at work in me."

"I performed no black magic on you. I took pity on you with a little nonsense—no more."

"You pity me, do you?" Ashman sounded as if he wanted to sob but hadn't the strength. "Everything is just material for your art, isn't it? Love. Blood. The soul. Just things you take and use without regard for their source."

"What can I do to help you?"

"It's that statue in your den of sin, isn't it?"

"You didn't mention it before."

"But I understand now. I see that wire figure in my dreams. It turns its empty head toward me, and looks at me without a face, and reaches out to me. I know what it wants. It wants my flesh."

Enoch could say nothing to deny Ashman's words.

Ashman continued, "What can you do for me, you ask? You can destroy that monstrosity."

"I can't."

"Can't, or you refuse?"

"I refuse to destroy my art."

"Then you'll destroy me."

"Nonsense. I'll take you to a doctor myself. Come and stay with me until you're well. Sleep and food will do you good, and I'll keep you away from the drink that's turning your mind to mush."

Ashman chuckled, a sound like broken bones clattering in his throat. "Ah, good doctor Enoch. Always the best of friends!" He gestured to the wounds on his forehead. "I'm Jewish, so I know that a golem is brought to life with this inscription. But do you also know how to shut the golem down? You erase one of these symbols and change the word 'truth' to the word 'death.' Did you know that part, too, Enoch? Did you?"

"I told you, it was only meant as play."

"Play, hm?" Ashman dipped into the shadows beside a sofa, and when he straightened he held a shotgun in both hands.

Enoch took a step back. "Will, don't be crude—this is beneath you."

"Home defense," Ashman explained. "To protect my art collection, of course."

"You know I can't destroy my artwork, but I'll help you in any way I can."

"Well, I admire your dedication to your craft. I guess you not only value it above the lives of your friends, but above your own life as well. Then the only other way you can help me is to get out. Get out, Enoch. You've cursed me enough."

"Will … "

"*Go!*" Ashman rasped, thrusting the shotgun barrel toward him.

So Enoch Coffin backed out of the room, and Ashman didn't follow. Before he let himself out into the narrow brick chasm of Sheafe Street, Enoch heard a pitiful wailing sound come from within the depths of Will Ashman's home, and its strange familiarity made him shudder.

VII

The creature poised in the center of the attic studio, thin as a weirdly anthropomorphic greyhound and crouched as if to spring upon its prey, was now fully clothed in its meager flesh of clay. Except, of course, for the face. Even the back of the misshapen, hairless head was covered, but where a face should have been there was still only a gaping, empty hole. A void.

Yet last night, Enoch had stood upon and crushed the penultimate block; the last block before the one to which this untamed aspect of the Faceless God had been exiled, stranded as if on a lonely island in that former archipelago of clay.

Tonight, Enoch Coffin was determined, when he sent his consciousness, his vital essence—his very spirit—into that realm of mist, he would join the avatar on the same block it perched upon. Surely it couldn't deny him. In that imprisoning pocket universe he had demonstrated the power of a god himself. It had nowhere to flee when he reached out to unveil the howling thing's visage.

As he sat at his work table with a blood-impregnated lump of clay resting before him, however, and began the mental exercises for sending his astral self into the beyond, he found himself distracted as if an insect buzzed at his ear. That nagging insect was Will Ashman. He hadn't heard from Ashman since he had gone to his home several days earlier, and he had made no further effort to contact the man himself, either. Enoch had tried to help the poor fool, and Ashman had rejected him. What more could he do for him—aside from destroying his art, which again was out of the question?

Irritated, Enoch tried to put the man out of his thoughts, and then to put irritation out of his thoughts as well. He must obtain a clarity of focus, a purity of concentration and purpose. Distraction wouldn't do, not when the object of his quest was so close he could almost touch it.

VIII

Mist billowed around him, so thick it was as if he were blindfolded, and he felt that he shouldn't move an inch lest he step off the platform upon which he had found himself and plummet. But plummet where? What lay below him? Perhaps only a yawning infinity of nothingness. Nothing but this white ethereal fog.

Then came that howl, that despairing wail of unfathomable pain, and even though it shocked Enoch—particularly since it originated from directly in front of him—at the same time it oriented and grounded him. The terrible cry even seemed to dispel the mist that separated him from its source. As the fog parted like ectoplasmic curtains, the creature was revealed hunkering just a few paces in front of him.

The avatar was not colossal after all, but only the size of a man. Or was he the size of a god, himself? It rested on all fours, the bony tips of its long fingers curled into the very material of the greenish-gray block they shared.

The thing's cry was sustained in a single ear-shattering, mind-blasting note of suffering. Under the bandages that completely obscured the front of its ovoid head, there was an elongated depression that was possibly a mouth gaping impossibly wide. The gauze was stretched across this opening like the skin of a drum, and it vibrated with the beast's noise. Furthermore, whereas on his most recent visits the gauze had only been splotched with blood, now the entire front of the bandages had been soaked through with dark red ichor.

Enoch had been riding on increasing waves of confidence each time he ventured into this little oblivion that had been created to hold the beast, but now that he was only steps away from it he felt as close to a feeling of fear as he would ever admit to. Who was to say the entity would indeed be as cowed and humbled as he had imagined it would be, once he stood directly before it, as if it might view him as its new master?

And now, too, hadn't he thoroughly freed it from its bonds? If it didn't destroy him, might it at the very least spring past him, finally liberated, and plunge through the mist into a different plane? Perhaps even the plane in which Enoch's own reality existed? If the beast escaped now because of him, would the Faceless God that had caged it here seek to punish him? Imprison him, next, in his own little oblivion?

He had come too far to worry about that now; the time for doubt had gone, back when he crushed that first block engraved with its binding spell. And the best way to deal with his fear of the creature was to ignore that fear altogether. So before his nervousness could increase, and his resolve waver, Enoch Coffin strode boldly forward, reached out his hand toward the bandage wound around the head of the skeletal being, and wrenched it away in one sharp motion.

With the blood-saturated bandages drooping from his hand like a flayed skin, Enoch Coffin stared at the visage revealed before him and cried out, "No! *No!*"

But it wasn't horror that had made him cry out, cry out so that the creature's own howl abruptly ceased and his took its place. No, it was anger he felt. Fury at being cheated of his prize.

He had hoped to prove that the Faceless God, at least in this bastard incarnation, did indeed possess a face but that no mortal had ever glimpsed it before. So it was a face he had anticipated uncovering. But not *this* face.

Back in his studio he had been distracted. His focus had been compromised. He had polluted the manifestation of this realm with his distorted vision, just as his friend's blood had polluted the clay and not enhanced it after all.

For the countenance that he had revealed, staring back at him with hopeless eyes in a shockingly skeletal yet still recognizable face, a face with the Hebrew word for "death" inscribed on its forehead, was that of his friend Will Ashman.

IX

Enoch Coffin was wrenched so abruptly from the fog-filled purgatory that he had to sit at his work table for a while until he felt less feeble and nauseated. From the corner of his eye, the nearly finished sculpture appeared to twist toward him slightly on its pedestal, but when he looked at it directly it was still, of course.

When he had his strength back he rose, but with uncertainty. Should he try calling? And if there were no answer, go to Sheafe Street in person? It was too late to call his friend's place of work. At last, Enoch decided to give an innocent-sounding call to the police.

"I'm concerned about my friend, Will Ashman," he explained to a detective he was finally transferred to. "I know he's been despondent over the recent suicide of his wife, and he hasn't answered my calls in days."

"Yeah, Ashman—on Sheafe Street, right?"

"Yes, that's him." Enoch was not surprised that the detective knew Will Ashman's name, or where he lived, and yet he had to *know* ...

"I'm sorry to tell you, sir, but your friend committed suicide, too, a couple nights ago."

The phone to his ear, Enoch turned his body to face toward the clay gargoyle again. "Oh Will. Poor, poor Will." He sighed. "How did he do it?"

"You really want to know?" said the policeman. "It was a shotgun. Must've put the barrel under his chin. The guys who responded to the call said he blew his whole face right off."

Enoch nodded, staring into the abyss that was the visage of the unfinished statue, and knowing that it would never be finished. In fact, just moments after he completed his phone call, Enoch Coffin set about destroying the tainted piece of artwork altogether.

Spectral Evidence

I

Enoch Coffin disliked two things about the "Witch City," as Salem, Massachusetts referred to itself for the sake of tourism. One was that the city had indeed made witchcraft a source of fame, when that fame was built upon the execution of twenty innocent people. The other thing that soured him was that in more recent times Salem had become infested with people only too eager to identify themselves as witches, who were to Enoch's mind no more witches than those innocents had been. Fakers, posers, goths, eccentrics. Even earnest and devoted pagans, whom he had more respect for, didn't seem to understand the sorts of witchcraft he himself had become familiar with, and even utilized, in his travels and in his art. But it wasn't that he found no charm in the city's year-round Halloween atmosphere, however tacky it might be. How could someone with his aesthetics be totally unmoved by a city that festooned and bedecked itself with images of death, the macabre, the supernatural? No, things were not always black or white. Not even when it came to magic.

Enoch didn't care for cars and avoided driving when he could. North Station was an acceptable distance on foot from his home in the North End of Boston, and from North Station it was only a thirty minute ride by train to Salem. Along the way, he sketched with a technical pen on a pad open across his knees. His model was an obese man, head shaved entirely bald, seated across the aisle from him, asleep with his head tilted back and mouth gaping wide. Enoch portrayed a monstrous old tree growing from the man's mouth, from which hung a crop of fruit, each one of them a miniature version of the sleeping man's face.

Bah—uninspired, but maybe he could add it to his selection of pieces on display at his destination today; an art show in Salem limited to the month of October, called *Gallery of the Grotesque.* He hadn't visited this place again since he had delivered his pieces to be included in the exhibit, and upon that occasion he had been sorry to even set foot a single time within its rented space. A series of linked rooms, their walls covered with dragons and vampires, zombies and more vampires. At first glance he had felt humiliated to be associated with it. But sometimes a balance had to be struck between art and commerce, and since Enoch was careful how he rationed the inheritance he primarily lived on, his art by necessity supplied an irregular source of additional income.

He hadn't really expected any of his pieces at the *Gallery of the Grotesque* to sell, the way he had priced them—though he would be damned if he underpriced them—but one had. And this was the reason for his return to Salem today. The buyer wanted to take possession of the artwork now, rather than wait for the exhibit to end next week, on Halloween. Furthermore, the man wanted to pay Enoch in person, so that he might meet face-to-face the artist who had so impressed him.

The commuter rail disgorged its passengers, and Enoch climbed a series of steps to the level of Bridge Street. The sky was bright blue, the air crisp but not biting, and the city with its quaint tree-lined streets, brick sidewalks, and many historic buildings seemed bent on coaxing Enoch into giving it another chance.

Still, with the city in the grip of its annual "Haunted Happenings," it wasn't long before its indigenous spooky folk and the influx of spooky pilgrims became manifest. Enoch gave an inward groan ... and yet, many of these creatures, both male and female (and often it was a challenge to differentiate), were as fetching as they were ludicrous in their dramatic black outfits, their abundance of improbable jewelry, their extreme hairstyles and makeup, their piercings and tattoos. Perhaps he would rent a room here in town and stay the night after his business had been conducted, so that he might partake a bit of the exotic fauna. Once again, Enoch Coffin was reminded that he was often drawn to that which repulsed him, and repulsed by that which attracted him. Once again, reminded that the only clear-cut black and white he knew was the relationship between ink and white paper.

II

When Enoch arrived at the rented shop space that housed the temporary *Gallery of the Grotesque*, the purchaser of his artwork was already there waiting for him, presently in conversation with one of the artists who had organized the showing. Introductions were made, after which the artist excused herself to return to her duties at the front admission desk, leaving Enoch and his new patron alone.

This person had been introduced to Enoch as Walter Mason, who appeared to be about thirty. "Appeared," because there was a curious ambiguity about him that allowed for the possibility that Mason was ten years younger, or ten years older. In addition, he was androgynous in appearance, even his soft voice lost between the masculine and feminine, his long black hair falling about a face so pale that Enoch wondered if the man wore whitening foundation. He had the look of a geisha who had let down her hair, and even cloaked his tall frame in a long black robe like a kimono. Ah, Salem.

"Oh, Mr. Coffin!" Mason cooed, at last slipping his hand from Enoch's own after having prolonged their handshake. The man wore long black velvet gloves that disappeared up the sleeves of his robe. "I cannot express my gratitude that you agreed to meet me in person! Your piece is so exquisite and so important to me—like a sacred thing!—that

I didn't even want to touch it with my own hands until you yourself removed it from the wall for me."

"I'm flattered," Enoch said politely.

"I'm not in possession of a bank account, so I trust that cash will be acceptable?" Mason reached inside the front of his robe and drew out a bundle of money, pressing it into Enoch's hands. "Three thousand dollars. Please count it."

"No need. Thank you." Enoch stuffed the wad into the pocket of his brown suede jacket. Though unchallenged, he somehow felt the need to explain, "I charged conservatively, considering that the work itself took over thirty hours in total."

"I can believe it—such an intensity of detail! Worth every penny; there's no need to explain. But I ask, is pen and ink your preferred medium? I see you represented here with oils, as well."

"Oils are my preferred medium, though I've sought versatility in regard to my art."

"And so you have achieved it! But I myself find your pen work, in the pieces represented here at least, to be the most impressive. Shall we move on, into the presence of your masterworks themselves?"

"After you."

They walked across polished wooden floorboards into another of the rooms, Mason's feet making sharp clacking footfalls under the flowing hem of his robe. Did stiletto heels account for some of his height?

They came to the white-painted wall where hung five of Enoch's artworks: two oils, an acrylic painting, and a duo of pen and ink drawings. Both pen and inks were similarly dense in detail, though one relied more on pointillism while the other utilized a crosshatching technique.

"Escher has nothing on you, sir!" Mason gushed, sweeping his arm toward the two drawings—the smallest of the five pieces—framed under glass. "I daresay, not even Piranesi with his *Carceri* etchings captures such a hellish sense of vast and otherworldly architecture ... such mind-bending geometries. Are you a trained architect, as he was?"

"I learned some drafting in school, but I never studied as an architect. You're very insightful; I will admit that Piranesi was one of my inspirations for these." Enoch didn't go on to reveal what other inspirations he might have had—such as his dreams.

"But they're very much your own, certainly! How did you envision such scenes? Did you sketch them out first, or just let your pen take you where it would?"

"The latter. I suppose I worked mostly from the subconscious." Again, Enoch felt disinclined to discuss the dreams he had experienced during the period in which he had worked on these two recent drawings, and several more in the same vein that he had opted not to include in the showing.

As if through fresh eyes, Enoch turned to face his drawings again, particularly focusing on the one with the obsessively intricate crosshatching that Mason had just acquired.

As Mason had indicated, both portrayed strange environments. The one done in pointillism illustrated an exterior view of a complex, gigantic city—seemingly abandoned and falling into ruin—while the one Mason had purchased revealed the interior, perhaps, of one of those cyclopean structures. Its ceiling soared impossibly high, while an overabundance of staircases and ramps crossed the scene, leading everywhere and nowhere. Shadows and light cut in from every direction, in angled planes and curved arches, creating an eye-straining interplay of black and white, line and absence of line—a maddening web of geometries.

No figures populated the exterior cityscape, but Enoch had placed a single person in the interior drawing, at its center, like a fly caught in that mad web. The figure was distant, barely a silhouette, apparently regarding the viewer as the viewer regarded it. Enoch couldn't even remember consciously deciding to include the lone inhabitant. As he had said, much of his approach to this series of drawings had been to trust his subconscious to take the reins.

But there had also been a recurring solitary figure in the dreams he had experienced, some weeks back, that had first inspired this pen and ink series. He remembered little more about the figure, though, than what he had captured here.

Mason cut into this thoughts with further praise. "Normally the guidelines of perspective anchor two-dimensional art in the laws of reality, but here you've used the mathematical laws of perspective subversively, against their own purpose. On a flat page, you've managed to convey dimensions beyond what can be plumbed!"

"You're very kind. You've articulated my intentions."

"My compliments are well deserved. But Mr. Coffin, may I impose upon you for one more favor? Could you, with the hands that gave life to this masterpiece, remove it from this wall and carry it to my home, and once there hang it again for me? My house is only a short, pleasant walk from here, I promise you. I feel that my own crude aura would only sully the magic of your creation. Call it superstition."

Once more Enoch gave his patron a polite smile. Was this the opening overture of a seduction? He was not yet desirous of Mason in that way, but he wouldn't rule out the possibility. Anyway, it wasn't a bad feeling to be appreciated for his work, nor a bad feeling to have three thousand dollars in his pocket, and so he replied, "Yes, certainly. Lead on."

Enoch took down his picture from the wall, and thus carrying it under one arm accompanied Mason outside, where they traversed the brick-paved sidewalks of Salem, upon which Mason's feet clacked sharply.

III

"How fortunate you are," Enoch observed, "to own such a lovely home, in such a location."

"Yes, yes," Mason agreed, "I am."

The house they arrived at was situated just down the street from the museum called the Witch House, formerly the abode of Judge Jonathan Corwin, who had been involved in the Salem witch trials.

Mason's house itself was narrow but long, with one of its ends facing onto Essex Street. Its roof was in the gambrel style, with two sloping surfaces to each side. There were three floors, including the attic. As they passed through a white picket fence to reach a door at the side of the house, a voice cried out behind them and they paused to look around.

"Mr. Mason," called an elderly woman from the thin strip of yard at the side of the house next door, separated by another length of white fence, a rake in her hands with which she had been gathering autumn leaves. "How has your uncle been? Still unwell?"

"Yes, yes, afraid so," Mason replied, smiling. "I'm still seeing to his needs. Hopefully he'll be up and around again soon."

"Please tell him I asked about him, will you?"

"Of course, of course, I will. Good day, Mrs. Howe."

The old woman waved, and Mason turned away. Enoch followed suit, and waited while his host unlocked the side door.

As Enoch started to follow Mason inside, he saw that the mailbox affixed beside the door was overflowing. He reached in, pulled out a thick handful of material, and glanced at a mailing label stuck to a coupon brochure, printed with the name SAMUEL CORWIN. When he was inside he held the bundle toward his patron. "You've been neglecting your uncle's mail, I'm afraid."

"Oh yes, yes, how forgetful I am," Mason said, accepting it and depositing it immediately onto a side table. "I'll go through it later."

"So it's not your house, then."

"Ah, no, I don't actually own it. My uncle has lived here in Salem for many years, and when he fell into ill health he summoned me to come and look after him, in return for which he takes care of my needs as well."

"Such as purchasing art?"

Mason's lips, too red in his pallid visage, pulled into a tight smile. "He doesn't care what interests I pursue with the money he so graciously grants me."

"Do you have a sizable collection?"

"I've only collected one item previously, but surely today marks a more valuable acquisition."

"Again, I'm flattered." Enoch held up the framed drawing. "So where did you intend to hang it?"

"My uncle provides me a room in the attic; I'd like to hang it there."

"The attic? Such a large house, and your uncle lives alone, but you stay in the attic?"

"Oh, it's a lovely large room in fine condition—you'll see. It's my own choice; my uncle gave me free rein. I happen to love attic rooms ... so artistic."

"Well," Enoch conceded, "my studio is in the attic of my home in Boston, and of course it's my favorite room in the house, so I can understand your sentiments."

"But let me show you," Mason said, leading Enoch toward a staircase.

"So your uncle must have been related to Judge Jonathan Corwin, then," Enoch said as he followed Mason, who clumped loudly up the stairs.

At the second floor, Mason turned toward his guest and smiled curiously.

"I saw your uncle's name on his mail," Enoch explained. "Corwin, not Mason."

"Yes ... he's my uncle on my mother's side. And yes, my uncle is a descendant of the judge. But we can't ourselves judge Corwin too harshly, since we're unsure today of the extent of his role in the witchcraft investigation, and what his feelings were on spectral evidence."

Enoch was familiar with the term. Spectral evidence was evidence not based upon hard fact, but upon visions and dreams. Spectral evidence at the Salem witch trials had consisted of such testimony as the alleged victims of the accused witches claiming that so-and-so had harassed them in a vision, in the form of an animal for instance. The Reverend Cotton Mather, who happened to be buried in the graveyard opposite Enoch's home in the North End of Boston, had recommended that spectral evidence be heard in the trials, but had advised that it could be the Devil himself in such dreams, merely pretending to be the accused witch.

Discussing this matter further, Mason said, "The Devil—ha. Humans always try to put their tiny anthropomorphic face upon the mysteries of the universe, eh, Mr. Coffin? I'm sure a sensitive soul like yourself, so obviously more finely attuned to the cosmos, understands how foolish such notions as the Devil are. The common ape confuses his own evil with the forces of the universe, in an attempt to place that evil outside himself, but the cosmos is not malign; the cosmos is indifferent. Cosmic entities would be no more evil than is a spider who traps a fly."

"You speak of humans as if to distance yourself from them."

"Ah, if only we could, eh, Mr. Coffin?" Mason smiled more broadly than he had as yet done, and Enoch could understand now why his smiles had been more subtle before. The man's small teeth appeared quite black, more so than decay would account for. Perhaps it was another intentional aspect of his dramatic appearance. Geishas covered their teeth with black wax, so that their teeth would not appear yellow in contrast with their white faces, so perhaps Mason was going for something of a geisha effect, after all.

They continued up the next flight of stairs, and when they arrived at the attic level Mason again turned to face Enoch and said, "As it so happens, on my father's side we're related to another person involved in the Salem witch trials, though her name is much more obscure. I believe a concentrated effort was made to eradicate mention of her from the record books."

"And who would that person be?"

"Her name was Keziah Mason, and though she hailed from Arkham she was one of those accused of witchcraft in Salem. She was no doubt the only authentic witch among those poor folk."

"Why do you say she was an authentic witch?"

"Well, in her testimony at the trial she made mention of curious practices that might be dubbed, for lack of a better word, magical. Such as utilizing, in her words, 'lines and curves that could be made to point out directions leading through the walls of space to other spaces beyond.' But she was not hung with the rest, because she mysteriously escaped from the jail. The Reverend Cotton Mather was quite perplexed, I understand, by what she left behind in her cell."

"Which was?"

"According to the only remaining document, which seems to have been suppressed, what Mather observed was, 'curves and angles smeared on the grey stone walls with some red, sticky fluid.'" Mason chuckled in that soft voice of his. "Perhaps in her own way, Keziah Mason was something of an artist, herself."

IV

"This is where I dream," Mason said oddly.

The attic had not been finished into an apartment as Enoch might have expected from Mason's words; its beams and rafters were open and bare, motes of dust swimming in rays of sunlight slanting in through its few windows. It did show signs that Mason inhabited it, but his bed was no more than a mattress without a box spring or frame, pushed against one wall. Candles had been burned in abundance upon an old steamer trunk, melted pools of wax standing in a profusion of saucers and other containers. Books were stacked about the room, many of them almost crumbling into dust. Such features as the candles and books, however, did in fact put Enoch very much in mind of his own house's attic.

Because of the house's gambrel roof, the angles of the long, single attic room were interesting. But most interesting was one corner in particular, not far from the mattress. Here, it was plain that newer pieces of wood had been nailed, spanning the space from one corner wall to the other, and from the floor to the sloping ceiling, in overlapping layers … but surely not for a practical purpose such as lending the roof further support. There were two-by-fours, wider planks, even lengths of thin doweling, crisscrossing in a kind of intricate wooden web. Further, lines had been painted upon these wooden pieces in a red pigment. The planks allowed a broader surface for some of these markings to form curves. Depending upon where one stood to regard the composition, these red lines intersected in different ways.

"So, you're an artist yourself," Enoch observed, "rather in the manner of your ancestor, Keziah. I have to admit, now, that I have heard of her history before."

Behind him, Mason said, "Really? But I shouldn't be surprised. You obviously have much arcane knowledge. You couldn't create such artwork, otherwise. It cannot be accident or mere intuition, your ability."

Where Enoch stood there was a concentrated icy draft, like a cold steel knife blade pressed flat against his leg even through the material of his trousers. Looking down at the ancient steamer trunk beside him, he noted a red light glowing from within, showing through cracks and peeking out here and there under the lid.

With a cocked eyebrow, he turned from the trunk to face Mason, and found that his host had shut the attic door. Painted upon its inner surface in the same red pigment was a large odd symbol of overlapping circles, lines, and tiny lettering in an alien script.

"If you would be so kind as to remove your drawing from its glass and frame," Mason said, as he pulled the long velvet glove from his right hand. In so doing, he revealed odd tattoos on both the upper surface and his palm. Red lines ran down each finger, top and bottom, and the natural grooves in his palm had been traced in red as well, though overlapping circles and more alien lettering had also been added. When he removed his other glove, Enoch saw that his left hand had been identically tattooed.

"Do you have a better frame to showcase it in?" Enoch asked, feigning innocence.

"Yes. There." Mason pointed beyond Enoch, at the wooden web in the corner. "I'd like you to nail the drawing in the center of the widest plank, there. I'll help direct you. You'll find a hammer and nails on the floor directly below."

"You can't do it yourself, because of your tattoos. Why, Mr. Mason?"

"I told you—I don't want to disturb your magic with my own."

"A magician like your ancestor, are you? A witch?"

Mason winced. "Such an ignorant term, Mr. Coffin, please. 'Witch.' It's no better than 'Devil.'" He then turned to confront the closed attic door, and spread the fingers of both hands in such a way that the lines on his digits matched the angles of certain lines on the symbol painted on the wood. When he pressed his hands to the surface, the red pigment there took on a fiery glow. It was a seal. A seam of weird red light now shone under the door, accompanied by another cold draft that speared into the room.

When Mason bared his black teeth in a smug grin, as if waiting for Enoch to show fear, the artist merely asked instead, "Where is your uncle?"

"Not far."

"Indeed." Enoch then whirled and with his arm swept most of the candles from the top of the steamer trunk. When he threw the lid open, the rest of the candles clattered to the floor. Red light burst up into Enoch's face, but it wasn't that which caused him to stumble back and shield his eyes with his arm. It was the frigid blast of arctic air that had been released. Still narrowing his eyes lest the icy air freeze them into balls of glass, he peered over his arm into the maw of the trunk.

Through plumes of churning vapor, which caught the ruby glow emanating from the impossibly deep throat of the trunk, Enoch made out a weirdly bent figure that appeared to be floating in a vividly red sea. Throughout this sea were strung a countless multitude of black cables, but the thickest cables appeared to pulse as if they were something organic. The pathetic figure snared in this black web and thus suspended in the crimson void was a nude elderly man, his mouth wide in a silent shriek and his eyes bulging in terror. Enoch knew that Samuel Corwin was still alive, trapped in that web like a fly, and staring back at him in helpless horror.

Mason came toward him and kicked the lid of the trunk shut. In doing so, the hem of his black silk robe rode up and his foot was revealed. It was a cloven hoof, tufts of black fur about his ankle.

"That will be quite enough of that," Mason said mildly. "Let's not be rude."

"You're being rather rude to your uncle, don't you think?"

"He's not my uncle. He's the descendant of one of those who persecuted my true ancestor, Keziah."

"I thought you said we mustn't judge old Jonathan Corwin too harshly because we aren't sure how much he had to do with the fates of the accused."

"Well," Mason chuckled, "just in case. Anyway, I had to have somewhere to stay; rents are expensive in this part of town."

"And why did you need to find a place in this particular town?"

"I had no choice; this is where I found myself. Thanks to you. It was your dreams that summoned me at first, Mr. Coffin—beckoned me to the window, if you will. Then you cinched it when you drew that." He pointed to the artwork in Enoch's hands. "You pulled me through the weave, along the lines and curves. You, playing with magic you only half understood, hooked me like an unwary fish and drew me into your wretched, limited mortal plane."

Enoch turned the drawing around in his hands to squint at it. Particularly, at the vague ant of a figure in its center. "So that's you."

"Yes. An unintentional portrait. Here." Mason moved to a crude shelf and took down a magnifying glance. As he returned to Enoch he continued, "It took me a number of days to follow the scent of your drawing, once I manifested in this realm from which my ancestor was spawned. When I tracked the energies to their source and viewed your creation, I understood how I had been brought here." He passed Enoch the magnifying glass.

Enoch accepted the implement and studied his own handiwork through its lens, but the figure was not that much more distinct: just a few strokes of his nib, a splotch of India ink, with a tiny open area suggesting where a white face would be. And yet, even as Enoch watched, he saw the rudimentary figure's long hair streaming as if blown in an arctic wind, its long black robe visibly stirring as well.

"What is it you want from me now," he asked, looking up, "that you feel compelled to seal me in this room with you?"

"I need you to reverse your artistic spell. I only want to return to my own realm and those who are like me—such as Keziah, who still lives and dwells in those other spaces. Unlike her, I was never part of this world, never fully human, nor would I want to be."

"You need only have asked. You didn't have to try to trap me here like you did your poor faux uncle. Just tell me what to do."

"As I say, you must nail your drawing at the nexus of my formula. I'll help direct its placement."

Enoch removed his pen and ink drawing from its glass-fronted frame, and then brought it to the corner where Mason had nailed his many crisscrossing lengths of wood, marked with their red lines and curves. Enoch knelt down to position the drawing against a broad central plank, and found he didn't really need Mason's direction. Painted tracks upon the wood aligned perfectly with certain angles in the drawing, formed by staircases and other architectural details that cut into the image from the edges of the paper. Several curved lines on the wood perfectly continued curves begun in the drawing by an arched doorway or a partially seen circular "rose window," such as one might find in a cathedral. Enoch could feel in his nerves an inaudible click as the lines of his drawing fell into place and the proper links were connected like electrical currents.

Holding the drawing against the wood with one hand, he picked up a nail and the hammer his host had indicated.

"A nail in each corner!" Mason instructed behind him. "Yes! Each corner must be bound!"

Enoch nailed the upper corners of his drawing to the central plank, and the bottom corners to another, narrower plank running parallel beneath it. He then rose, still holding the hammer causally, though now he had a crude weapon.

"A pleasure to see an artist such as you at work," Mason told him. "Despite the inconveniences you've caused me, my admiration for your ability is sincere. Now, if you'd kindly move aside."

"Don't you want me to remove you from the drawing? Maybe with a brush and some white correction fluid ... "

"Now that the final puzzle piece is secure, your work is done. At last, I can touch it myself."

As Enoch watched, the creature that had taken the name Walter Mason knelt before his strange construction in the corner and carefully positioned both hands over the pen and ink drawing, spreading his ten fingers just so. When he seemed satisfied with their alignment, he pressed his palms forward, making physical contact with the drawing. The red lines tattooed along every digit continued various angles that Enoch had inked in.

And then, every red line Mason had painted along the wooden pieces began to glow, creating a net of fiery strands so bright that Mason's form became merely a silhouette. From out of the attic corner came such an intense, blasting cold wind that Enoch involuntarily stepped back and again covered his face with his arm. The wide-brimmed slouch hat he favored was blown off his head and his hair was ruffled by the roaring gust.

But the arctic wind quickly died away, and the luminous scarlet web dimmed to its natural state. When Enoch lowered his arm, Walter Mason was no longer in the attic room.

He moved closer to his drawing and crouched down to examine it, having again taken up the magnifying glass. Peering through the lens, he saw that the vague dark figure standing in the center of his drawing of an immense, otherworldly chamber had vanished.

Enoch turned toward the steamer trunk, approached it and once again opened the lid. There was no longer any red-glowing void, nor icy vapors. The uncanny portal had reverted to a mere musty and empty old steamer trunk. Poor innocent Samuel Corwin was irretrievable now, and Enoch Coffin preferred not to speculate on his fate. It wouldn't be the first time a miscarriage of justice had taken place in the Witch City.

He used the claw end of the hammer to pry the nails from the four corners of his drawing, and then replaced it in its frame. He'd bring it home with him, instead of returning it to the gallery, lest questions were asked.

Enoch was not rattled by the experience he had just undergone. In fact, he was pleased that today's excursion to Salem had been rather more interesting than he had anticipated. He was quite gratified that one of his drawings had proved so potent. Though to be honest, he was also a bit relieved that this drawing was the only one in the series of pen and inks in which he had incorporated a figure.

The three thousand dollars in his pocket wasn't detrimental to his mood, either, even if it did come from an old man perhaps forever ensnared in the spider web of a vengeful part-human entity.

Enoch moved to the door upon which the seal had been painted, but the symbol no longer glowed crimson. Red light and a freezing draft no longer seeped in beneath the door. Enoch turned the knob and stepped from the room without any unsavory consequences.

Once again in the street, and hurrying away lest the neighbor woman notice him again and mention him should there ever be an investigation into the disappearance of Samuel Corwin, Enoch took note of the goth-types he saw walking along Essex Street here and there. Yes, Salem was full of their ilk.

Yet how many of them, he wondered, had not come here as tourists from other cities or states, but as visitors from someplace much, much farther away than that?

Every Exquisite Thing

I

For painting in oils, which was his favorite artistic medium, Enoch Coffin preferred not to buy paint in tubes but to create his own. To achieve this, he purchased little jars of dry pigment that he mixed with walnut oil (which cut down on the yellowing engendered over time by linseed oil). But he would also add his own unique ingredients to the recipe, which he felt imparted additional power to his work. Sometimes quite considerable power. Some of the ingredients he required, according to obscure grimoires in his library—such as a facsimile of the Voynich manuscript—were for him best found in Boston's Chinatown district.

Enoch always made a full day of his Chinatown excursions, riding in early from his home in the North End on the subway system's Orange Line. He would visit a Vietnamese restaurant for a bowl of *pho*—beef noodle soup—and a cup of strong *ca phe sua nong* thick with sweetened condensed milk. Or maybe some Chinese *dim sum* instead. Before the ride home, he'd stop at the corner *Hing Shing Pastry* bakery for some pastries filled with lotus seed or red bean paste. Life was as much for the sensual pleasures of the moment as it was for learning what lay before and after life, and Enoch didn't believe one needed to starve for one's art, in any sense of the word.

Ah, but he loved this little tease of Asia, which reminded him of travels he had taken when his finances, or the generosity of patrons, had allowed. Strolling here past arrays of exotic fruit on the sidewalk, or spying live chickens pacing about in a building's vestibule, put him in mind of exploring the back streets of Seoul, where someone had once spat blood at him from a balcony, and upon looking up he had glimpsed a furtive figure with the obsidian face of a demon. Up sprang memories of Vietnam—of riding a ferry across a wide black river in the wee hours of the morning on his way to visit the Phuoc Dien temple complex by the Cambodian border. He had been intrigued to find that young transvestite prostitutes plied their trade on either shore and upon the ferry itself, and in flirting with one of these beguiling creatures he had peeked into its bra to find it stuffed with toilet paper.

And so it was that Enoch raised an eyebrow in appreciation, albeit tinged with a bit of confusion, when he entered his favorite Chinatown apothecary and found a beautiful woman tending the back room, instead of the wizened old man who owned the tiny establishment. The stranger stood behind the counter where he had only seen elderly Shun situated in the past. Behind the woman, the small room's back wall was lined ceiling to floor with wooden drawers labeled in both Chinese calligraphy and Vietnamese lettering.

The woman's eyes were already locked on Enoch's when he entered, as if his arrival had been anticipated, though he never called ahead prior to a visit here. "Hello," she said in accented but accomplished English, "may I help you?"

"Ah, I was looking for my friend, Shun," Enoch explained.

"Oh, I'm sorry, but my father passed away about a month ago."

"What? Oh no ... I had no idea. I'm terribly sorry." Enoch had liked Shun, but he fretted more about obtaining the materials he needed to enhance his paints. "Your father, you say? I never knew Shun had any children. So did he train you in his special craft?"

"Yes, he did; very thoroughly. I'm sure he sensed the end was coming."

Enoch judged the woman to be in her mid to late thirties. She was tall, with wavy black hair framing a pale handsome face. Her long nose, strong jaw, and composed mouth gave her an aristocratic bearing, but her eyes struck him as deeply sad. It was the sadness of her eyes that most accounted for her beauty. Enoch recalled that Oscar Wilde had said, "Behind every exquisite thing that exists there is something tragic."

He wondered how long she had studied with her father, because he'd never seen her in any of his previous visits to the herbalist. He believed he would have remembered her.

Enoch said, "Well, what is your name, my dear?"

"Jiao."

He explained in as little detail as possible, feeling a bit self conscious, how he added special ingredients to his paints to "empower" his art. The woman nodded as she listened, as if this were the most normal of concepts. When he had finished, Enoch said, "So I have a bit of a shopping list today, Jiao."

"Please begin." She smiled politely. Her smile was as sad as her eyes.

He leaned forward on the counter between them, and one by one related the materials he needed, having by now memorized them. He watched as the woman named Jiao went from drawer to drawer, filling small brown paper lunch bags with dried leaves, seeds, or what looked like twigs and bark. Into one bag she dropped a number of tiny mummified seahorses. She stapled the bags shut when finished, and soon ten of these stood in a row on the counter. She gathered them all into a plastic shopping bag for him.

"Very good," Enoch said, watching the woman's face carefully. "Now, what I need are some of the more obscure ingredients Shun kept upstairs. Such as his 'Essential Saltes.'"

Jiao held his stare for several beats. "He brought you upstairs? He gave you Essential Saltes?"

"Yes. He never told you?"

"No."

"I assure you he did, or else I wouldn't know any of this."

Jiao nodded slowly. "That's true. What is your name?"

"Enoch Coffin."

"Very well, Mr. Coffin. I'll take you upstairs."

Jiao came out from around the counter, and Enoch followed her into the main part of the shop. She spoke to a young worker in Chinese, and apparently he wasn't expecting to see her beside him, for he looked around with a startled gasp. Enoch had the impression the lad was afraid of his new boss. Apparently she told him to keep an eye on the back room, and that she was taking a customer upstairs. The boy, whom Enoch recalled having seen on earlier visits, nodded quickly with understanding.

Then, Enoch was following Jiao outside the shop to the street and another entrance to the building. Within, they found a shadowy staircase and Jiao led him to the familiar third floor, where she unlocked the door Shun had always unlocked for him, no doubt with the very same key.

II

The apartment was murky, its shades pulled and drapes drawn, its air a mix of exotic scents. Incense, yes, but other odors unidentifiable, and not all of them pleasant. As he trailed Jiao into a central room perhaps intended as a dining room, Enoch said, "I need to paint you."

The woman stopped, and turned to meet his avid gaze. She was restraining a smile, but was it one of pleasure or derision? She said, "Why do you say that?"

"Well, aside from the obvious reason, that you're strikingly lovely, it's an intuition of mine—and I've come to trust my artistic intuitions more than I trust the rising and setting of the sun."

"I see. And I suppose you would want to paint me in the nude."

"You mean you nude, or me nude?"

"Very funny."

"I wouldn't protest if you were willing, but I wouldn't insist upon it."

"Hm. You're very handsome yourself, Mr. Coffin. Has anyone ever painted your portrait?"

"Me? Oh no, I'd never permit that. I'm like those savages who are afraid a photograph will steal their soul."

Neither consenting to nor declining Enoch's request, and still holding that enigmatic little smile, Jiao moved across the room to an antique Chinese kitchen cabinet. Normally this would have housed dishes and utensils in the upper section and food in the lower, but instead Shun had stocked the hundred-year-old cabinet with cures, potions, and concoctions not available to his common customers.

While Jiao opened its cupboards, Enoch turned toward an altar he didn't recall having seen in the apartment before. It seemed to represent the practice of ancestor worship, featuring as it did a framed old black-and-white photo portrait of a handsome young Asian man, before which were arranged flowers, offerings of fruit, and joss sticks burnt down to their yellow stems. "Who is this dashing young fellow?" Enoch asked his host.

"My husband," Jiao replied.

"Oh—and here I thought the photo was quite old. I'm sorry to learn you're a widow. What losses you've suffered."

"Yes," Jiao said, facing him now and holding a glass container close to her chest. She had removed it from the cabinet. "You said you needed the Essential Saltes of the *con rit*?"

"Yes." As they had ascended the stairs, he had told her that much. *Con rit* was the name the Vietnamese had given to a legendary sea creature with a fifty-foot-long segmented body like that of a centipede. A rotting specimen was said to have washed ashore in 1883, and Shun possessed a bottle containing some of that carcass's distilled Saltes. Enoch told his host, "When painting a seascape, I like to add a touch of the *con rit's* essence to the mix. In the same way that, when painting a forest, I mix vegetable matter with my paints, or add cemetery soil to my hues when I render a graveyard scene."

Jiao held out the container she carried, and now Enoch could see that it was empty but for a dusty residue. "And my father sold you the Saltes of human beings as well, did he not? Such as these?"

"I can't read the label," Enoch said, gesturing toward the bottle she held, "but yes ... yes, he did. Sometimes I add them to the flesh tones with which I portray the living or the dead—whatever that painting calls for. But also, there are times when I use them throughout the entire painting, whatever its subject, if these Saltes represent the crystallized remains of some great artist or poet, so that their psychometric force might be imparted to my own work. Your father managed to collect quite an array of specimens in his travels. He was a singularly gifted alchemist. As an artist, I am an alchemist myself. He understood my motivations, and my needs."

"But did he sell you any of the contents of *this* jar?" Jiao asked in an insistent tone, further extending the labeled empty container.

"As I told you, I don't know. One jar looks the same as the others to my eye. Why do you ask? Whose remains did that contain?"

Jiao took in a long breath in preparation to speak, but she was cut off by a loud thud above their heads and looked up sharply. Enoch glanced at the ceiling. It sounded to him as if someone in the apartment above had dropped something heavy on the floor.

Enoch returned his gaze to his host, and looking strangely stricken, she resumed, "My father did indeed gather quite a collection of human remains, sometimes already rendered by other alchemists into their Essential Saltes. But most of these remains he himself distilled."

"So he boasted to me. As I say, I'm aware he accumulated arcane knowledge."

"You are familiar with the Cultural Revolution, that swept my country from the sixties into the seventies?"

"Yes. It was a terrible time."

Jiao snorted a bitter laugh at his understatement. "Theories vary on how many people lost their lives in that time of savagery. I have heard anywhere between one to twenty million lives lost. In Guangxi there were public ceremonies, banquets, in which people were cannibalized.

Of course during this dark time, artists were persecuted. Some managed to hide their art under the floorboards of their homes, and return many years later to retrieve it."

"It's all very horrid."

"This jar, here, once held the remains of an artist named Song Yi. Yi's art was not shocking or challenging. He painted simple rustic scenes of people at work, people laughing and living. Lovely portraits. But forty-three years ago, he was handed over to the authorities by a traitor he believed was a friend. This friend told them that Yi was subversive and dangerous, and so at the age of thirty-eight, Song Yi was publicly beaten until he died from his injuries."

Enoch said, "Yes … yes, I know. I do know this one's history."

"You do."

"Your father sold me some of this artist's Saltes on several occasions, so that I might use them in my own art. In so doing, I believed some of his essence —"

The bottle slipped through Jiao's hands then, struck the floor and shattered into several large pieces.

"What is it?" Enoch asked. The woman was visibly trembling now.

"It is evil, what Shun did. Evil, what you did, too."

"Look, Jiao, I'm sorry you don't approve of what I've done for my art, or what your father did for his own purposes. Not that I ever understood all his purposes. I thought you might carry on in his footsteps. If I was mistaken, and you'd rather not sell me any of the materials from this cabinet, then I'll go."

"Now I understand everything," Jiao said as if she hadn't heard him, sounding close to tears. "Now I know what went wrong."

"What are you talking about?"

"I should show you. Come with me."

"Where are we going?"

Jiao pointed above her. "Upstairs."

III

The apartment upstairs, when Jiao had unlocked it and let him inside, proved even gloomier than the one below, but as if to compensate for this there were other stimuli to assail Enoch's senses. A profound heightening of the odd, unpleasant odors he had detected downstairs, and a distant, pitiful moaning. He supposed it *might be* a human being making that sound.

Jiao led him through the apartment, and he shuffled along carefully lest he bump his shins or trip in the dark. The moaning, increasing in volume though still muffled, seemed to guide them. Were there garbled words? Why was the voice so horribly, inhumanly *wet*-sounding?

They came to a short hallway, and Jiao positioned herself to one side of a closed door, into the wood of which a narrow horizontal gap had been sawed out, at face level. Enoch noted another modification to the door: a hasp screwed into the wood, so that the door could be padlocked from the outside.

In the murk, he couldn't make out Jiao's face as much more than a ghostly smear, but Enoch felt the weight of her stare. "Look inside," she told him in a flat voice.

As if reluctant to turn his back to her, Enoch hesitated, but then moved to the slit cut into the door. Warily, he leaned his face close to it. He held his breath against the stench.

The small chamber was no doubt intended as a bedroom, though it was empty of furnishings aside from a bare mattress on the floor. Boards had been nailed over the single window, so that only a few chinks of light penetrated the gloom. But as Enoch peered at a pale, indistinct shape sprawled on the mattress, his eyes became a bit more acclimated. And as if the shape on the mattress had just awoken and seen his eyes at the slit in the door, it suddenly stirred with weird, agitated movements.

"Good Lord," Enoch muttered.

The thing that rose up, as best it could, from the foul mattress was without clothing, and Enoch wasn't sure if he was grateful for the darkness that obscured the thing's form, or more unnerved by the fact that he couldn't quite make sense of what he was seeing.

It should have been a human, that much was certain, but it had either been altered from that state or had never been able to achieve it. Half the chest was missing, and one arm with it, the creature so shockingly compromised that it should not even be alive. Its pelvis was askew, its legs disproportionate, one skeletal and the other a bloated knobby mass, apparently with no foot at its end. And the head … if that translucent, gelatinous blob could be called a head …

The monstrosity hobbled toward the door with a awkward limp, rushing at Enoch as if it meant to burst straight through the wood to get at him. He backed away, and a moment later it thudded into the door and rattled it in its frame. Fingers curled in the slit, but the pulpy hands were too swollen to squeeze through.

Just before backing away, Enoch had caught a glimpse of the thing's visage. Only a glimpse, and yet he had the keen eyes of an artist. That face, though it seemed to have lost one eye under a bulge of its lumpen head, was the same face from the black-and-white portrait on the altar downstairs.

"That photo I asked you about," Enoch said. "You said it was your husband. Is this creature your husband, then?"

"I lied," Jiao replied. "My husband was Shun."

Enoch switched his gaze from the fingers scrabbling in the peephole to the woman standing opposite him. "Shun wasn't your father?"

"My husband, Mr. Coffin. Over forty years ago, during the Cultural Revolution, I met a handsome young artist named Song Yi. He was a beautiful soul—nothing like my cruel husband. We fell in love. He painted me, as you have asked to do. You briefly charmed me with your request. You reminded me of him. And yes, he painted me in the nude. One day, my husband discovered this painting hidden amongst my things."

Enoch glanced toward the door. It was all coming together now. "The man in the altar photo. That was Song Yi, not Shun."

"Yes."

"So this creature, in this room … "

"Shun turned Yi over to the authorities, and after Yi was beaten to death Shun managed to steal his body. He had perfected his evil magic even then. Perhaps it was sheer spite, some malicious gratification, that inspired him to practice his arts on Yi. He reduced my lover's body down to its Essential Saltes."

"And yours, too … am I right, Jiao?"

"After he strangled me in a fit of rage, Shun told everyone I'd run off and left him. Yes, Mr. Coffin, my husband practiced his alchemy on my dead body as well. Maybe he gloated over the two bottles that contained Yi and myself, in the decades that followed."

"So how then did you become reconstituted?"

"Shun grew old, and perhaps sentimental. As he confronted his own mortality, maybe he felt guilt for what he had done to me. And so, the lonely necromancer raised his wife from the dead."

The wet, bestial voice behind its door blurted out an inarticulate cry, as if reacting to her words.

"So Shun resurrected Song Yi, as well?"

"No. He sold Song Yi, bit by bit … to *you*. I had no idea, until this day. Enough of Yi's Saltes remained that I suspected nothing when I set about resurrecting him myself. Because you see, Mr. Coffin, my husband had trained me to be his assistant herbalist. And his assistant in his demonic experiments, as well."

Enoch looked to the peephole in the door and saw one eye there peering out at him. One eye with an Asian epicanthic fold … one eye that hinted at a living, human mind somewhere behind it. An artist's eye. He could understand why the woman hadn't destroyed the abomination.

"I'm sure Shun was secretly amused selling you pinches of my lover's essence," Jiao said. "Sadistically amused. But what of you, Mr. Coffin?

Didn't you ever pause to consider your own actions?"

"My dear, I never thought that anyone would ever want to restore this man."

"Perhaps you should have entertained that possibility."

"Perhaps I should have," he allowed.

Jiao reached toward the peephole in the door, and squeezed her slim hand inside to run her fingertips along the creature's cheek. It let out a soft, pained groan. It was the first sound this being had uttered ... because the moaning Enoch had heard, and which hadn't ceased, originated behind another closed and padlocked door in the hallway. It too had a slot sawed into it.

Enoch gestured toward this second door. "And your other tenant?"

"Who do you think?"

Enoch stepped to the door and drew close to its peephole. This room too, benefitted from a few slivers of light through the boards covering its solitary window. Here too was only a soiled bare mattress on the floorboards. Here too, an uncanny pallid occupant. But this creature couldn't rise to its legs, for it had none. It dragged its abbreviated lower half after it, flopping crazily about the room on its misshapen forelimbs as if searching endlessly for a means of escape. Perhaps sensing Enoch at the slot, it whipped its head around and its noises became more plaintive. The artist recognized its wizened face, however distorted.

"Enoch!" the tortured figure gurgled in its awful voice. He could only just understand it. *"Enoch ... help me ..."*

The ruined thing crawled to the door and thumped its rudimentary, flipper-like forelimbs against the wood, but couldn't rise to the level of the peephole.

"I'm sorry, Shun," Enoch spoke through the door, "but this isn't my story. I'm afraid I'm only a customer."

"Enoch! Enoch ... help me! Help meee!"

Enoch turned back to face Jiao. "I suppose I should be going."

IV

The young man whom Jiao had left in charge of the shop in her absence rang up Enoch's purchases at the front counter. Jiao had disappeared, but just as Enoch was prepared to leave she returned to the shop from outside. In both hands she carried an object inside a plastic shopping bag. It was obviously a container of some kind. A jar.

She extended it to Enoch, and he accepted it. The beautiful woman with her mysterious, sad eyes explained, "I'm afraid I won't be able to provide you with any more Essential Saltes in the future, Mr. Coffin, but I'll give you some just this last time."

"I understand."

"Consider them a gift," she said, smiling. "With them, I think you could paint a very dark and demonic vision indeed, if that's what suits you."

"Whose are they?" he asked, though he knew he didn't need to.

"Unused bits of my beloved husband, of course."

Returning to the North End of Boston on the Orange Line that evening, munching some flaky pastries filled with lotus seed paste from the *Hing Shing Pastry* bakery—and with the jar of Saltes in his knapsack with his other prizes—Enoch Coffin felt regret indeed that his favorite apothecary would no longer make available to him the rarest of the ingredients he favored for his customized paints. But even more, perhaps, he regretted that he had not been able to bring himself to make a request of the apothecary's new proprietor.

He had little doubt she would have denied him, yet still he wished he had asked her if he could come back to her home in the future, in order to paint two portraits.

As striking as Jiao was herself, Enoch's interest had shifted to two other models even more unique, more remarkable, more in agreement with his taste in subject matter.

But then, Shun's establishment had always been a source of terrible wonders—and one person's tragic horrors are another person's exquisite things.

Impossible Color

I

Enoch Coffin accepted that he must suffer for his art. He also accepted that sometimes other people must suffer for his art, as well.

Though Trent was an exceedingly handsome young man, with a thick mop of dirty-blond hair spilling across his eyes, Enoch had him posed nude in the most grotesque of positions, looking like a gargoyle struggling against its stony nature in the hopes of flight. Enoch had kept Trent in this pose for over an hour, as he sat in the youth's favorite armchair sketching him in charcoal. He could have finished long ago, but he was punishing the boy for his insolence. Not that he minded gazing at his uncomfortable model, either.

"I thought the idea of a sketch is that it's fast," Trent complained, without turning his head when he addressed Enoch. The last time he had moved significantly, Enoch had jumped up from the armchair and kicked him in the hindquarters.

"How would you know anything about sketching?" Enoch replied. "You, whose hand has only ever known the feel of a computer mouse?"

They were in Trent's apartment in Brookline, Massachusetts, home of the New England Institute of Art, where Trent was a student. Enoch liked downtown Brookline, with its diversity of restaurants, nice little shops and bookstores, its civilized and artistic atmosphere, but it was in Boston's Museum of Fine Arts that they had first met and struck up a conversation several months earlier. Trent's father was a successful Boston optometrist, and paid not only for his son's schooling but this comfortable apartment as well.

"I think this one's complete," Enoch sighed casually, perusing his handiwork.

"Thank God!" Trent began to rise from his twisted crouch.

"Wait! I'm starting a new one with a sanguine crayon."

"I don't think so!" Trent said, straightening up with a pained expression, as if gargoyle-like his limbs had indeed begun to ossify. "What's a sanguine crayon, anyway?"

"It's the end of the world," Enoch muttered.

"Well, do you know what vector graphics are?"

"If Goya made do without your vector graphics, I'm sure I can as well."

"I tell you, someday digital art will make paintbrushes and your sanguine crayons as obsolete as e-book readers are making physical books obsolete. Really, Enoch, I wish you'd let me show you the art program I use. I think once you got past your inhibitions, you'd be intoxicated by the possibilities."

"Inhibitions? You nasty pup—I should boot your little white ass again." Enoch set his pad and charcoal stick aside. "I don't want a computer to cross my doorway, but I've seen enough digital art and it isn't that I haven't been impressed. As in any medium, some artists are more gifted with these tools than others. But it's simply not my religion. I need paint on my hands—I want to smell it. I want to feel clay shaped between my palms. Next you'll be telling me that internet porn will make sex between two human beings obsolete."

Standing naked before the the older man, thrusting his pelvis forward as he massaged his cramped lower back, Trent smiled seductively and said, "Now that's one thing I *don't* want to become obsolete."

Enoch rose from the chair to stretch his own body. "So what are you patching together now from the ether?"

"Patching together," Trent snorted. "What I'm into now is 'forbidden colors.'"

"*Forbidden Colors*—the novel by Mishima?"

The younger artist laughed. "No. They're also called 'impossible colors.' They're colors that supposedly can't be seen under normal light conditions, because of the way our brains process information from our rods and cones, which is called the opponent process. But under certain experimental conditions that challenge this process, test subjects have been able to see colors they couldn't name—like yellow-blue. Not yellow and blue blending into green, but a color that looks both yellow and blue *at the same time.* And the same with red and green, which are two other opponent colors. Imagine a color that appears both red *and* green."

"Are you sure you're talking about real colors, and not just tricking the eye with illusion?"

"Aren't all colors illusion? Just frequencies of light ... immaterial things?"

"So you're trying to create such an impossible color on your computer?"

"Yes! It's my obsession now. Imagine being the first artist to render a work of art in colors no one has ever seen before! Maybe you can't achieve this with your old smelly oil paints, Enoch, or else it would have been done centuries ago, but with new technology why shouldn't we be able to figure out how to teach the eye to see new colors without test conditions?"

"Teach the eye? The eye is a machine. Can you teach your hand to feel scent?"

"Oh Enoch, and here I thought you were a true adventurer of the arts!"

"It's one thing to talk, brat, and another to achieve. Anyway, to me you're still talking about earthly colors. Red. Green. Red *and* green. How about a color that has nothing analogous, nothing to compare it with at all?"

"Sure, why not?" Trent agreed enthusiastically. "That too. Maybe that can be achieved. That's what I'm after."

Enoch shrugged. "Well … it is an exciting concept, certainly."

"Here, let me show you my latest test." Without bothering to don his clothing again, Trent moved to a desk upon which his computer system was set up, and leaned over it to tap at his keyboard. Enoch came to stand beside him.

On the computer's monitor, against a black background standing shoulder-to-shoulder, were two identical human silhouettes, one red and one green. Trent explained, "The red and green have to be the same brightness, and just the right opposing hues. I've been trying this with a white background, too, to see if it makes any difference. Anyway, you see that white X on their chests? Now, if you cross your eyes and combine those two Xs … "

Enoch barked a laugh. "Cross my eyes? My dear, do you really expect people to come into a gallery and cross their eyes to view a piece of art? Maybe if they stand on their head it would work even better."

Trent turned to glare at his guest. "Fuck you, Enoch. I would never laugh at any artistic project of yours. This is just a test! Maybe you're intimidated by my ambition. Or too proud to open that dusty old mind of yours."

"Pah." Enoch strode across the room, retrieved his sketch pad and his slouch hat, and fitted the latter on his head. "Cross your eyes now, my boy, and you'll see two of me leaving. But I'm afraid we're both composed of the same hues."

II

It was three months before Enoch Coffin heard from the art student again. By that time he'd put Trent out of his mind altogether, engrossed as he was in his own art projects. But then one night, while he was working on a painting in the attic studio of his narrow little house on Boston's Charter Street, Trent called. Enoch hated being disturbed while working, and always screened his calls, but when he heard Trent's excited tone he couldn't help himself. And it was the words even more than the tone that made him pick up, for what Trent had said was: "Enoch—I think I've found my impossible color!"

‡

"I've always got my antennae up," Trent said. "Always trawling the net."

"Of course. You and your precious internet."

Trent ignored the older man's disparagement; they'd been over such things before, tiresomely. "I found out about this estate sale … an eccentric old character in Swampscott named Charles Gardner. A real hoarder, but instead of hoarding piles of newspapers and worthless shit like that, this guy collected all kinds of weird antiques, rare books, artwork from obscure artists all over the world. They said his house was floor to ceiling with his treasures; there were just barely paths through it all. And what first caught my eye was that this guy's family originally came from nearby Arkham. And you know all those stories out of Arkham … "

"Some intimately," Enoch replied. He sipped the coffee Trent had served him. He liked his coffee the way he liked his lovers: varied. Today he had asked for it black.

Trent was pacing the floor of his Brookline apartment excitedly, jabbering a mile a minute as if stimulated by some drug more potent than coffee. Enoch knew the drug well. It was the muse.

Trent went on, "Well, I saw a very interesting object listed for sale so I decided to contact the agent about it, and this agent is also a local historian so she knows her stuff. It seems an ancestor of Gardner's had a pretty strange thing happen on his farm, back in 1882. A meteor—*apparently* a meteor—crashed on this farmer's land. At the core of the meteor people found a smooth sphere of a color that was, according to a contemporary newspaper account, 'almost impossible to describe.' *Hm?*" Trent smiled provocatively. "The sphere had some funny properties, such as 'attacking silicon compounds.' But the fallen object's worst property seems to have been radiation, which took its toll not only on the farmer's livestock, but on his own wife and sons as well … and eventually poisoned the poor guy himself. When locals came to investigate the deaths, they witnessed a beam of light radiate from the property's well—a beam of light of a color that was said to be an 'unfamiliar hue.'"

"Interesting," Enoch admitted.

"I guess this was one very freaky light show, and really rattled these guys. Anyway, supposedly the meteor and the strange sphere inside eventually disintegrated without a trace, and the old farmhouse is long gone. The agent told me the area where the farm stood is even today a dead plot of land where nothing will grow, and no one has ever built anything there again. Maybe that in itself isn't enough to corroborate such a story, huh? Ahh … but then there's *this*."

Trent turned toward a side table and lifted a riveted metal box, tarnished dark with age. He raised its hinged lid, and turned back toward Enoch as if offering a cigar from a humidor. Instead, what Enoch saw inside the box was a pile of glass squares.

"What are these?" he inquired.

"The farmhouse had casement windows composed of multiple small panes, as was the style back in the day. It was from this window that the witnesses watched that weird light show erupt from the dead farmer's well. Someone had the presence of mind to rescue these panes, and they got passed down into the hands of old man Gardner. Someone with an eye for the unique. Someone who understood they were a treasure worth preserving, whereas another person might have thrown them away. Even the estate sale agent, who recognized them as a historical curiosity, doesn't suspect their potential value both scientifically and, more importantly to me, artistically."

"May I?" Enoch poised a hand over the proffered box.

Trent grinned, his eyes seeming illuminated from within. "Yes, Enoch … hold one to the light. Look *through* it."

Enoch picked up the topmost square of glass, and as his host had suggested raised it to a nearby window through which glowed bright, prosaic sunlight. Trent watched his friend's handsome face, upon which the brows soon gathered and sensuous mouth turned down in a contemplative scowl. Enoch angled the glass slightly, this way then that, and next pivoted in his chair to hold the little pane up to the artificial light of a wall lamp. Again, he shifted the glass slightly to observe its subtle effects.

Trent said, "There's a kind of iridescence, isn't there? Like the oily colors in a soap bubble. It's faint, but it's there, isn't it? Imprinted on the glass somehow, the way they say lightning can etch a photograph onto glass. And glass is silica, is it not? Didn't they say that the funny globe had an odd effect on silicon? But you tell me now, Enoch. *What color is that?*"

It was as the young artist had said: the effect was delicate, but undeniable. Enoch set aside the pane to select another one, then a third. The anomalous quality was present in all of them—a subtle iridescence. But what color or colors indeed? Enoch opened his mouth as if to suggest a hue, but quickly closed it. Once again he started to speak, once again stopped himself. "I don't know," he conceded at last. "My God ... there's a ghost of color trapped in this glass, but I'll be damned if I can put a name to it. It's not related to any known color, and that's just not something you can envision with your imagination, the way you can imagine how another planet might look, and the life upon it. This is something that we've been denied, even with all the countless sights our world has to show us. It shouldn't be possible, but —"

"Yes," Trent cut him off. "*Yes.* Impossible color."

Enoch rose from his chair, and now it was his turn to pace the living room, as he again and again gazed upon the glass square he held before windows, then artificial light sources, back and forth. Having set down the metal box again, Trent watched him, and at last Enoch faced the student and said, "So what are you attempting to do with this find?"

"In regard to my art? I'm not sure yet. Just because we can see it doesn't mean we can copy this effect with paint. I've been trying to think of a way to record it somehow. Get it into my computer. Maybe find a means of scanning the glass ... or if not that, photograph the glass and—if that captures the quality—then scan the photograph. If I can't replicate the color with physical pigment, maybe I can move it onto a virtual palette."

"You have enough of these panes—you could still pursue the scientific possibilities as you pursue you art."

"Enoch, you disappoint me more and more! You, the pure old-fashioned artist, the man of personal integrity, thinking of money that could be made from this?"

"Artists do have to eat, young man; pappy can't carry you forever. Never mind that for now. You have enough of these that you can let *me* have one of them." Enoch slipped the pane into the pocket of his brown suede jacket.

"Hey!"

"Don't worry, I am indeed a man of integrity; I won't try selling your miraculous discovery myself."

"But you may find a way to incorporate it into your art before I do!"

"Me? With my primitive smelly paints? Oh I doubt it. But still, it's captured my imagination. I want to study it further. You won't deny me, will you? Perhaps I'll discover something that might even aid you in your own pursuits."

Trent sighed, then shrugged. He knew the older man was right. But also, he was just afraid enough of the odd artist Enoch Coffin that he didn't care to oppose him.

III

Before he began, Enoch propped the pane on the sill of an attic window so that sunlight might stream through it. Misty suggestions of color spread upon the worn floorboards. Dust motes swam in the beam like alien microorganisms. He stepped into this beam himself, reverently, as if into the glow through a cathedral's window. This caused him to wonder what his late father Donovon Coffin—a stained glass artisan— might have composed from pieces of this glass.

Enoch held out his artist's hands like receptive instruments that might somehow, intuitively, detect and *grasp* the proper frequency of light. He watched the pastel illumination play across the skin of his hungry appendages.

He realized it would most likely prove a fruitless—the word was *impossible*—endeavor, but with this appropriated prize as his inspiration he set out to duplicate the pane's strange tint in a conventional painting. On that first day he tried watercolors, for their translucence and delicacy, but the next afternoon he switched to oils, which he preferred. Yet both approaches resulted in the same: a compounded muddiness that was nothing like the effect trapped in the glass.

For both paintings Enoch had used the same subject matter: a stone well in a rural setting, created solely from his imagination, and in both paintings he portrayed this well in the deep of night. Uncanny light in a bright, vaporous column churned straight upward into the sky, where it bored through a ceiling of clouds and reflected upon their underbellies. The result in each rendering was not unlike the erupting mushroom cloud of a nuclear explosion, and was all the more ominous for that. They were not at all a bad pair of paintings ... they just didn't reveal anything like the color he was attempting to replicate.

That hue was so elusive in the glass's faint tint—what he wouldn't give to see it in greater, purer intensity! The thought drove him on in his frustrating attempts, and it was this that leant more power to the scene in the oil painting, which he kept working at stubbornly. For dramatic effect Enoch ended up adding sinister trees with their leaves all burnt to ash and the ends of their denuded branches sheathed in glowing luminescence. Branches that appeared to have become sentient, reaching futilely toward the sky as if to hold onto that nameless force, as it returned to the cosmos from which it had plummeted like the essence of Lucifer.

Eerie green phosphorescence like luminous rot, glowing on the grass around the well and the underbellies of those clouds ...

No!

A blue phosphorescence, then ...

No!

An orange kind of glow ... a purple and orange kind of glow ...

No and no. Failure and failure. In the end he could only concentrate on the setting itself. His uncanny pillar of light was a cheat ... green blending into blue into purple into orange. All terrestrial colors. Never had the limits of his art shackled and chafed him so. Illusion and lies, that was all he was good at, and not so good after all. In the end he flung his mess of a palette away from him in self loathing.

IV

On the third day following their last encounter, Trent phoned Enoch and they compared notes. Enoch reluctantly described his frustrations with his twin paintings, expecting Trent to use this as fuel to criticize Enoch's outdated artistic methods, but the younger man actually expressed keen interest in having a look at the art when he had a chance. "It sounds like your intuitions are attuned to the scene," Trent remarked, "if not the color. Myself, I've tried photographing the glass with my digital camera, then moving the pictures into my art software and stealing the color with cloning, adding it to a custom palette, other techniques ... but they all seem to lose something in translation. The color either disappears altogether or get changed into other colors, from the common spectrum."

"Maybe what we're seeing is a head trick ... a mirage ..."

"Oh Enoch, that we're failing to capture this phenomenon doesn't mean it doesn't exist! We have to be more humble than that."

"If we were humble we'd never be trying to reproduce this color in the first place."

"Well, if lightning can make pictures, then we can do it. What are we if not bundles of lightning in bags of skin?"

Enoch smiled at the phone. "Sometimes I remember why I decided to be friends with you."

"I'm flattered. Well, anyway, my father is working on something for me that might broaden my artistic vision."

"Your father?"

"You shall see, when it's ready ... you shall see."

‡

The next day, Enoch mounted the steps to the attic with uncertainty as to what he might do next to approach the matter of the otherworldly color. He was reluctant to concede defeat, though, as long as he knew the younger artist was still pursuing his own methods. The pane beckoned yet taunted him, like a glass microscope slide containing a species of life that had yet to be identified. As he reached for the door to his studio, he wondered if there were some type of photoreactive paper that he might spread on the floor in the projected beam from the pane, which might accept a transfer of the color. Not a way to work freely with the color, perhaps, but a start along the path of directing and controlling it.

As it turned out, he found his daunting challenge had already been dismissed for him. He was certain he had left the small square pane leaning on the window sill. Now it was gone. When he approached the window, all he discovered was a fine sprinkling of glittering dust on the sill and partly spilled onto the floorboards.

Within minutes, Enoch was calling Trent in Brookline. But the student didn't pick up. Was he attending class? Enoch left a message for him.

"My boy, I suspect there was good reason your eccentric old man

Gardner kept the panes in that metal box, which I further suspect might be made of lead. I just found my sample of glass reduced to dust. I'm not lying, if you find that hard to swallow. I don't know if it was exposure to light, or the air, or what else that might account for this, but I remind you of the story of the meteor you related, and the sphere within it. You told me after a time both of them dissolved, leaving nothing behind."

A beep, as the allotted message time ran out. Enoch set down the phone and turned to contemplate the sparkling dust. Each grain seemed to trap a particle of weird light as its nucleus. Though he had handled the pane by its edges quite a bit, he was now reluctant to make contact with its possibly irradiated remains. He swept up the dust carefully, poured it into an empty pill bottle of light-resistant brown plastic, sealed that in an airtight sandwich bag, and stored the package away in a dark drawer.

Later that afternoon he called Trent again. When there was no answer, he chose not to leave a second message. But Trent still didn't pick up his phone when Enoch tried two more times that evening.

Several days passed silently and Enoch didn't attempt phoning Trent again. Either the young artist was making no progress and didn't want to talk about it, or making progress and hoarding his discoveries jealously. Enoch wasn't one for collaboration—his vision was too personal, his ego too great—so he didn't care much one way or the other. He wasn't going to beg for attention like the pathetic needy creatures that often haunted his own privacy, so he engrossed himself in his various ongoing projects.

Then, one night in the wee hours, a call came. Enoch was still awake, not at all unusually, in his attic bent over his scarred old work table. With a palette knife he had scooped some gel medium, used in conjunction with acrylic paints, from a container and spread it on a small canvas panel. The gel was thick but would dry clear. He made a little concavity with the knife in the center of the goop, then into this hollow he poured the fine grit of a drinking glass that he had smashed with a hammer after he'd wrapped it in an old towel. He then mixed the granules throughout the gel evenly and spread it across the panel to gauge its texture, and so that he might gauge the effect when it dried.

The call interrupted him in the midst of this experiment, but when he heard Trent's voice he picked up. He almost didn't recognize that voice at first, however, and he couldn't make out the words. The student sounded drunk perhaps, his voice slurred, weak and hoarse.

"So," Enoch sneered into the phone, "it deigns to call me at last, talking in its sleep."

"Yes, sleep," croaked the distant, strained voice. "We are all asleep. Our eyes are closed. We do not see."

"And I do not see what you're babbling about."

"Even as you sit there in your loft listening to me now, you don't see the aura your body emanates, Enoch. Not the way I am seeing my own aura at this moment. Like me, fire laps from your skin, flutters and coruscates, twines around your limbs like spectral eels, in ever-changing colors that have no words to label them in any human tongue. Everywhere in your loft, every object organic or inorganic gives off a different aura of different hue. Those old dead floorboards are awash in a glow that even were they gilded would not compare! An ant on your floor is an iridescent scarab to bring tears to one's eyes! But you of course are the source of most of this glorious light, this terrible color. I know, as even now I wave my hand in the air before my face, and watch the swaths and ribbons it weaves in its wake. To think that you and I sought to paint these impossible colors upon canvas! We are painting these colors upon the air with every step we take! Flames billow from your mouth with every word and breath! Beams flare from those gorgeous eyes of yours! And around your head, in a corona, in a halo: rippling colors to put an aurora borealis to shame!"

At first Enoch thought his friend was merely ranting, but the more he listened the more his instincts told him Trent was speaking the truth, if only the truth of madness. "What have you discovered?" he demanded.

"Too much," that whispery voice rasped. "Isn't that the way? When Icarus touched the blaze of the sun?"

"Tell me what you've learned and stop waxing poetic."

"When you and I cease waxing poetic we will both cease to be. Our flame will have extinguished."

"I'll come see you in the morning."

"You left a message that your piece of glass disintegrated?"

"More or less."

"That's good, Enoch. It's better that way, my friend."

"And yours?" No answer. "And yours, Trent? Hello?"

"No. I keep them in their Pandora's box."

"I'm tired of your vague and suggestive talk. I want to come see you right now."

"The trains aren't running now, Enoch."

"I have my crappy old pickup truck."

"Are you concerned for me or just curious about what I've seen?"

"Both. I'm coming."

"If you must. When you get here, let yourself in. The door is unlocked."

V

It was an hour like purgatory, the streets of Brookline all but deserted, and Enoch parked the beat-up pickup truck he drove when he had to in a free spot a little distant from Trent's apartment building, walking the rest of the way. His clomping footsteps had a lonely resonance.

He found the apartment unlocked as promised, but inside it was unlit as well. He made his way into the living room carefully, reaching out his receptive hands in front of him and trying not to trip or bump into anything, eventually following a feeble glow of flickering light. He found Trent sunk back in his favorite armchair, with several candles burning on surfaces around him. One candle stood beside the familiar riveted metal box.

"Oh, look at you!" exclaimed the shadowy seated figure, in a ghostly choked voice. "How you *burn!* And to think I once found your eyes beautiful when they were merely blue!"

"Can I put on a light?"

"I'd rather you didn't. I don't think I could stand it."

Enoch stood over his friend. Though the gloom was thick and cloaked the young man, candlelight was reflected in the lenses of a pair of spectacles he wore. Enoch had never known Trent to wear glasses before—and certainly not glasses with lenses that flashed with such remarkable color.

"The special aid you directed your father the optometrist to fashion for you," Enoch observed.

"Yes, and they broadened my artistic vision as I had hoped ... and then some. I'm sorry I can't bequeath them to you, my friend. I can't do that to you."

"What do you mean?"

"I told my parents I was going away to visit a friend for a while, so they wouldn't come here and see me this way. I don't want them to find these glasses. I don't want my father to look through them again. I'm glad you did come tonight, Enoch. Please, you must promise me something."

"Promise you what?"

"You must swear to me, as my friend, swear as a man of integrity, that you will smash to tiny bits every pane of glass in that lead box. And when you've done that, you must promise me you'll smash these spectacles, too."

Enoch Coffin was silent for several long moments, but at last said, "If that's your wish, then I promise you."

Did he see a black crescent open in the vague, pale smudge of a face? "Thank you, dear friend."

"But what's wrong with you? What's happened?"

"What happened to old man Gardner's ancestor, and his wife, and his sons? The color demands a high price for its glory. You're familiar with many an old frightening tome, aren't you? So you must know the Bible."

"It's not my favorite frightening tome."

"I shouldn't think so," Trent hissed, his wispy voice fainter by the second. "But therein it says, 'The sun was risen upon the earth when Lot entered into Zoar. Then the Lord rained upon Sodom and upon Gomorrah brimstone and fire from the Lord out of heaven; And he overthrew those cities, and all the plain, and all the inhabitants of the cities, and that which grew upon the ground. But his wife looked back from behind him, and she became a pillar of salt.'"

Enoch nodded solemnly. "I understand."

Trent didn't add comment to that, to acknowledge that Enoch gleaned what was happening. Several more drawn-out moments ticked past, in which Enoch found himself mesmerized by the light dancing in the lenses Trent wore. At last, he stepped forward to cross the remaining distance between them, and reached out to remove the spectacles from that shadowy visage.

Briefly, when he pulled the glasses away, two hollow pits were revealed behind them, black tunnels bored far back into the student's skull. Enoch thought he heard a final sigh ... and then the top half of Trent's head collapsed and crumpled down into the hollow of the lower half. Enoch stepped back, still holding the spectacles. He heard more than saw the rest of the disintegration, rustling sounds like sifting sand. Some larger bits thumped softly onto the floor.

VI

Enoch kept his word. When he brought the heavy lead box of little window panes to his house in the North End, he smashed every one of them, pulverized them to a fine powder. The lenses of the spectacles, too.

Then he mixed these glittering, weirdly incandescent granules into the gel medium, and began a new painting depicting the scene at the well. Normally he didn't care for acrylic paints, which he felt didn't blend as well as oils and dried too quickly for his taste, but in this instance owing to his use of the gel medium it was the right choice.

Again he portrayed a night scene, twisted trees straining to grope at the cosmos, light rushing up from the old stone well in a soundless volcanic blast. But instead of blending terrestrial colors to hint at this unearthly light, he used the gel, which would dry clear but prove a binding medium for the countless scintillating particles of glass, each like the cell of a body that could not be fully comprehended with the puny, reptilian human brain.

He would not be able to show this painting for very long at any one time, if he hoped to preserve it. Private showings, then, never a public exhibit. Any long exposure might be detrimental to the painting ... and the viewer as well.

He experienced a deep gratification that he had succeeded in besting the challenge, though a bit of guilt for feeling triumphant where Trent had failed. Well, in a sense it had been a collaborative effort, much as Enoch normally avoided such.

He had painted this scene on a much smaller canvas than usual. One that could fit inside a riveted metal box.

Shadow Puppets

I

Enoch Coffin had met some of these artists before—unfortunately. He even recognized some of the attendees who were not artists, from other exhibitions, including his own. This being the case, he was forced to put up with much small talk before the night's event. Repeatedly he was asked what project or projects he was currently pursuing himself. He fended off most of these questions very quickly, as they were largely just obligatory politeness, though he did converse more at length with a few individuals who seemed to hold a sincere interest in his work.

An aged woman with more paint on her face than some of Enoch's canvases, who had been listening in on his conversation with one of the more tolerable guests, cut in with the admiring comment, "Young man, you put me in mind of that actor … hm … he was in Stone's film *Platoon*."

"Gawd, not that Sheen person, I should hope," Enoch said dryly, raising his wine glass to his lips.

"No, no … another character in that one."

"Must be that scar-faced bastard you're thinking of," said a voice behind Enoch.

He turned toward the speaker, and molded his lips into another of tonight's artificial smiles. "Ah, hello, Dane. The man of the hour."

This evening Dane van der Sloot was artist, gallery owner, and host all in one, the venue being his own home in Bar Harbor, Maine. Enoch didn't think Dane's income as an artist could account for the impressive house; he'd heard the man was a widower, his wealthy wife having perished in a freak accident a few years back, her heart apparently having given out when she made the odd decision to swim in the chilly waters off Acadia National Park's Sand Beach, late one summer evening. Odd, because later her family had insisted the woman had never learned to swim.

"Enoch," Dane said with a nod. "Frankly I'm surprised that you accepted my invitation and came all this way. I feared you'd decline, but thought I'd give it a shot anyway. I'm glad I did ... thank you."

"Mr. Coffin has traveled the world," said the person he had been conversing with. "Maine isn't all that far from Massachusetts—true?"

It was far enough when one's vehicle—in this case Enoch's battered old pickup—was of dubious reliability, but he didn't care to divulge such personal details. Enoch replied, "It's a beautiful area. I've been to Acadia National Park in the past."

Enoch didn't add, though it might be implied, that he wouldn't have driven six hours (not counting rest stops) for Dane's show alone. September was a lovely time of year in Maine, offering a balance of golden warmth and invigorating chill, and past the high tourist season of summer. Still, even now from the pink granite summit of Cadillac Mountain one could count on spotting some large cruise ship or other prowling amongst the Porcupine Islands, their shaggy humps suggesting the backs of a pod of great aquatic animals. Thus, the streets of quaint Bar Harbor would be filled with tourists from the UK and elsewhere. Enoch had detected a British accent or two among tonight's attendees of Dane's art presentation.

"Why do you work from Maine, if I might ask?" the painted grande dame asked Dane, now running her wine-lubricated gaze up and down his tall frame, garbed in a crisp black suit and black turtleneck. "Why not someplace more ... sophisticated, like New York?"

"Well, I'm from this state originally, my dear," Dane replied with patient good cheer. "But I did pursue my career in New York for many a year, actually … before they kicked me out." He laughed to show he was joking, though Enoch knew it was not entirely a joke. "I decided to return to my roots. Where else in the world—and I ask you this, Enoch, you being the great world traveler and all—where else can one encounter such a perfect marriage of forest, mountain, and ocean? It's like a magnificent nexus point of all the elemental power Nature could devise. The forces of Earth are pure here, resources just waiting to be tapped into. I am here precisely because it is the antithesis of New York, or Mr. Coffin's own Boston."

"But most of the art scene here," the woman continued, with a bright red sneer, "seems to consist mainly of lobsters and lighthouses painted on wooden plaques for tourists in Bermuda shorts."

"All the more reason for me to be here!" Dane exclaimed, clapping his large hands together. "To enlighten!"

"But you're preaching to the choir, aren't you, Dane?" Enoch couldn't resist commenting. "This showing isn't open to the general public. It's by special invitation only, so I'd say you must feel we honored guests are already sufficiently enlightened to appreciate whatever it is you plan to reveal to us tonight."

"Enoch," Dane returned, his eyes glimmering, "there is always room for further enlightenment."

"I see. Very well." Enoch spread his hands. "I await epiphany, then."

"Oh, I think you'll find this right up your dark alley, Enoch. We aren't all that different, you and I, even if I did overhear that you once rather ungenerously referred to me as a 'sad aging goth' and a 'cruel and pretentious boor.'"

The grande dame looked to Enoch with a stifled gasp, as if expecting a fist fight to break out.

Enoch wasn't about to deny or apologize for his words, so he smiled, sipped his wine again, and said, "A boor perhaps, Dane, but never boring."

"I'll accept that as a compliment of sorts, Enoch. But do you still consider me cruel? Isn't Nature itself cruel?"

The man was undoubtedly cruel, even by Enoch's standards, and it was his trouble with animal rights groups and the law that had chased the artist out of New York state as much as any tree-hugging impulse. Even while in New York, Dane's work had often ostensibly addressed Nature as a theme. The trouble had come from using living things as part of his mixed media. A typical piece would be *The Game of Life and Death*, a glass labyrinth containing a single white mouse and a large starved rat, an interactive artwork in which two attendees of the exhibit would slide open or lower in place any variety of partitions, as would benefit the animal they had chosen as their avatar. In *Ouroboros*, a snake with a live mouse fastened securely to its tail would thus swallow its own tail, finally expiring as a tightened O. Fish, birds, lobsters, and ultimately cats all factored into his artworks. Those who vehemently protested Dane's work had asked when he would move on to placing human babies in his glass tanks.

"Well," Enoch responded, "it's curious to comment on the suffering to be found in the world, by inflicting suffering yourself."

"Ah, so you came all this way simply to judge me and feel superior. I see. We've had a bit of a competitive relationship, haven't we, you and I? Especially since I began my studies of the occult. I think you felt threatened then, as if you feared I had entered into your own territory … and might outdo you."

"I understood you were delving into esoteric knowledge, Dane, but I've never seen it manifested in your … *art*." Enoch placed a derogatory accent on the word "art."

"Ah, but tonight you will see my new body of work." Dane pushed back his sleeve to glance at a wristwatch with a black face. "And I had better get ready … the show is about to start."

II

The title of Dane's presentation was *Shadow Play*, and the reference to "play" made Enoch wonder if this were to be a performance art type of thing. So far no physical art was on display other than the house's customary collection. The group of attendees had assembled at the circumference of a large room with not a stick of furniture nor a stitch of rug upon its honey-hued floorboards. It would take up too much space for them all to sit down, so they stood in a tight ring close to the equally barren walls. Enoch thought of the O of the dead snake in *Ouroboros*, and wondered playfully if glass walls might appear out of nowhere as a result of Dane's outré studies, trapping all his guests and making them into the artwork themselves.

At least *that* Enoch might have to applaud.

Dane emerged from a curtained doorway, pushing a wheeled cart covered with a black cloth toward the center of the room. He was not only dressed all in black, but wearing black eyeliner. Enoch muttered to the person beside him, "The eternal goth. Embrace what you are, I guess. Maybe he's finally ready to be honest with himself, and his art."

"Shh!" the person shushed him, watching their host raptly.

"Hmph," Enoch grunted, refocusing on Dane as the man swept the black silk cloth from the cart like a magician unveiling some cheap illusion.

Sitting atop the cart was a good-sized glass fish tank with an open top. Instead of containing water, however, it was filled to the brim with what appeared to be an opaque fluid, black as India ink.

Then Dane swept one hand above the tank, tracing strange symbols in the air. It might seem to the others a theatrical, even ridiculous bit of showmanship, but Enoch recognized one or two of the symbols the artist formed. They were sigils of conjuration ... one of them representing the "Dragon's Head," or "ascending node."

Turning slowly as he spoke, so that his eyes might sweep the faces of all gathered around him, the showman intoned, "Are we ape or apex? We are told we should be humble in the face of the Creator, but the Creator is Nature, and humans are the pinnacle of natural creation. Though we started from humble origins ..."

A flourish of his hand, and the concentrated black fluid resting in the aquarium shot upwards, hovering in the air. In a mere blink, the inky matter spread outward, became a pulsing elongated shape with a single whip-like appendage. Enoch thought of it as a giant protozoan.

Oohs and aahs from the audience. Dane continued. "Nature flexed her muscles, tested new forms, squeezed them from the air with her sheer force of will."

The pulsing shape elongated further, coiled in the air now as a gigantic segmented worm. Around him, Enoch was aware that some people were cringing, recoiling, even shifting behind others in fear. He noted now that the floating, pliable black substance held an iridescence like oil.

"Nature realized she was God," Dane said, "and she found she had a taste for godhood."

The shape altered, took on the appearance of a man-sized fish swimming in place, but remained entirely black. Even its eyes—mere representations. Enoch had recognized this material already for what it was, and knew that its own eyes if they were to manifest would be glowing greenish orbs.

Unconsciously he rubbed at an odd tickling sensation on his right arm, that originated down deep in his nerves.

Dane prattled on, but Enoch doubted the others were listening any more closely than he was. They all watched in awe, confusion, and anxiety as the levitating black matter changed form repeatedly. Each time Dane made some odd gestures to command or direct it. The fish developed legs and became an oversized replica of a frog, right down to its throbbing throat sack, though none of these animal manifestations uttered a peep. The frog transformed into a lizard, black as a silhouette or a sharply defined shadow, then the lizard into a rat with a furry coat— each hair an extrusion of that obsidian substance. The rat became a monkey, appearing to sit on its haunches in midair.

It didn't take a genius to see where this was headed.

"Then Nature," said Dane, "made Man in her own image. Because *all* life is her own image. She shaped us … and now with the power she gave us, we shape her. Shape all aspects of this world. We are Nature! We are the Creator!" He wove a mystical sign in the air beside the monkey, like a conductor dramatically orchestrating a crescendo. "*I* am the Creator!"

The strange niggling sensation in Enoch's flesh had become a real distraction, and even as he starting rolling up his right sleeve to reveal the spot he realized what was happening. *Of course!*

Recently he had been to Innsmouth, Massachusetts. There, in an impulsive artistic mood, he had used his switchblade knife to open an old wound in his arm, a scar that formed a cryptic symbol. One of the locals—her lineage not entirely human, and thus versed in the arcane herself—had used a tiny portion of shoggoth matter to heal the wound, leaving a black mole upon his skin there.

Shoggoth matter. It was reacting to the proximity of Dane's living clay, which was undoubtedly a shoggoth under his enchantment. Shoggoths … the army of the Deep Ones. The servants of the otherworldly Elder Things, servants that Enoch had read had ultimately turned against their masters and annihilated them. And here was Dane, only a fairly recent explorer into esoteric arts, daring to exert his mastery over one of those terrible entities!

By now Enoch had rolled up his sleeve enough to discover more than a mole. The raised black spot had extruded a tiny, thin tendril that wavered in the air, as if reaching out to the levitating, morphing blob.

Dane's gestures caught Enoch's attention, and he looked up to find the artist repeating the same motions again and again. And yet, the shoggoth suddenly seemed disinclined to obey him. The monkey had not become a human, which was obviously the intended climax of the performance. In fact, the monkey's shape was growing unstable, corrupted, as weird and disturbing distortions pulsated across its body. It twitched with terrible spasms, its tail flicking as if it were being electrocuted.

The hair-like growth reaching from Enoch's arm, unnoticed by any but himself, was making similar erratic movements.

On a sudden impulse—an instinctive impulse, as if another force controlled his body—Enoch stepped forward and waved his right arm in the air, tracing a sigil of his own. It was the "Dragon's Tail," or "descending node." A banishment.

Instantly heeding his command, the shoggoth lost its tortured form and dropped down into the glass fish tank from which it had risen. Once more at rest, it again appeared as a benign black fluid.

Dane glared at Enoch, looking ready to burst into convulsions himself as he fought to suppress his rage, but he covered the aquarium with the black silk cloth again, and in a strained voice improvised some concluding words.

"And what is Nature's ultimate form—the apex of her genius? Need I show you, dear friends? You need only turn to look at the person standing beside you. Or you need only look at me. *We* are the climax of this presentation, my friends ... you, and I."

With that, he turned to push the wagon toward the curtained doorway, while his audience—freed from their stunned state, and probably relieved that his incomprehensible black putty was being removed—burst into wild applause.

III

A short time later Dane took Enoch aside in the kitchen, and in a low voice growled, "Were you trying to make me look like a fool? Steal my thunder, Enoch? I wasn't finished ... you cut me off right at my fucking climax! You interfered in my art!"

"Are you mad? You didn't see what was happening? Your pet was rebelling."

"Yes! Because you were commanding it to resist me!"

Not consciously, Enoch wanted to say, but he didn't care to reveal the truth about the shoggoth tissue wed to his own flesh. He only said, "Nonsense—it chose to disobey you. Luckily I've been at this longer and broke down its will. You should thank me for that; there's no telling what that thing might have done in a few minutes more."

"I've never experienced any trouble like this until you came here."

"Per your invitation," Enoch reminded him.

"You were competing with me!" Dane persisted. "Trying to show me up at my own presentation!"

"What are you talking about? It's you who's trying to compete with me—that's why you asked me here. To show off. To show *me* up. Anyway, don't worry; I'm sure no one but you understands what I did, any more than they understand the nature of your parlor tricks. But I'll tell you, Dane … you might get off on playing God, but you are in way over your head with this creature. Even with my knowledge I'd never try to master a shoggoth!"

Two other guests drifted into the kitchen at that point. In a more composed tone, Dane asked Enoch to stay on after the others had left. Enoch didn't care to be alone in that house with the artist and his familiar, though, so he made excuses about being overtired and needing to get to bed.

"Are you staying here in Bar Harbor?" Dane asked.

"No," Enoch thought it prudent to lie, "I took a motel room in Ellsworth. It was cheaper."

"Meet me for breakfast tomorrow, will you?" Dane persisted, some of his polished charm having returned, at least on the surface.

Enoch consented, curious to understand how Dane had summoned this entity.

And so, as agreed upon, the next morning the two artists sat across from each other in a nice little spot in downtown Bar Harbor, both with blueberry pancakes in front of them. Attired all in black as always, and with his hair gelled into careful disarray, Dane revealed, "I have a friend at the College of the Atlantic here in town. Hurricane Irene didn't do too much damage up this way last month, not like Vermont saw, but after the storm some odd debris had washed ashore on one of the Porcupine Islands. It was spotted from a boat, and so my friend and other researchers from the college went in to investigate. They thought it was going to be a whale carcass. Well, have you ever heard those stories about mysterious 'globsters,' as they're called? Blob-like rotting bodies that wash up and sometimes go unidentified?"

"You mean to suggest those are shoggoths?"

"Well, this one was. It was huge. My friend showed me pictures. You don't think I could manage to control a healthy, full-sized shoggoth, do you? What I have is the living tissue that my friend excised from the hulk before the rest of it decomposed, broke down without leaving a trace. Why it sickened in the first place, we may never know."

"You and your friend are close enough that he knew this thing might appeal to you?"

"*She*," Dane corrected, "and yes, we are. Close enough that she would accept a generous payment for the sample she salvaged, and for claiming to her superiors that *all* of the mysterious globster disintegrated."

"So it's only been a month since you learned how to command that thing, and devised your performance?"

"Strike while the iron is hot, I say. Who can tell when the fragment of the creature I own might also sicken and die?"

"Or regenerate to full size," Enoch warned.

"Coffin, you're just jealous that I'm doing this and you aren't. Look, I know you despise me. But even you have to admit that I've achieved brilliant results controlling this creature, without the use of telepathy as some of their masters are alleged to have employed."

"I won't say I'm not impressed. And whether I despise you or not, it doesn't mean I want to see that thing twist your head off. I'll have you know that's said to be their signature means of killing."

"Yes, yes," Dane waved at the air, "I've read all that." He sipped his coffee, eyeing Enoch intensely over the rim of his mug. When he set it down, he said, "I still think that you sabotaged my work last night."

Enoch sighed and wagged his head. "Look, as I say, your audience has no idea your performance wasn't meant to end the way it did, and you can always stage more of your ... shoggoth art down the road."

"Oh, you can be assured I'm not done with my little pet. But you can also be assured you won't be appearing at any future presentations of mine. You can deny it all you like, but I'm sure you caused the beast to become recalcitrant, and then you made a grand gesture of saving the day by banishing it back to its container. Bravo, Enoch, bravo." He clapped his hands. "Perhaps we should simply become collaborators, hm?"

"Dane, I'm telling you, it's dangerous thinking to believe I caused the creature to become uncooperative."

"Of course you'd try to dissuade me, being so afraid that I'll outshine you, and all."

"Gawd, you think you matter so much to me, but I'm done wasting my time on you, believe me. I'm going to enjoy my stay a few days longer and leave you to your own devices. You can take all the chances you like—though I pity the people around you. I hope a week from now I don't see newspaper reports of a whole troop of vengeful protoplasmic monsters emerging from the sea to reclaim their lost sibling." Enoch forked the last bit of pancake into his mouth, washed it down with a final sip of coffee, and dug out his wallet to pay for their meal. "Now, if you'll excuse me I'll take my leave. Good luck to you, Dane. I'd watch out, if I were you."

Dane nodded, smiled, and said, "You might want to watch out, too, Enoch."

IV

That afternoon Enoch drove his pickup into Acadia National Park and left it in a parking lot, walked down to Jordan Pond with its lovely view of the humped twin mountains called the Bubbles, then went on to the Jordan Pond House restaurant, where he sat out on the lawn drinking more coffee and enjoying the popovers the place was famous for. While partaking of this light lunch he wrote notes to friends on several postcards he'd bought in the restaurant's adjacent gift shop. When he was finished, he decided he'd like to hike some more, so he continued along the trail that looped the water's edge, slouch hat clamped on his head and walking stick in hand.

Afternoon advanced, the lowering light slanting in through the trees in dazzling fragments, the air refreshingly brisk. Enoch had hiked a good distance, and thought it best to pick up the pace so as to return to his vehicle and leave the park for his bed and breakfast in Bar Harbor, not wanting to be out in a pitch black forest when evening fell. He wasn't sure how prevalent they were or where they were dispersed, but he'd heard there were black bears and bobcats within the park's limits.

Because day was on the wane he encountered fewer people; now, only one couple walking in the opposite direction, and one pair of bicycles shot past him. Even still, several times he was compelled to stop where the trees thinned at the pond's edge, and admire the thousands of small fish that seemed to hang suspended in the clear, clean water.

On one of these occasions when he turned to gaze into the pond, he caught a glimpse of a larger dark form passing below the surface, but decided it must only be a dense shoal of those little fish, or a distortion of the shifting water. He had had the impression of a shark cruising along, but that was impossible in land-locked Jordan Pond.

The artist had walked a bit further on when a burbling disturbance of the water to his side actually startled him, and caused him to stop and study it again. The splashing eruption quickly subsided, but it left him unsettled ... until he realized that this unsettling feeling also had to do with the tickling sensation deep within his right forearm.

Enoch swiftly rolled back his sleeve to see that the black alien matter fused with his flesh had once again extended a tendril, which wiggled in the air like a hair-thin finger—pointing toward the water of Jordan Pond.

"That bastard," Enoch murmured, turning away and hastening his pace along the trail even more. Black bears and bobcats were now the least of his worries.

Ahead of Enoch, from behind a tree, a man stepped onto the trail directly in his path.

With evening imminent, the figure was merely a silhouette, but Enoch knew that tall frame, the sharp shoulders of its expensive black suit, the post-goth spiky hair.

"Sorry, Dane, but I forgot my six guns today," Enoch said. "Or do you care to duel with paintbrushes?"

The figure did not answer with words. There was, however, another kind of response. A green orb of light opened in the center of its chest. A moment later, several others surfaced across the shadowy form. More and more followed. And yet the figure had not advanced ... yet.

"So Dane wanted me to see the intended ending of his show, eh?" Enoch said to the phantom. "His self-portrait. And it's a fitting one—as black as his tiny soul."

Now, at last, the human-like outline took a step forward, but when Enoch raised his walking stick before him it stopped in its tracks.

"Be gone, poor creature," he commanded, using the walking stick like a sorcerer's staff to draw a series of runes in the air, including that which conveyed the "Dragon's Tail." "You don't really have any beef with me. I'm not the one who's enslaved and degraded you, and you know it."

Enoch was certain that the shoggoth cells wired into his own substance added to the potency he needed. And sure enough, the green eyes glowing like a constellation of fungous stars upon the surface of the figure one by one blinked out of existence. Then the featureless obsidian figure turned and dashed into the forest, rather than return to the water of the pond. In the deepening gloom, it instantly slipped from view.

V

The following evening, in the Bangor Daily News, Enoch read that local artist Dane van der Sloot had been discovered dead in his home by a female friend who worked as a researcher at the College of the Atlantic. Nothing had been stolen, apparently, but the home was found in great disorder as if a desperate struggle had taken place from room to room. The artist had been beheaded, but the details of this matter were not divulged, except to say that his head had not yet been recovered.

"Oh how terribly predictable," Enoch sighed, folding the paper away and reclining on the comfy mattress in his room at the bed and breakfast. "You should have admitted it, you sad fool; you just can't compete with me."

After the threat that Dane had directed at him in the park, he felt no sympathy for the artist's fate. In fact, he would have gladly paid admission to attend Dane's final performance: scurrying about his beautiful house like a small white mouse pursued by a starving rat.

Fearless Symmetry

I

(From the personal journal of Enoch Donovon Coffin)

I was not at all pleased when the journalist from the monthly Boston arts scene magazine—covering my little exhibition—gave a smarmy smile as he suggested that I was patterning myself after Richard Upton Pickman.

The gallery in question is a wee thing located in the narrow brick chasm that is one-way Prince Street, in Boston's North End ... just a few small rooms that were once an apartment, their walls painted cream and the floorboards polished to an amber gloss. The gallery owner also owns the Italian restaurant next door, needless to say one of numerous in this neighborhood. I frequent her eatery and her art showings alike, and she has taken a shine to me; hence the invitation to exhibit my own work. She also offered to hang my paintings on the walls of her restaurant—that is, until she viewed my art for the first time and wisely decided against that concept, lest she discourage her clientele's appetite. She's a cute enough little dumpling, but doesn't stir my own appetites.

The young reporter had given his name as Joel Knox, and in answer to his comment—or accusation—I said, "Certainly I have been *inspired* by that artist. But if I've patterned myself after him, then you must also say I've patterned myself after Bosch, Bruegel, Blake, Dali, Giger, Beksiński,

Kahlo, Bacon, Ernst, De Chirico, Escher, Kubin, Topor ..."

When he saw that I had no intention of stopping this litany on my own, and particularly since I'm sure the smug little ass didn't recognize half these names, he regurgitated a name he did know. "I'm partial to Pollock, myself."

"Hm," I grunted, "yes ... perhaps the best of the chimpanzee artists."

"Well, I'm sure you have other favorites, but I mention Pickman because the similarities are obvious. Both of you pursuing your work here in the North End. Both of you seeking to shock your audience with extremely grotesque imagery executed in a highly realistic style ..."

I'm sure I winced. "*Shock*. You trivialize my work."

"Oh, but it isn't your intention to be shocking, Mr. Coffin? To be controversial? I'm reminded of an artist I did an article on who patches together maps of the USA and the American flag from bits of human skin, taken from people who donated their bodies in good faith to *science*. But he only uses White people's skin, because it's a statement, you see, on America's sins. He also claims his work is not meant to be incendiary, or sensationalistic." Knox chuckled. "I've never interviewed such a hypocrite. One can't have their cake and eat it, too. Why not just unapologetically admit, 'Yes, you bet, I want people to feel a thrill of revulsion. I want to shock the living shit out of people.' Isn't there more honor in being truthful to oneself, without any pretentious bullshit?"

"I trust you're speaking of this other fellow ... not me," I said calmly.

"Yes, of course. I'm just making a general observation."

"Hm," I said. "I don't know or care about this person you mention, who does sound more calculating than corpse artists such as Witkin and von Hagens—who are, as you say, honest and up front with their morbid and beautiful work. But at the risk of sounding like I'm spouting 'pretentious bullshit,' those who work from a darker palette are always going to be accused by some as merely attempting to draw attention through offensive effects. Is von Hagens' work merely educational? Of course not. Is it meant to provoke? I should think so. Is he having his cake and eating it, too? Maybe. Is that dishonest, or is the work simply functioning on multiple levels? Why not stop putting the artist on trial and focus on the art itself, and what it's saying?"

"Aren't the art and the artist one and the same?"

"Now that's a more provocative question than I might have given you credit for, young man."

"So what is *your* art saying, Mr. Coffin? Tell me."

"Ask my art, is what I'm telling you. Go on … commune with it." I waved my arm toward the paintings framed upon the walls around us.

"Are you afraid to just tell me straight what your themes are? Your aesthetic, your motivations and intentions and inspirations?"

"Ahh," I sighed, "you want me to encapsulate all that into one or two facile lines you can use as a caption beneath a photo of one of my paintings?"

"If I can find a painting of yours the magazine won't be afraid to publish a photograph of." He smirked.

"Well, let's just say I'm a reporter—like you. Does a reporter only impart, 'Today I saw a puppy frolicking in the summer sun?' No. Reporters tell us that blood gurgles in the gutter. That brains slide down the windshield … "

"No, no, no," Knox cut me off, waving a hand. "We may need to hear that dark events have happened, but we don't always need someone holding those bits of brain under our nose, and then on top of that trying to convince us there's a *beauty* in those brains."

"Well as you can see, I sometimes achieve a visceral effect, though I should hope not even you would dismiss me as a gore-hound. But to me, there is undeniable beauty in the knotted form of the human brain."

"But it's how that brain came to be exposed … how it's presented …"

"How indeed. I suppose one is either attuned to terrible beauty or one isn't. Though I should hope you would try to *open* yourself to such beauty."

"I'm open enough to appreciate that your technique is beautiful. Just as Pickman described himself, primarily you're a *realist*. Or at least, you pretend you've seen some of these things you portray."

Now it was my turn to smile. "What makes you think any of these images are pretend?"

For a beat or two the journalist almost looked afraid, as if he were willing to open himself just a little more and believe me, but then up came the protective screen of his grin. "Anyway, so you're sensitive to the comparison with Pickman. It hit a nerve. You want to be known as an individual. Well, not to offend, but I still say it's plain to see. Look at these, for instance!"

He pointed to a nearby pair of oils. The painting on the left was rendered during a trip to Vietnam, extrapolated from a battered old photograph I was shown. It portrays three Viet Cong soldiers glaring back at the viewer, behind them an opening into a tunnel network of the type employed throughout the war. Lying at their feet is a nude albino carcass, shot a number of times. With its canine aspect the corpse suggests a large hairless baboon, and yet the feet appear to be oddly hoof-like. The gallery card accompanying this piece gave its title: *The Tunnel Rat*.

On the right, a painting entitled *The Dig*. The name refers to Boston's disastrous "Big Dig," the costliest highway project in the history of this country, which even resulted in a number of well publicized deaths. Less well known is that one worker vanished during the project, leaving his family to wonder if he was accidentally buried alive, or if he ran away to start a new life somewhere. My painting depicts a terrified worker in a hardhat being pulled into a rough opening in exposed ancient masonry by several pairs of unnaturally white, simian arms. The faces of his attackers are mostly obscured in the shadows, but their eyes glow like those of hyenas caught in infrared light.

One of the visitors to my exhibition had praised me for my political metaphor ... he seemed quite proud that he had gleaned a statement in my painting about the whole Big Dig debacle; its consumption of time, money, and blood. I have been accused of cruelty by more than one acquaintance, certainly by more than one lover, but I could not divest this poor chap of his satisfaction, and so I'd thanked him for his insightfulness.

But my current and less enthusiastic companion asked, "These paintings in particular aren't influenced by Pickman?"

Perhaps out of mounting defensiveness I spoke too freely. "They are influenced by my living across the street from Copp's Hill Burying Ground. By living above a system of obsolete tunnels that most people in this city would never suspect the existence of. Pickman did not invent those tunnels, and they and their inhabitants are not his alone to represent."

"*Inhabitants?*" The fellow wagged his head. "Mr. Coffin ... I'm not trying to be antagonistic, here, but the similarities between you and Pickman can *not* be denied! Come on now, what else do you have in common with him? I heard he had a strained relationship with his father, who lived in Salem. What was your upbringing like?"

"I can't vouch for what you say about Pickman and his father," I replied evasively. "Of course the father might have been disturbed by his son's art—but then, why would he take possession of such infamous pieces as *Ghoul Feeding* after his son's disappearance? Perhaps you're only speculating unfairly about Mr. Pickman." I took a step closer to the man, and he took a step back, his shoulder nearly brushing one of my framed works. "And it would be unfair, and unwise, to speculate on my own family matters."

"Sorry," Knox stammered, "I didn't mean ... " But his words trailed off when he looked over his shoulder, saw the frightful visage of one of my typically outré portraits only inches from his nose, and jerked away from it with a little gasp.

I snorted with amusement. Yes, I had to admit, if only to myself ... there *is* something to be said for the shocking.

That evening when I returned to my nearby house on Charter Street, my encounter with young Joel Knox stuck with me. As if still debating with him in my mind, I thought of Blake's words: "What immortal hand or eye, dare frame thy fearful symmetry?"

If one believes in a Creator, then one must recognize Him as an artist of many terrifying works. Fearful things that one would think He created quite fearlessly.

My young critic was blinded by morals, I felt, and morality has no place in art. Would he object to a painting of a tiger, tiger, burning bright, in the forests of the night? Ah, but a tiger has no morals. A tiger is a work of terrible beauty. Should other creatures that rend and feast on flesh not be considered manifestations of terrible beauty, just because they are more obscure?

The little puke did hit a nerve with me. But not so much about Pickman, as about my own father.

II

(From the article Ghoulish Legacies: The Art of Donovon and Enoch Coffin, *by Joel Knox)*

I'm sure I never would have been driven to investigate the matter of Enoch Coffin's family had it not been for his hostility about the subject, at the scene of his exhibition. The next day I returned to Prince Street, but this time to interview the gallery's owner, Marie Lavoria. I met her over espresso in her small but noteworthy restaurant, *Ristorante Lavoria*, next door to the gallery. Owing to the shocking (yes, I said it, *shocking*) quality of Coffin's work, I was curious as to why this wholesome-seeming woman should be such a supporter. When she spoke of him in glowing— bordering on gushing—terms, I suspected that the attraction might extend beyond the art to the artist himself. Ms. Lavoria didn't seem to be so intimate with Coffin as to possess great detail on his upbringing, but there were a few tantalizing tidbits she had learned in conversation with her newfound friend, and in her enthusiasm she innocently gave them up to this fellow "fan" of her hero's work.

She said, "When I told Enoch my father was a mason who dabbled in sculpture, thus inspiring my own interest in art, he told me his father Donovon Coffin was a very gifted stained glass artisan, whose work could be found in churches and private homes throughout New England. He also crafted beautiful glass lampshades in the fluid Art Nouveau style, but also the more linear and symmetrical Art Deco style. He was a great admirer of the stained glass work of Frank Lloyd Wright. Enoch said his father was always experimenting with style and technique, and achieved some very striking and original effects."

"How fascinating that the senior Coffin was also an artist, then," I replied, "but one who pursued more beautiful modes of expression. I wonder what went wrong with the son that he took on such a darker outlook."

"Well," said Ms. Lavoria, as if hesitating to add to her revelation, "Donovon's church work was always praised for its execution, but there was some controversy about the subject matter he chose, which was apparently often a bit gruesome. John the Baptist's severed head presented to Herod on a platter … St. Bartholomew flayed alive, with his own skin draped over his arm … St. Sebastian almost erotically pierced with arrows … and of course, explicitly bloody depictions of the Savior in His sufferings. Enoch said that children looking up at some of these artworks burst into tears and thereafter refused to return to church, and even some adults complained at being unnerved the way light would glow weirdly in the eyes of various figures. There were even complaints, maybe unfounded but maybe not, that there was hidden imagery—I guess you might compare it to subliminal imagery—such as demonic faces leering from seemingly innocent designs. More than once Donovon was asked to remove and substitute one of his creations, and as his reputation started to become tainted, increasingly his artworks were outright refused. Finally, he stopped getting church commissions, making just enough of a living off his other work."

"How fascinating. I guess the apple didn't fall far from the tree, after all. So where did the elder Coffin grow up and ply his trade?"

"Oh—in the very same house on Charter Street that Enoch lives in today."

III

(From the personal journal of Donovon Abraham Coffin)

I am home again, after my demeaning incarceration. If there were any chance of me fashioning windows for a church in Massachusetts again, my arrest has exploded it.

Fools. They of course thought I meant to rob that grave in the Copp's Hill Burying Ground, across the street from my own abode. Rob it! Rob it of what? A handful of dust? But I couldn't tell them the truth, could I? That there are tunnels below the graveyard, a whole ant's nest of tunnels through this area of the city, in which those hungry *others* dwell. I couldn't reveal the truth about that old blue slate, with its image of a winged angel of death seated on a block bearing the words *Memento Mori*, a scythe in one hand and the other pointing downwards. Yes, pointing down *there*—a hidden sign, like those I incorporate in my own glasswork, so as to communicate with the perceptive and sensitive explorers of this world who are not satisfied by the spiritual pabulum they feed the sheep, those sheep I terrify with their own blood-drenched faith! No, I knew that figure pointing at the earth was a signpost left by a kindred soul. I knew that there was no body in that plot to be robbed! Had they not interrupted me, I would have revealed a hidden trapdoor, perhaps taking me into a section of the tunnels walled off from the rest, with steps leading down further … maybe even leading me to what I seek!

A door into the Dreamlands.

No, I had to lie, of course. I told them I sought a skull to use as a model in my art, for a piece portraying Mary Magdalene contemplating a skull after the manner of Gustave Dore. Ha. They seemed to buy my explanation, though it didn't enhance their feelings toward me, and they warned that if I were caught at such activities again I'd be shipped off to Danvers State Hospital.

This is why I must resist my compulsion to locate a secret passage in the cemetery again. I must at least wait until a sufficient period of time has passed, as frustrating as that may be.

But ah! I am making progress with my very own Dream Lens, I feel, and may not need a prosaic trapdoor at all. If my efforts are rewarded, I will be able to see into the Dreamlands at will!

And not only see, but in seeing, part the veils and open a portal—so that I might pass bodily into that other realm as the Ghouls themselves do.

IV

(From the personal journal of Enoch Donovon Coffin)

It was a beautiful afternoon for a stroll in the graveyard, with the lowering sun glowing through the overhanging autumnal foliage, painted leaves scuffed up by our feet and swirling about our shoulders like fiery infernal ash. Marie Lavoria must have felt it was quite the romantic setting indeed. I kept my paws in the pockets of my suede jacket lest she try to hold my hand.

We stopped every now and then to read the inscription on this or that slate, tilting in their rows in the Copp's Hill Burying Ground. Marie smiled and reached up to me, and I nearly flinched away, but she merely plucked a leaf that had alighted on the brim of my slouch hat. She then squatted down before a headstone so as to read its engraved script.

"*Sacred to the memory of Miss Mercy Jones ... Aged 20 and 6 months.*"

"How specific. But when you die at so young an age, I suppose one need be grateful for a few extra months."

"Yes—so young. I wonder if she ever got to experience love." Marie rose and again smiled up into my face. "How about you, Enoch? Have you ever experienced love?"

"I experience love every day."

She raised her eyebrows.

"The love of my art," I went on. "I'm afraid it leaves me little room for other forms."

She looked a bit crestfallen, and said, "But I've seen you in the company of a number of different people in my restaurant." She was polite enough not to mention she had observed me in the company of both genders, and then some.

"My name is Enoch, not Eunuch, my dear." I winked. "When one is hungry, one must dine. A restaurateur must understand that."

Marie blushed a little and looked away, but she was also smiling again. "I understand that hunger," she admitted, no doubt still holding on to the hope that she and I might share a special feast of our own one of these days.

We continued strolling, and she asked, "What about your parents? You never felt the urge to marry, as they did? Surely your father loved your mother."

"He did indeed. He loved her so that it split his heart."

"Really?" My companion came to a halt again, intrigued. "Is that why you're afraid to love?"

"I said nothing of fear. But perhaps I'm reluctant to be distracted by the pain or pleasure of such conventional pursuits, when I have my calling to attend to."

"But how was your father hurt? Did your mother pass away at a young age?"

"Lebanah Coffin was a beautiful creature. He portrayed her in his glasswork numerous times, and she even graces a few churches ... as an angel. She was an albino, with flowing white hair and skin white as a blank canvas, and uncanny eyes with pink irises. Her feet were

94

deformed, however. They could be said to have resembled the feet of Chinese women who had bound their feet tightly for too many years. One might say they were even ... hoof-like."

"Oh! From an injury?"

"A congenital deformity," I replied. "Yes ... something in her *genes*." Ah, if only my innocent friend understood the full ramifications of such a genetic lineage!

"So what happened? Did she leave him for another man?"

"She did leave him, yes, but to follow her destiny. It was time for her to *change*."

"Change? You mean, she felt she needed to discover herself?"

"Something like that."

"But she left you, too! Her only child!"

"She had no choice. She didn't want to hurt me, or my father."

"I don't understand."

I began walking again, and Marie was forced to hurry to catch up to me. "I suppose I seek her in my art at times," I mumbled. More to myself, really. "But it wasn't enough for my father to immortalize her beauty in his own art. He sought to find her again. His dream was that he might join her somehow."

The key word—the word that surely escaped poor mystified Marie—being *dream* ...

V

(*From the article* Ghoulish Legacies: The Art of Donovon and Enoch Coffin, *by Joel Knox*)

I was very happy that I returned to *Ristorante Lavoria* for lunch after another visit to Enoch Coffin's latest exhibition, in the course of researching this article. Not only was the fare excellent, but I met Marie Lavoria again and she had some fresh material to share regarding her favorite artist's childhood. The sad matter of his abandonment by his mother when he was just a wee sprout, and the father's apparent obsession with her.

"Sounds like maybe she had some issues," Ms. Lavoria confided in a whisper, tapping her temple with a finger. "Oh, but please, don't quote me on that ... I wouldn't want to hurt Enoch."

"Of course," I assured her.

I was more intrigued than ever, and now determined to interview Coffin again before I put this piece together. To that end, I phoned the man via the number Ms. Lavoria provided. Even though she cautioned that the artist shunned the telephone, he picked up when he heard my voice. I asked him if I might interview him in his own home, so as to view his studio and more examples of his art.

"Of course," Coffin said. "When would you like?"

"Well, you live on Charter Street, correct? I'm just a short ways away, here on Prince Street. I could walk right on over if you're available."

"Certainly, please do. I'll put a pot of coffee on."

VI

(From the personal journal of Donovon Abraham Coffin)

Many have fleetingly and flittingly visited the realm called the Dreamlands—naturally, in dream—but did not remember afterwards, or did not appreciate what they had experienced if they did retain a fragment of remembrance. But there are those adepts who have reached the Dreamlands purposely, intentionally questing, by projecting their essence while in a hypnotic state or meditative self-entrancement. They descended the seventy steps to the cavern of flame. And I have tried to find those steps ... oh yes, I've tried. Yet my talent doesn't lie in lucid dreaming, or astral projection. My talent lies in my love of art, a love I have sought to instill in the mind of my young son. He is all I have left of my darling wife. I will not be content with that, however, so long as my art might serve me.

My Lebanah was more knowledgeable in arcane matters than I, more *attuned* to them, but we had learned some things together, and since her departure I have furthered those studies on my own. Driven no longer merely by a sense of curiosity as an artist—an artistic curiosity as scientific as it was mystical—but now by a desperation of the spirit. So I have learned what I could, wherever and however I could, with a kind of *violence* of need.

Oh, I would be lying if I said I only want to find my way again to my beloved's side. I am forever an artist/seeker. How could I not dream of creating artworks modeled—from *life*—after the blank-faced wheeling Night-gaunts ... the strangely leaping Ghasts? And in the background, the looming Tower of Koth? Those oversensitive hypocrites who no longer want my work casting its multi-hued light into their silly hovels of worship have no idea that if I had my way, those windows would not portray tortured saints but Gugs with fanged vertical grins! Titanic, winged Shantaks!

Yes, as a pilgrim of the Dreamlands I know my Lebanah has changed ... transformed as does the butterfly to fulfill her true nature. But though her beauty has altered, I am sure it has altered to a beauty of another sort. A terrible beauty.

Yet I have not sought her by literally venturing into the tunnels below these streets, where the dangers are too acute and the rewards too limited. That nesting place is only the intermediary zone between here and the Ghouls' true home. And it is *that* place of wonders I seek.

In my seeking, I had encountered rumors that in the Sesqua Valley, in the Pacific Northwest, there was a Dream Lens secreted in the basement of an old home, a lens that had been guarded by generations of one family. A great lens that allowed one to peer directly into the Dreamlands. Yes! This I must see, and duplicate with all my skills! So I ventured to that strange valley, to the town situated in the shadows of twin-peaked Mount Selta, a town where the veils are thin the way they are in a place like Arkham or Dunwich. But my quest proved fruitless. The weird locals with their silvery eyes and, often, suggestively deformed countenances mistrusted me ... professed to know nothing of any such Dream Lens. I begged, bribed, even threatened, all to no avail.

I did not return to Massachusetts with a sense of defeat, however, but only a new determination.

If I could not copy the alleged Sesquan Dream Lens, then I would design one all my own.

VII

(*From the article* Ghoulish Legacies: The Art of Donovon and Enoch Coffin, *by Joel Knox*)

Coffin greeted me quite cordially at his door facing onto the old North End street, and admitted me into his narrow little home. Not unexpectedly, I was immediately struck by the décor, though to go into it at length would require another article all its own. Suffice it to say I was surprised to find that the grotesque—though certainly in evidence, and *very* grotesque—did not outweigh the beautiful, and he really does seem to be a man of diverse, eclectic tastes. Though how much of the décor could be credited to him, as opposed to the parents who owned the house before him, I couldn't then gauge.

Noting my fascination and occasional revulsion as I took in my surroundings, he proceeded to conduct a little tour for me. In the comfortable parlor with its leather furniture and overflowing bookshelves, amongst his own paintings hanging on the walls—some of which I can't imagine any gallery in the city would consent to display, nor any sane person wish to purchase—I spotted a painting that was unmistakably the work of Richard Upton Pickman. Unsurprisingly, it presented a number of ghastly nude figures with distended dog-like features, white-skinned and blotchy with greenish mold or infection, clambering out of a freshly dug grave in what was clearly the Copp's Hill Burying Ground. The title, I read, was *A New Doorway*. I grinned at Coffin. "I see a Pickman here, but nothing by any of those other heroes you listed for me at the gallery."

"Actually, it was my father who acquired that piece," Coffin revealed.

"And he must have done these, himself," I observed, sweeping my arm toward the room's two windows, both of which were of brilliantly colored stained glass. For the first time I focused my full attention on them, and was quite frankly stunned when I did. Perhaps I'm not sufficiently familiar with this craft, but I didn't know such complex work was possible. One of them was so intricately ordered and symmetrical I was put in mind of the mirrored view through a kaleidoscope. The other was a swirling chaos like thorny nebulae that reminded me somehow of a fractal image. Looking too long at either one of them brought on a kind of dizziness, or vertigo, as if I might plunge through them into a cosmic void from which I might not return. At last I had to look away, muttering inarticulately, "Remarkable."

A circuit of the ground floor alone was already too much to take in, but my host let me catch my breath by inviting me to sit at a dining room table for coffee. I asked him, "Do you live here alone?"

"Except for my friends." He waved at a nearby credenza, on the marble top of which stood a bizarre array of objects, including a limbless anatomical model made of wax with intricately painted internal organs, a pallid heart (dog? pig? human?) preserved in a block of Lucite with a tangle of long black worms emerging from its split sides, a deformed human fetus with strangely fish-like features crammed in a bottle of alcohol, and a coiled snake rearing its head inside a bottle of yellowish fluid.

I pointed to the last item. "Is that drinkable?" I asked.

"That's a matter of opinion. It's a cobra preserved in rice wine. I picked it up in Vietnam."

"What does it taste like?"

"It tastes like a cobra preserved in rice wine. Care for a glass?"

"I'll stick to the coffee, thanks." I watched the artist dump spoonful after spoonful of sugar into his own cup. "Have a little coffee with your sugar," I joked.

Coffin smiled at me oddly. "Amusing. I've never heard that joke before."

"Sorry," I chuckled. "I'm sure you haven't."

"I see you brought your laptop."

"I had it with me earlier; I like to write on the run. In coffee shops and so forth."

"And in Italian restaurants?"

"Hm?"

"After you called, our mutual friend Marie Lavoria rang me and admitted rather sheepishly that you had been interviewing her about my family. Silly girl even gave you my phone number and precise street address." Coffin had been stirring his coffee now for an unusually long time, though maybe it was just to dissolve the unusual quantity of sugar. "I can't be angry with her ... she's innocent to the point of ignorance ... though I did gently suggest that she should be less free with information I might share with her, in the future."

"Well, I know you sort of suggested at the gallery that you would rather I didn't speculate on your family ..."

"I don't think I 'sort of' suggested that; I thought I was quite clear."

"But I'm not speculating, Mr. Coffin. I'm here to ask you straight out. Tell me about your father, Donovon Coffin. Tell me about his art, and how it influenced you. You can deny Pickman all you want, but denying your father's hand in what you do —"

"Would you like to see?" he cut me off.

"Hm?"

"See his art studio for yourself. My own studio is in the attic, and we can look at that, too, of course. But since you're unrelenting on this topic, I'd rather tell you about him myself than have you pry around clumsily and assemble an inaccurate or unbalanced story. Thus, if you are so determined, let me show you what remains of my father's workplace." Coffin drained his coffee, including the sugary sludge at the bottom, and clinked the cup down in its saucer. "His studio was in the basement."

VIII

(From the personal journal of Enoch Donovon Coffin)

I led my guest to the door to the cellar, but with my hand on the knob I turned to face him. "Before I show you my father's workplace, and the culmination of all his skills and efforts—a caveat."

"Which is?"

"You're on a path to investigate my father, and so it's inevitable that in digging deeper you'll uncover certain facts. Certain ... unsavory, scandalous stories. As I say, I fear that in focusing on these details in your article—taking them out of context, exhibiting them in unfair proportion—you'll besmirch my father's name. And, by extension, my own. But it's more a matter of a son's loyalty than an artist's pride. Otherwise I might not share with you the thing that I've decided to reveal. I entrust this experience to you so that you might see my father less as a madman, and more as the tainted genius he truly was."

"I appreciate that you're willing to give me a broader understanding of your father, so I agree to treat him fairly in my article."

What a sincere look he gave me. Did I believe him? Not fully, I'm afraid, but all I could do was try to impress upon him my strongly-felt desires. If I couldn't stop him, I must at least try to educate him. But this family matter touched a vulnerable place in me, one I do not easily share, and I'm not sure if he understood the level of anger I was forcing myself to restrain. I do not like feeling vulnerable or angry, emotions that amount to a loss of self control, and yet I felt myself holding back growling fury like a dog straining at its leash.

"Before we descend, I'll tell you what you'd soon enough discover on your own. My father, for all his brilliant efforts, wasn't satisfied with the outcome of his experiments. One night he stole into the Copp's Hill Burying Ground, to a plot he felt bore a secret message inscribed in its slate, and began digging in the earth there. Despite the late hour, he was spotted and arrested. He had been arrested briefly for the same crime, once before. This time he was incarcerated at that sprawling monstrosity, the Danvers State Hospital. Father suffered a complete breakdown there. He began to only eat meat ... and then, begged for only uncooked meat. He stopped communicating with words, just howled and growled like a wild beast."

"Oh my ... well, uh, I'm sorry," my guest stammered uncomfortably.

"On one occasion he attacked an orderly, biting him quite badly on the face and neck. They put him on certain antipsychotic drugs, and eventually these seemed to be effective. Maybe that caused the staff to become lax in their attention, because ultimately my father escaped from the hospital ... and disappeared. There is no official record of his fate beyond that."

"Oh! My God, that's ... wow." Then the word "official" obviously sank in. "The authorities never learned his fate, but do *you* know where he ended up? What happened to him?"

I turned the knob, and opened the basement door on its old squealing hinges. "This way," I instructed, starting down the stairs.

I led Knox into the basement of my little house, the former house of my parents, with its ceiling of old exposed beams and walls of red brick squeezing out a cake frosting of crumbling mortar. Immediately his attention became focused on the bizarre display featured at the center of the largest room. Overlooked were the various sturdy wooden tables, and the large light table with its milky glass top, upon which my father had worked his craft. The young man also seemed to overlook my own spare easel, which I had left set up here, for I did not exclusively work within my studio in the attic. He was so distracted, he didn't even acknowledge the unfinished painting propped upon that easel.

He also didn't appear to notice the axe leaning against one brick wall, in case of emergencies. I abhor guns.

"What was this thing originally … a well?" Knox asked, walking tentatively around the low stone base rising from the cement floor.

"While other families in this neighborhood long ago paid people to cover over the openings in their basements—especially after strange rumors of attacks and disappearances—my father actually paid workmen to remove the heavy cap from this ancient well. He had already built his Dream Lens, as he called this construction, so he and the workmen then fastened it in place over the opening." I didn't add that my father had directed the operation to take place quickly, before anything below might come through.

Knox was in the process of taking in the construction that I had called the Dream Lens. It was a convex hemisphere, a web of lead that held in place many individual sections of glass of various sizes and colors, in totality forming no obvious pattern. The hues were subdued, however, not bright primary colors as one would expect in a stained glass composition. Faint, sickly-looking tints of gray and amber and sepia, absinthe green and urine yellow and ghostly blue.

In addition, around the perimeter of the lens were a number of apparatuses on hinged arms. Some looked like magnifying glasses, others like telescopes. Several were strong lamps, with differently colored filters over them to change the tincture of their beams, though presently none of them were turned on.

"Father tried various combinations of color … of magnification. Different types of crystal for the lenses. And of course, different sorts of spells to imbue the device with outré potency."

Knox looked up at me, his expression torn between admiration for my father's craftsmanship and revulsion at this seeming monument to his insanity. "To achieve *what?*"

"Enoch? Enoch, are you down there?" called a familiar voice from the head of the stairs.

Oh Gawd, when would I learn to lock my front door?

"Is that Marie Lavoria?" the journalist asked.

"Yes," I sighed. "Let me go up there and see what the silly wench wants."

"Mind if I stay here and get down some impressions while they're fresh?" The man had carried his precious laptop downstairs with him, under his arm. He placed it on one of the work benches and opened it.

"Yes, go ahead. I'll explain the Dream Lens ... perhaps ... when I return. I may even let you look through it, on one more condition. That you do not report what you see through it."

"What?"

"If I should permit you to experience my father's achievements, you must swear to me on your word of honor you will not reveal what the Dream Lens can do, nor what you see."

"But ... I don't understand."

"Enoch? I hear you down there!" Marie called, sounding agitated. "Please!"

I groaned, and gestured at Knox's portable contraption. "Just play with your toy and I'll be back in two shakes of a Night-gaunt's tail."

"A ... what?"

But I left him to attend to my other unwanted guest.

‡

Apparently not content with having admitted to me over the phone that she had spoken with Joel Knox about my parents, Marie had come to apologize in person, bearing the gifts of a bottle of Pinot Noir and a box of the Sicilian cannoli she knew I adored. And no doubt, she hoped, the gift of her own voluptuous self. To spare her further guilt, or perhaps out of some vague premonition, I didn't reveal to her that the writer was at that moment tapping away at his computer in my very own cellar. I sent her away as quickly as I was able to extricate myself from her moist eyes and babbled apologies, which wasn't quickly enough to suit me. Naturally I accepted the wine and cannoli, to placate her, and with thoughts of sharing them politely with the arrogant brat in my basement—to which I finally returned.

IX

(From the personal journal of Donovon Abraham Coffin)

I have failed in parting the veils, but not utterly. That is to say, I have not opened a gash through which my embodied consciousness might enter into the Dreamlands—the realm of my beloved. But with my sleeve, so to speak, I have cleaned dirt from the window panes of reality. I am sure I have peered into the Dreamlands, but into other planes as well, which I had not intended to gaze upon. Different panels of glass, in conjunction with a variety of incantations and sigils traced in the air, have yielded different results. They are but murky, fleeting visions. One might think they had only imagined they'd seen something, or misinterpreted what they did see. The additional instruments help focus the images somewhat, enlarge or clarify them. I have to angle the lamps just so. And then, if the fates are kind, I am peeping through a keyhole ...

Who could consider this a failure? I will admit with all humility it is brilliance, even when it is accidental brilliance (for what artist isn't well acquainted with, and reliant upon, pure serendipity?). But it is not the goal I seek.

... Even as I marvel at the barely discernible yet heart-clenching sight of a prowling shape tall as a mountain, a silhouette against the stars, its twin dog-like heads surmounted by headgear like a bishop's miter— surely a scene of the Dreamlands.

... Even as, holding my breath lest I jiggle the scope just a fraction and banish the image, I spy upon a herd of amorphous black hulks congregated about an underground lake, constellations of green eyes blinking in and out of existence across their heaving, pulsing forms.

... Even when, through another of the colored windows, acting like a television screen receiving transmissions from some other dimension, I watch a swarm of arthropod beings glide through the infinity of space, their ribbed wings spread wide like sails.

The cosmos itself taunts me, as if to say: "You think the matters of your puny human heart have any significance in the face of *all this?*"

But more men than I have suffered under the magnificence of the stars, for there is a cosmos just as vast inside our puny human hearts!

These glimpses of alien vistas are failures, I say. Magical, miraculous failures the likes of which other men would sell their souls to achieve. But these visions do not put me in my lover's arms!

There has been one serendipitous outcome, however, that granted me an especially remarkable gift. It may be the closest I come to my goal. It may have to suffice ... oh, though the word "suffice" rakes its claws through my soul!

I was gazing through the hexagonal green pane, as viewed through the brass spyglass and with the pale green filter fitted on the nearest lamp. And down there in the tunnel, three figures scuttled into view. Pale as creatures that had never known the light. Naked and furtive, and gazing back at me with wary curiosity. But they were beautiful! They were humans! They were more beautiful than humans ... beautiful as *gods!* And one of them—yes!—one of them was my very own Lebanah!

They peered up at me only a few moments, then shifted position as they meant to scurry away into the tunnel again. I shifted, too, before they could flee. I wanted to call out to her! Tears welled in my eyes!

It wasn't the tears distorting my vision, though, that accounted for the change in what I saw. It was moving to another panel of glass that did it—this one the amber octagon. Through this pane, the effect was entirely different.

Before they disappeared into the darkness of their honeycomb beneath the city, I saw the three figures in their true form. This time, the green blotches of mold on their white flesh. Their animal-like countenances. Their glowing feral eyes.

I fell against the Dream Lens, embracing it with my spread arms, wracked with sobs.

"Come back!" I sobbed. "Come back! Let me see you a minute longer!"

Why didn't she stay, so that I might gaze upon her at greater length? Does she love her tribe more than me, now?

No, I don't think that's it. The thing is, she doesn't realize I unwittingly imparted this occult attribute to one section of glass. She doesn't realize that through it, I can see her and her fellows as they once were.

She is ashamed that I should see her as she is now.

But she must come back—she must! For I am a failure ... a failure ... and a view of my darling through the keyhole is all that I have left of her. This illusion, this lie, this teasing memory.

No! I will not let that suffice.

Even if I have to return to Copp's Hill with my shovel, and again seek my path through the realm of the worms.

X

(From the personal journal of Enoch Donovon Coffin)

When I reentered my basement, it was to be confronted with a tableau that was for a moment too much to process. Multiple details clamored for my attention. There was Joel Knox's laptop computer, open on one of the work tables with its screen glowing and covered in text: his article in progress. Not far from that, also open upon the same table, was my father's journal, and I cursed myself for forgetting that I had left it there.

I had left the Dream Lens' lamps turned off, but I saw that one of them had been switched on ... the one with a green filter, positioned above one particular panel of glass that was also tinted pale green, and hexagonal in shape.

When he had first circled the Dream Lens, examining it, Knox must have noticed that at its base the dome was hinged on one side, and locked in place with two bolts on the other. I knew he had noted this feature, because the Dream Lens now stood open like a large hatch. Knox had undone its bolts, which I myself had never dared attempt.

Finally, there was Knox himself, standing before the opened hatch defiantly and gripping the long handle of my axe.

"You evil son of a bitch!" he spat.

"I am something of a son of a bitch, in ways you may not know, but I'd advise you to clear away from that hatch and let me lock it again."

"The hell I will, you bastard!"

"What are you saying, Knox? I tell you, move away from that opening!"

"I read a little of your father's diary. All insanity. There, I said it— *insanity!* An insanity you've clearly inherited. But I thought I'd have a look anyway ... and that's when I saw your prisoner!"

"My ... prisoner?"

"How long have you had that poor girl in that pit, you psychopath? I'm going to call the police down here and get that wretched creature out of there!"

Terrible awareness had dawned, and I took a step toward the young journalist. "Knox, get away from there!"

"No!" He brandished the axe threateningly. "One more step and I'll put this in your skull!" His eyes were wild. "You imprisoned her so she could model for you, huh?" He nodded toward my painting on its easel. At some point he had noticed it, after all. But one thing he hadn't done was call the police already. His cell phone was still in the pocket of his jacket, which he had left upstairs in my parlor.

"Knox!" I shouted.

"All your noble talk about art," he raged. "Now I understand you, and your sick father, too!" He demanded: "What did you intend to do to her when the painting was complete? Kill her? Chop her up with this axe? *Eat* her, you monster?"

I lunged forward then, in an attempt to seize the axe's handle and grapple for it.

I was too late. I don't know if the creature sprang upward on its own, or if another one or two of its kind gave it a boost, but I saw a pair of unnaturally white, simian arms like those I had rendered in my painting *The Dig* reach up from below and grasp Knox's ankles. He was wrenched off his feet, falling in such a way that his belly slammed hard against the rim of the hatchway. The force of impact caused him to let go of the axe, which clattered to the floor. He scrabbled to hold on to the rim, and for a moment his eyes locked on mine in a horror so profound I wish I had captured it in a photograph. I would have loved to paint it.

Then, he was dragged below, and I heard a frenzy of high-pitched screaming, and the deeper tones of savage snarling. Finally, the shrieks gave way to a ghastly gurgling, as one hears from a man choking on his own blood.

I scooped up the axe, dreading that I might have to use it, but the beast below was satisfied with its prey and didn't make a second leap. I took hold of the lifted hatch and eased it back down to its base, then shoved the two strong bolts in place.

I fell away from the Dream Lens, panting. As infuriated as I had been with my guest, I hadn't wanted *this* to happen. If he had sworn himself to secrecy, I had thought to tantalize the writer with a glimpse into the Dreamlands, or one of the other alien worlds my father's device could penetrate, but I hadn't planned on showing him the creatures that dwell below these streets. Perhaps the familiar, tinted light of the lamp had attracted them. Attracted *her*.

Having regained my composure, I went to bend over the fellow's computer and read the last words he had written:

' *... if you are so determined, let me show you what remains of my* *father's workplace." Coffin drained his coffee, including the sugary sludge at the bottom, and clinked the cup down in its saucer. "His studio was in the basement."'*

"Sugary sludge," I muttered. "Ever the disapproving wretch, this one."

I turned from the device, and went to the Dream Lens. I reached out to switch off the lamp with the green filter over its bulb, but I could not resist the imp of the perverse and brought my eye close to the spyglass on its jointed arm. Through its quartz lens, I gazed through the green-tinted hexagonal panel and thus into the ancient brick tunnel below.

She was still there, her slender nude figure crouched over a torn scarecrow that had once been a man. Thankfully, in this light the blood appeared black, but there was much black. Sensing me above, she tilted up her face to peer back at me. I was struck, as always, by the impossibly beautiful face that my father had long ago fallen in love with. The face he had given to angels in the stained glass windows of churches throughout New England. Her long white hair wild in her face, and her lips and chin smeared with glistening blackness.

Minus the blood, it was identical to the face of my oil portrait in progress.

"Oh, Mother," I admonished her sadly.

XI

(From the personal journal of Donovon Abraham Coffin)

Failure, and failure again. But I have succeeded, at least, in escaping from their madhouse and returning here. Yet how much longer can I evade them? They may have already come here looking for me, and will no doubt do so again. Therefore, I haven't much time.

My dear son Enoch has been in the care of his aunts. I trust those spinster sisters will raise him well. They love art, and books, and I'm sure they will nurture him. I hope they will see that this journal reaches his hands.

Yes, I hope you are reading this, my beloved son.

I am proud of you. The proudest moment of my life, apart from my wedding day and the day you were born, was when I came down into the basement and found you had switched on one of the lamps of the Dream Lens. With a pad and pencil, you were sketching a flock of weird, crab-like beings with membranous wings soaring through the place between stars. You looked startled and ashamed, but I reassured you. Of course, I forbade you from looking into the Dream Lens unattended again—until you were ready—but my praise for your drawing was sincere. It was remarkable! You will be the artist I wish I had been. You will succeed where I could not.

Forgive me for abandoning you, my son, but I hope you understand my love for your mother. If I can not use the Dream Lens to join her in the Dreamlands as a fellow citizen of that realm, then I will lift the Lens aside and descend bodily into the brick and mortar labyrinth below.

If I can not join your mother's pack, then what I want is for her to dismantle me with her own hands ... consume me with her own teeth ... digest me in her own belly until we are conjoined. Until I am part of her ... one with her ... forever.

(*Note: Joel Knox's proposed magazine article,* Ghoulish Legacies: The Art of Donovon and Enoch Coffin, *remains unfinished and unpublished.—EC*)

The Brothel in the North End

The house, built in 1910 but nowadays called a condo, was on Hull Street in Boston's North End ... a nondescript row house fused with a line of such units, forming a quaint wall of red brick. The street was so narrow that cars could only pass along it in one direction. Across the street from this wall of brick condos, and the row of cars parked tightly in front of them, was the Copp's Hill Burying Ground.

On the other side of the ancient cemetery, on Charter Street, was the domicile of the controversial artist Enoch Coffin. The owner of the house on Hull Street, aware of Coffin's interest in painting extraordinary subject matter, once invited Coffin to visit and paint whatever he saw that captured his fancy. Coffin was promised he would discover a wealth of inspiration for his grotesque work. However, upon realizing what went on at that address, the artist turned down the request of his company.

The owner of the house on Hull Street, a man named William Aiken, was insulted by this rejection. Being permitted entrance to his home was an honor that his guests paid great sums for. But then, Aiken supposed Coffin was jaded. His guests had never seen anything like what he had to offer behind that unremarkable and inscrutable door of his.

A stone-lined tunnel ran beneath Hull Street, under the line of expensive parked cars, unbeknownst to Aiken's neighbors in the condos wedged cheek to jowl against his own. This cramped tunnel communicated between Aiken's basement and an ant-like series of

113

earthen tunnels beneath the cemetery. He kept the door to that tunnel tightly locked on his side, however, only unbolting it when he had hired men with him. Hired men with guns. And he only unbolted it when it was time to summon the females.

It was in his basement that he had created his brothel.

Oh, Aiken's guests were jaded, too, in their own way. Money had bought them women of every race and shape and age. Children, both female and male. Money had permitted some of his customers the luxury of snuffing the life from their fleshly toys. But even the most jaded of them had never, before coming to the house on Hull Street, lain with a being that was not human.

These bestial subterranean beings, white as albino cave animals, were encrusted with dirt, with blood from the dogs and homeless people they fed upon, encrusted with the decay of the long-dead corpses they crunched their semi-canine jaws into, encrusted with mold and their sweat. They stank, and that was part of their appeal for Aiken's wealthy patrons, who lived their lives among people with showered, perfumed, neatly attired bodies that belied their inner filth.

The females would be lured from the tunnel, fitted with muzzles and bound with restraints at wrist and ankle to prevent them from giving in to their nature in the throes of passion, but they were not forced to engage in these sexual acts. In payment for their acquiescence, before they were tied down they attacked and feasted upon the sacrifices the brothel customers had brought with them: human escorts, who had been led down into Aiken's soundproofed basement, unaware of what their johns truly had in mind for them.

After they had been sated, the lean and carnal female ghouls—their naked white breasts slathered in blood, their sharp-boned faces masked in gore, shreds of flesh crammed between the ragged teeth hidden behind their muzzles—willingly laid down on the three hospital beds Aiken had arranged in his basement. He only ever accepted up to three customers into his brothel at any one time. Only up to three ghouls were permitted through the door. Aiken didn't want to worry about too many escorts being reported missing at any one time. More importantly, he didn't want his hired men to have to watch over more than three ghouls at any one time. There was always the threat that their sacrifices would not be enough to satisfy them, once their bloodlust was stoked.

Aiken took precautions against the ghouls, but ultimately he didn't take sufficient precautions against his hired men. One night one of them, feeling he hadn't been paid adequately for his services, and that he had been verbally abused by his employer, sneaked back into the basement alone before he left the residence on Hull Street, and unbolted that door to the tunnel under the street.

Despite their arrangement, the ghouls couldn't resist their nature any longer … it was too long between the sacrifices Aiken offered them. And the males had grown jealous of the meals their females were offered.

The next time Aiken ventured alone into his basement, he became the last of the sacrifices in the brothel in the North End.

The Mummified Hand

Outsiders were drawn to the forested Sesqua Valley, in the shadow of twin-peaked Mount Selta in the Pacific Northwest, as if they converged there along psychic ley lines. They heard how the veil between worlds was thin there, maybe rubbed thinner by many an incantation and evocation, from Sesquan and outsider alike. There was a cemetery in Sesqua Valley devoted to these outsiders: the poets and artists, the junkies and would-be sorcerers, who had a way of ending in that dirt. But Emmett was a native, despite having spent some time outside the Valley. It was a kind of tradition that young Sesquans did this; it was like the Rumspringa of the Amish and Mennonites. Ironically, the other five waited for his return there in the Valley, though they were themselves outsiders.

By bus, Emmett was currently returning to Sesqua from Sea-Tac Airport in Seattle. He'd flown to Sea-Tac from Logan Airport, in Boston.

In Boston, Emmett had visited the home of the artist, Enoch Coffin. Coffin, who was spoken of as a seeker of mysteries, who painted the things he found—whether people believed the miracles and monstrosities on his canvases were based on reality, or not.

Emmett had been warned that Coffin was mourning the recent death of a dear friend, a writer, and probably wouldn't see him, being a private person at the best of times. However, when Emmett came around, and Coffin met him at the door of his narrow house on Charter Street, in Boston's North End—directly across from the Copp's Hill Burying

Ground—the artist went quickly from gruff to intrigued.

He said, "You're from the Sequa Valley."

"Yes, sir!" Emmett said. "Have you been there?"

"I have. As my father, also an artist, visited there before me. Anyway ... you have the Sesqua look. It's unmistakable, if one has seen it before." The eccentric artist referred to certain aspects of Emmett's face that one might consider deformities—here being perhaps lupine, there perhaps frog-like. But most striking of all, of course, was the odd silvery sheen of Emmett's eyes. Many people he'd met outside the Valley had assumed he was wearing contact lenses.

Coffin admitted him, made him coffee while Emmett explained—to an extent—what he and his five friends sought to achieve. In Coffin, he had felt he'd find a sympathetic ear; or at least, that he wouldn't be mocked.

"We want to stand upon the Plateau of Leng," Emmett told him. "We want to enter the Dreamlands."

And yet Coffin did mock him a little, as he set his coffee in front of him, but this was just Coffin's way. "Then I suggest you ... fall asleep."

Emmett nodded. "That's one way. We all go there, if only briefly, that way ... and mistake it for the usual nonsense of dream. But there are other ways, as I'm sure you know. Lucid dreaming, astral projection. The use of certain drugs ... "

"Which, of course, can surely *delude* one into thinking they've traveled to the Dreamlands."

"True ... if one were uninformed, impulsive, and careless in how they took that approach. Also, in my own Sesqua Valley, it's widely known that there's a portal called the Dream Lens, in the basement of a certain home, but the people who've lived there for generations guard that portal *rigidly*. The latest guardian isn't even a Sesquan. Her husband was, but he was killed in a mishap related to the portal, and she's watched over it ever since and won't let even us other Sesquans near it."

"I know that. Years ago, my father went to the Valley to see the Dream

Lens. He was a stained glass artist, and hoped to create something like it himself."

"Ah! But they wouldn't show it to him?"

"No," Coffin said, seating himself opposite his guest.

Emmett twisted in his chair to look around him at all the strange paintings, and decorations, and artifacts that filled the room's every vertical and horizontal surface. "I was told you had an astonishing collection of items you've brought back from your travels."

"Though I try to vet my friends and confidants carefully," Coffin said, "it seems there will never be a lack of gossip about me. Ah, but would I really have it any other way?" He sipped his extra-sweet coffee with pinky extended dramatically.

Emmett faced him again. "We heard you possess a hand, in a box. A mummified hand. Supposedly, this hand was from a priest belonging to a cult from Leng."

Coffin watched him over his cup's rim, waiting for him to go on.

Emmett did. "I wouldn't ask you to defile this artifact for us, by giving me some fragments from it, except that I was told you've already shaved bits from it, to mix into your pigments for several of your paintings ... to give them strange effects."

"Only one painting," Coffin corrected him.

"Was it of Leng? Do you have it here?" Emmett looked around him again.

"Yes, and no. It was a commission, for another wide-eyed soul like yourself. So ... you want some pieces from that holy relic, do you?"

"Six small shavings ... the size of a thumbnail would do. I'm prepared to pay you, though I have to admit I can't pay many thousands. I'm hoping you'll have a little pity on a group of like-minded explorers of the unknown, bored like you with the stultifying limits of this earthly existence."

The artist snorted. "What a well-practiced spiel." He looked Emmett up and down. "I'll give them to you for nothing, if you'll agree to pose for me, my beautiful beastly friend."

"Pose for a painting? Of course—I'd be honored!"

"Pose for me in bed, *and* for a painting."

"Ah!" said Emmett, grinning. "Well ... I guess I'd be up for that, too."

And so the artist and the Sesquan conducted their business, and when Emmett went on his way—to head back to his friends, waiting for him in the Valley—it was with six flakes shaved from the palm of the mummified hand of the alleged Leng cultist, stored in a little wooden box Coffin had given him.

Coffin stood in his doorway, watched the young man climb into a cab that carried him away, and he chuckled. For his father, though denied a look at the Sesqua Valley Dream Lens, had constructed one of his own in the basement of the house that Enoch Coffin had inherited and now dwelt in. And though it did not actually form a portal, this lens nevertheless allowed one to see into other realms ... and so it was that Enoch Coffin had painted his landscape of Leng from life.

‡

They sat in a circle on the bare floor of the attic in Emmett's humble home, which he too had inherited from his parents ... who two years ago, being aged and ill, had stripped nude and walked hand-in-hand into a particularly thick night mist. Never to be seen again.

In black paint the group had meticulously rendered a geometric formula on the floor, and the six of them—also naked—sat within sections of this. In his hands, Emmett held a bowl containing a murky fluid. One of the constituents of this concoction was datura, from the plant called "the devil's trumpet."

Holding this bowl above his groin, officiating despite his youth because he was the lone Sesquan among them, Emmett looked around at the other five slowly—from one to the next—and addressed them.

He said in a reverent tone, "We know there are many stories, not all the same. They don't even, all of them, place Leng in the same location. Which is all the more incentive to *find* that place, for our essence to *walk* that place, so that we might *know* that place.

"Sometimes we hear of a race of bestial, goat-like beings who dwell on Leng, and perhaps those beings are Sesquans who long ago crossed there before us." He had also secretly wondered the opposite: if Sesquans were the descendants of these goat-beings, who had ventured here from the Dreamlands. But that theory didn't suit him now, so he went on, "The *Necronomicon* tells us that dwelling upon Leng is a cult of cannibals." He smiled and nodded around at them, one to the next. "To commune with that cult, let us too partake of human flesh now. The flesh, I believe, of one of their very members. In so doing, perhaps we will cross time and *become* them. Perhaps that cult was *us*, all along."

He dipped his fingers into the dark solution, lifted from it a dripping, now sodden flake from the mummified hand in the possession of Enoch Coffin of Massachusetts. Emmett placed this morsel on his tongue ... and he swallowed it. He then passed the bowl to the person on his left. It continued around, clockwise. His communion was repeated.

When the bowl had made its circuit and returned to him, minus the bits of withered flesh, he set it behind him and rested his hands upon his crossed legs. He stared straight ahead, as if fixedly, yet unfocused upon anything material. He even ignored the face of his lover, directly opposite.

He lost sense of passing time. Well, that was appropriate, wasn't it? Was it just the discomfort of sitting nude on the planks of this hard, cold floor that was causing his body to feel increasingly stiff? And the lights of the six candles placed between the six members of their group ... could their flames possibly be changing in character, becoming preternaturally bright, or was it the datura that caused their light to burn his eyes and make him want to close them? But he resisted that impulse. They were not going to sleep their way into the Dreamlands.

Oh! Were the others seeing this now, too? But he didn't want to speak to ask them … afraid to break this spell, to banish this materializing portal.

For that was what it had to be, floating above the center of the circle that their own bodies were a part of, like the indispensable gears of a clock. What had manifested was a great black gem, slowly rotating. It was a trigonal trapezohedron, with six rhombic faces. Its facets glistened like obsidian.

Entranced, without questioning why he did so, Emmett lifted his right arm, reaching his hand toward the hovering gem. He raised up from his seated position, leaned forward on his knees until he could touch it. He did so.

The gem did not feel glassy to the touch, as he had expected. It was like gelatin, unresisting, and his fingers slid into its substance, and then his entire hand, and then he was screaming, as his hand was sucked away at the wrist. He drew back a stump, its end blackened and cauterized and steaming with icy vapor.

But the key had been inserted into the lock, so to speak, and the door was flung open. A great black flower—at least, that was how his mind hallucinated or interpreted it—bloomed open and filled the room. Or were those petals the unfolding facets of the gem? In any case, the six of them and their painted circle were engulfed in this blooming darkness and all six candles were extinguished at once in its living breath.

In the resulting utter blackness—in the moment of their transition— delirious and terrified, anguished and ecstatic, Emmett thought, "That was *my* hand. It was *my* hand Coffin came in possession of. *My* hand we all tasted."

The Lunar Gate

(From the journal of Enoch Donovon Coffin)

I

I feel I am not a man of this time. That is not to say I feel I am of any time, but rather that I have existed outside of any conventional current through which the common shoals of humanity have flitted their fins toward their extinguishment. I will admit I have an affinity for the ways of old, that I have affected archaic manners of speech, and even of technique when it comes to my art. (I shall die with a paintbrush, not a mouse, in my hand ... unless it is a mouse feasting on my hand.) My embracement of outmoded things does not mean I wistfully wish to have lived in some "better" time, but merely that certain aesthetics resonant with me; sifted gold nuggets of the past that are agreeable, comfortable, sublime. In many ways the arts may have been more refined in the past, even if certain social conditions were less so. The fact is, an individual of my unique character, esoteric studies, and shall we say debauched tastes for pleasure would not have been welcomed in the common social circles of the past few centuries, and might well have been hanged as a witch.

There are millions walking this sorry ball, still, who would call hysterically for my death if they could but witness my acts this very night, in my attic studio. Those who would bury me under an avalanche of religious tomes, drown me in cascades of holy water. They, more than me, dwell in the past; the darkest times of ignorance and superstition. Yes, they sense there are wonders and mysteries in this universe, but they're like lost sheep trying to read a signpost, sheep too low to the ground to truly scan the cosmos for these wonders—to make out, as it were, the *actual* configurations in the stars. Like children who see horses and dragons in cloud formations, looming over our existence they think they discern a bearded old White man, whereas I see the churning black vortex that exhaled us out and will inhale us back in one day, as a dreamer breathing in its sleep. The most frightening thing isn't the idea of a Creator who becomes angry at us if we disobey Him; it's that the forces of creation don't care in the slightest about us, if they recognize us at all.

Yes, I am a creature out of time, dwelling in my own stream, rather like those creatures that swarm in the air in my attic even now, as I take a break from my painting to scribble in this journal. Earlier tonight, on the worn old boards of the floor I drew a circle with chalk, then various lines and curves cutting into this circle, and finally symbols at the meeting places of these pathways like the nodes of a circuit. Upon drawing the last symbol, upward from this circle beamed a cylinder of light, looking like sunlight though outside it was well past midnight. Like dust motes floating through a shaft of said sunlight, whitish-translucent insects swam in the air, wriggling their legs, reminding me of the sea monkeys, or brine shrimp, an aunt had gifted me with as a child—one of the dear sister aunts who had raised me after the disappearance of my tormented artist father. Of course, these animals are not brine shrimp nor any other animal known to earthly biologists.

I am in the process of rendering an oil painting, a portrait for a client who sought out my services. As the canvas is sizable, 4x6 feet, instead of using my old standup easel I've clamped the canvas to a wall-mounted setup of my own devising, created cheaply from a large piece of particle board attached to arms with brackets that allow me to extend the board and tilt its angle. The painting portrays my client, an attractive blue-blooded Bostonian of thirty-eight, seated in front of a mirror contemplating her reflection, which is apt because this person's narcissism is as palpable as her disdain for me. (I suppose she was offended that I resisted her sexual overtures at our first meeting.) She sat for me here in my studio on two occasions and so that part of the painting is finished, and now I've been enhancing the background. That is, the background as seen in the mirror's reflection.

I have been using a long-handled brush, dipping it into the column of uncanny light radiating from my floor and guiding one of those swimming creatures onto its bristles, then gently withdrawing the brush's tip from the light. I have to move quickly from the light to the canvas, before the creature dissolves in this other environment, but not so quickly as to dislodge it. I then smear the creature, and the paint it has become stuck to, onto the surface of the canvas, mashing the animal into the painting so that no sign of it is noticeable in the *conscious* sense.

But with each specimen I add to the background, the painting becomes more imbued with an aura of wrongness. I know this, because I can even feel it myself. Staring at the painting as I work on it fills me with a kind of revulsion, and it would mystify me if I didn't know the cause, because the painting itself is beautiful. That was very important: I want my client to see that I have portrayed her in a very flattering way, in both versions of her in the composition, so that when the painting causes her weird, undefinable discomfort she won't be able to pin the blame on me. Maybe if she hadn't been so contemptuous toward me, and if she had paid me a fairer price for this work (did she think her body would offset that?), I would be working on something that would fulfill her brittle need to reaffirm her fleeting beauty, as she had intended.

I am a generous artist, however. I am giving her seemingly innocuous painting some rather unique special effects, added free of charge! Quite an improvement on hiding skulls and the word SEX in ice cubes and such in subliminal advertising.

Ah, the things I do to alleviate boredom when my financial situation necessitates that I take on such commissions.

I like to think my outré techniques are unique, not mere gimmickry. Some years ago, on the one-year anniversary of the Boston Marathon terrorist attack, I participated in an art show reflecting on the perseverance of my home of Boston in the face of violence and crime. I added human blood (my own that time, I swear!) to my paint, along with other enhancements. Some who viewed my painting openly wept, though my intention was only to move people, not upset them. Perhaps too much blood; art is an inexact science, and I'm always learning. In any case, the painting was auctioned off, the proceeds going to the families of the bombing victims, because I am not entirely mercenary.

I think I'll only add one or two more of my poor little collaborators to this piece, before I kneel down, smudge away one of the nodal symbols at the periphery of the circle, and banish the tube of light. After all, the effect should be subtle ... not drive one insane. This has been a fascinating experiment for me, and I would like to take the effect further one day, no doubt for a personal piece.

The long-handled brush keeps my hand from getting too close to the light, by the way. I surely wouldn't want one of those bugs getting onto, or into, my skin.

II

I watched the young woman from across the street, with some degree of amusement and a touch of interest, the latter mostly due to her extreme beauty, obvious even from a discreet distance. She stood at the door to my humble abode, while for my part I leaned against a lamppost at the brick-walled, tapered end of Copp's Hill Burying Ground, which jutted like the prow of a ship bearing only a cargo of the dead.

She rang the bell (not knowing that it was long past functioning), waited, rang it again, and as her frustration clearly mounted resorted to banging on my door. When that, too, elicited no response she moved to her left, to one of the pair of ground floor windows that look out onto the exceedingly narrow street I dwell on, and rapped her knuckles on the glass. I could all but hear her internal sigh.

At last she looked about her, as if questioning if she were at the address she sought, and spotted me where I lounged. I tipped the brim of my slouch hat at her and shifted my position a little to point at the sign affixed to the lamppost that read DO NOT ENTER. The sign referred to one-way Snow Hill Street, behind me, but I wondered if she took my meaning. Surprise visitors are seldom welcome, unless I am already acquainted with them. Especially these days, when I have felt more reclusive than in the past.

"You aren't Enoch Coffin, are you?" the beautiful young stranger called over to me. "The artist?"

"As opposed to some other Enoch Coffin?"

"Actually, when I looked you up online I did find some other Enoch Coffins," she replied, crossing the street to me since I hadn't done so to join her. "One died in 1761, another in 1814 ... "

"Yes, and there have been others," I replied. "One gave up the ghost in 1736, another in 1675 ... "

"Maybe they've all been you," she teased, smiling as she sought my eyes in the shadow of my hat. "And you pretend you've died so you can start a fresh existence."

"My secret is out! Now, my dear ... I'll take one box of the peanut butter patties, and one of the thin mints. I like the lemon ones, too, but I must preserve my slim girlish figure." I lay a hand upon my abdomen.

The lovely face contorted. "Excuse me?"

"Oh, so you're not selling cookies? I don't see any copies of *The Watchtower*, either. So ... I am both disappointed and relieved."

If she *had* been selling the Savior door to door, depending on my mood I might actually have invited her in. I'd done so recently with a pair of women—one White, one Black—whose mild and friendly manner had inspired civility in me. Alas, when they'd followed me into my parlor the White lady had outright gasped at the paintings hung there, most of which were of course by my own hand, though there was the one by Richard Upton Pickman that my father had come into possession of. On that day, the ladies in question had babbled some excuses and quickly departed. Oh well … I'd tried to be nice.

My uninvited visitor finally caught on to my jokes and gave a patient smile. "I'm not a Girl Scout or JW, Mr. Coffin. I hoped I could have a word with you. I'm sorry to have come to your home like this, but I couldn't find a phone number or email address for you."

"What is the nature of your visit, Miss … ?"

"Maeve Cawley," she stated. "It has to do with art."

"Can you be more specific?"

Whatever weak smile she'd manifested abandoned her face utterly. "A series of paintings you've been doing for my stepfather, Jacob Orne."

"Ah ha," said I. I stepped past her, crossing to my front door while carrying by their handles the several plastic bags of items I'd picked up at a corner convenience store some blocks away. It was an unseasonably warm day for October, pleasant weather for a walk. The woman who'd identified herself as Maeve followed after me, as I knew she would. "Usually Mr. Orne sends someone else; that pretty but sullen and charmless boy." I stopped suddenly at my door and turned to her. "Come to think of it, you rather resemble him."

This striking woman had long, lush dark hair, complemented by thick dark eyebrows that offset the lightness of her cat-like green eyes. The smooth freshness of her face and lips put her in her mid twenties, whereas the untalkative green-eyed boy who had come to my home on several occasions to collect finished paintings for Jacob Orne I had figured to be just out of his teens.

"You mean Aidan," Maeve said. "Yes, he's my brother. Have you seen him lately?"

"Seen him lately? Not since he collected the last painting your stepfather sent him for. Am I to gather from your statement, then, that *you* haven't seen him lately?"

"Neither me nor my mother have seen Aidan since the eleventh. My stepfather claims not to have seen him, either."

I noted her use of the word *claimed*. "Well, my question then is: have you come to speak to me about my work for your stepfather, or to ask me about your missing brother?"

"Both, Mr. Coffin."

I produced my keys to unlock my front door. "I think you had best come inside then, Miss Cawley."

III

I have to admit I welcomed the tasteful perfume my guest wafted into my living space with her. However much I cherish my solitude—especially in recent years, as I say—I have always enjoyed the company of other people. They have offered intellectual and artistic stimulation at the best of times, or at least provided sexual diversion, for after all I am a fleshly entity. Some friends and acquaintances have been quite charming, others comically amusing—though often in a tragic way. Isn't there sadness to all clowns? There was certainly an aura of sadness to this young creature, or at least of deep anxiety.

I have sadness of my own, but it is of an intensely personal nature, seldom even revealed to myself. The death of my dear writer friend of Seattle a few years back was really a blow, and then there are of course the tragic and mysterious ends of both my parents. It was this familial type of loss that made me sympathetic to Maeve Cawley's concern for her missing sibling. Coming to grips with my own losses has been partly responsible for my withdrawal from socializing—and even from traveling, since my visit to the Sesqua Valley in the Pacific Northwest a dozen years ago. How time flies, as they say! Sadly, I find that once you allow yourself to become mired in one place, the cement only seems to further harden.

Of course, my quasi-retirement from the world at large also had to do with the inevitable wear of age, having well passed the half-century mark, and the effects many of my more interesting experiences abroad had had on me. I was a walking collection of scars, though many of them were psychical ... and of those, not necessarily unwelcome reconfigurations of my mind and essence. Some of the physical wounds had been self-inflicted, though not out of self harm. The bit of shoggoth matter wedded to my arm, to heal a sigil I'd impulsively carved in my flesh with my switchblade whilst visiting the remarkable town of Innsmouth, had long been fully absorbed by now, though at the time I'd been assured that its effects would remain with me for the balance of my life—which I was also assured, back then, would be prolonged as a result of that cellular integration. If that were the case, I could only hope that the years ahead rekindled my physical and creative energies, for I felt there had been a real lapse in the latter ... my recent experiments with extradimensional critters notwithstanding. After all, look at the mundane piece those poor things had been sacrificed for. I had to admit to myself that I'd been selling my very soul, as it were, for bread money ... and creating less and less work that was truly *inspired*.

That is, until I received the commissions from Jacob Orne. In tackling that series I had finally created something very much like my work of old.

"Alas," said I, carrying a tray of coffee and cake into my living room and setting it down on a little table, "I had no Girl Scout cookies."

I found my guest standing before one of my framed oils, staring at it with less horror than those unfortunate JW ladies I mentioned before, though I wouldn't go so far as to call it admiration. Wonderment, perhaps.

"I'd know your style anywhere, after seeing the four paintings you've done for my stepfather."

"Four so far," I said, taking a seat.

She turned abruptly to me. "Where is the fifth?"

"Unfinished, in the basement."

She looked down at the floor in front of her. How curious human behavior is. Did she expect that some superhero's X-ray vision would permit her to see into the chamber below?

I continued, "When you said you were that boy's sister I feared you had come to claim the last painting prematurely, but that isn't the case, is it?"

Maeve Cawley came toward me. With her apparently shapely figure attired in black jacket, skirt, and nylons she looked very business-like, or as if dressed for a funeral. She sat opposite me but didn't touch the refreshments, leaning forward with those amazing eyes beaming earnestly from under their dark brows. "Have you been to my stepfather's house in Eastborough, to see how he's displayed them?"

"I have not been to his house in Eastborough," I replied, spooning a generous helping of sugar into my black coffee. Luckily the butter cake wasn't too sweet, to offset it; my indulgences do have their limits, or so I tell myself. "I have never met Jacob Orne in person. When your brother—whose name I never knew until you told me—first came here and sat where you are now sitting, he had a laptop with him through which I conversed with Mr. Orne, though he had the camera turned off so that I only heard his voice. That was when he hired me to paint his five not-so-easy pieces. I assume it wasn't through young Aidan that you found my house, if the scamp has flown the coop?"

"I had to track you down on my own." I must have arched an eyebrow at her, because she added, "Pardon the expression."

"On the subject of Aidan Cawley, I can only tell you I haven't seen him nor heard from him since he came for the fourth painting, once it had dried sufficiently. That would have been, oh, the fifth, wouldn't it? It was a Saturday. And so you say less than a week later he went off somewhere?"

"Apparently."

"Have you talked to the police?"

131

"Not yet. My mother's discouraged me from doing so. She says he's just in a mood and will come back around when he's ready."

"And might that not be the easiest answer? He does come across as the moody sort. Perhaps he tired of running your stepdaddy's errands."

"Mr. Coffin," said my guest, "he didn't take his laptop with him. Even his phone was left in his bedroom."

"He lives with you and your mother and Mr. Orne in Eastborough?"

"He does, but I live in Worcester, where I work."

"Ah yes, Worcester. They have a nice little art museum there. It's been too long since my last visit."

Maeve sighed wearily, as if tiring of my frivolities. As I say, she exuded an air of anxiety. "Mr. Coffin, I want to ask you … to *beg* you … not to complete that fifth painting for my stepfather."

I had to chuckle in surprise. "Not finish it? I could hardly do that, could I? I am to be paid three thousand dollars for that painting, as I was paid for each of those that preceded it. Further, it is part of a set, meant to complete it. Your stepfather would, I'm certain, feel cheated and outraged if I didn't deliver the final piece. And why would you even ask me this?"

"It's hard to explain, Mr. Coffin, because I don't know why, really, he commissioned you to do this series in the first place. Only … there's a terrible *wrongness* to the room where he's hung them; you can feel it. My mother let him use one of the upstairs bedrooms to hang them in, one painting on each of its five walls. Well, it's his house anyway, isn't it? He had Aidan paint the walls and ceiling black for him, and there's nothing else in the room but a little stand at the center, where he's placed a globe of the moon."

"That does sound like an interesting setup, smacking of occult practices. Are the walls of equal length?"

"No? Is that significant?"

"Not necessarily; I'm only curious … trying to picture it. It sounds like a striking manner in which to mount my artwork, though it's odd that it's hidden away in some upstairs room. But this supposed wrongness you claim to sense … might you only be experiencing an uncomfortable reaction to my admittedly bizarre work? To the uncanny subject matter the paintings portray?"

I will say here that the unearthly landscapes in question contained no unusual components in the mix, such as my extradimensional arthropod friends, though as I'd worked on them I had wished I owned a piece of moon rock to pulverize and sprinkle in for flavor.

"As weird as those images are," Maeve insisted, "it's more than that. You would have to know my stepfather more to understand. There's a wrongness about *him*."

"Ah, I see. So the two of you are not close."

"God forbid."

"Your mother must have seen something in the man."

"He has a certain charisma ... and a lot of money. When my father passed away my mother was in a rough spot. My stepfather comes from money; I don't know that he himself has ever worked a day in his life. When he was younger he spent much of his time traveling the world, getting up to God knows what."

"He sounds like someone I know."

"I hope you're not speaking of yourself, because I'd hate to think you'd do some of the things he's done. Some of which he's been investigated for."

"Oh? Well, I am all ears." I munched cake as though it were popcorn.

Maeve drew in a long breath as if to prepare herself for some major revelation. "You've never researched him online?"

"Though I occasionally use the library's computers, I do not own one myself, nor do I have a little smart phone grafted to my hands like most people." I didn't add that I had years ago disposed of the laptop an earlier guest named Joel Knox had left behind in my home after his own, er, disappearance, lest the damnable thing be traced to me through some technical means beyond my backward understanding.

So Maeve proceeded with her revelation, and it caused me to rather lose my appetite for butter cake.

IV

"For some ungodly reason—I guess, simply because there's no bottom to the depths of human depravity—four years ago my stepfather's first wife was arrested for activities associated with an online group of monkey haters."

"Monkey ... haters?"

"Yes," said Maeve, growing ever more intense. I thought she might begin trembling. "Heidi Orne belonged to a chat group of about twenty known people, who sent money to her as the group's ringleader to obtain photos and videos of the torture of long-tailed macaques, mostly babies, being held in Thailand. A country, by the way, that my stepfather has traveled to frequently in the past. For sex tourism, I wouldn't doubt. Anyway, these monkeys would be psychologically tormented, and then physically. Allowed to heal, then tortured again. With hammers, screwdrivers, sexually mutilated, splashed with acid, set on fire ... "

I raised a palm. "I get the idea."

"So even your taste for horrors has its limits, Mr. Coffin?"

I bristled somewhat at this question. "Missy, I have never, nor ever would, approve of the suffering of any innocent, vulnerable animal. Even those I eat. And that includes humans, who are the least deserving of such concern—as your story surely proves." I wouldn't even draw out the suffering of an insect, extradimensional or otherwise, and was more likely to catch spiders and such in my house and set them free outside. I stressed, "Just to clarify: I have an affinity for the Other ... not for evil."

She sighed deeply. "Why monkeys, I don't know, but I suspect it's because they're like human infants. For their videos, these monsters would even dress them up in little outfits. You could see how broken their souls were ... the exhausted misery in their faces." Maeve paused to collect herself a bit. "I saw a brief segment of video on a news site. No physical torture was shown, thank God, but one monkey was pulled out and talked to and teased by some fucker. There was even a kid, a son I guess, moving through the scene in the background. The next generation of monster. I don't care how much they need the money there."

"It is indeed unthinkable. As the 'Prince of Preachers' Charles Spurgeon once said, 'You cannot slander human nature; it is worse than words can paint it.' I wouldn't doubt these same people would torture human infants for money ... or just for the kicks alone. And perhaps they do."

"Heidi Orne had pet cockatiels, and a little dog, and yet she was arrested and charged with uploading more than twenty images and a hundred thirty videos of monkey torture to this forum."

"Was she given jail time?"

"As the group's leader she was facing five years behind bars, but while she out on bail and waiting for her trial date she ended her own life. *Apparently* she self-immolated in the backyard of the house where two years later my mother took the woman's place—as Jacob Orne's second wife."

That word again: apparently. "And what of him, and the investigation you mentioned?"

"He claimed to know nothing of his first wife's activities, and when she was arrested she swore up and down to the authorities that he had nothing to do with it. If you can believe that."

"I have to say I'm dubious. So he was never charged, himself. And what of those fiends in Thailand?"

"I doubt they'll ever see justice. Anyway, I find it hard to believe that my stepfather didn't know what was going on. I think it's likely from his foreign adventures that he was the one who set up the entertainment in the first place. Rich folks and their jaded tastes and all. You see the headlines ... or do you not have a TV, either?"

"There may be an old one gathering dust around here somewhere. Well ... thank you for brightening my day, Miss Cawley. All I can say is, I hope that fate catches up with those who remain unpunished, and may they ... 'self-immolate,' as well. Or that someone else 'self-immolates' them."

"As I suspect happened with Heidi Orne."

"And how much of this is your mother aware of? Is she not a little nervous about this past investigation into her hubby, and her predecessor's demise?"

"She hasn't admitted such to me. Maybe, maybe not. There have been other investigations, too, about other matters, but you know how it is with money. It helps lubricate you to slide out of tight situations."

"Until the day it doesn't. As you know from the headlines."

Maeve blurted suddenly, with tears coming to her eyes, "Mr. Coffin, I'll give you five thousand dollars to destroy that last painting,"

I reached across the table to take her hand, but she pulled back from this old geezer's touch. "I cannot, missy; so sorry. Go forth and tell your mother to divorce her creepy husband. She'll get a lot of that sweet money in the settlement, if she needs it so badly."

"My mother is a sad drunk," she choked.

"Been there, done that."

Oh, and that's another reason why I'd been in the state I was in for the past decade plus. I'd never minded a good beer, glass of wine, or whiskey. The trouble was, of late I minded it even less.

Maeve rose from her seat, her coffee untouched. Had she feared the debauched artist might drug her, then pose her unconscious body for a painting in the nude? I was hardly *that* wicked a demon. In any case, she said in a hurt and accusing tone, "I guess I hoped if you refused to stop working on that last painting, you'd at least want to help me find Aidan because you're gay, yourself."

"Gay? Well, I suppose I'm not always somber, but I don't know if I ever get that giddy." I smiled sympathetically at the child. "My dear, I dislike labels. They're so limiting."

"I have a few labels for you, but I'll save them for another time. Good day, Mr. Coffin."

I followed her to the door she had banged on so ardently earlier, and there she turned to face me a last time, saying, "If you won't destroy that last painting, looks like maybe I'll just have to destroy the other four, to keep my stepfather from continuing with whatever it is he has in mind."

I am sure I gasped audibly. "Don't you dare! Those represent my best work in years!"

"They're not your possessions anymore; you've accepted your blood money for them."

"You are the dramatic one, aren't you? Look, if I hear anything from your brother I will let you know immediately. I'll even ask around about him, if I can think of a relevant place to do so ... though as I say, he didn't even tell me his name, much less anything else about him, such as him being gay. Give me your phone number."

Begrudgingly Maeve recited it for me, and I produced a neglected charcoal pencil I still carried in my jacket for impromptu sketching and wrote the number on a receipt from a liquor store I had stuffed in another pocket. Then, out she stepped from my abode and I stood a few moments in the doorway watching her walk up Charter Street to wherever she had managed to find a place to park her car. At last, I shut and bolted the door.

Foolish in my old age, I felt a touch of guilt that today I planned to return to work on the painting awaiting me in my basement. But return to it I must.

V

If by chance I should someday disappear under enigmatic circumstances, as did my parents before me, and all that remains of my voice—besides that which my brushes and pens articulate—is this journal, I herein declare to you its discoverer that the greatest achievement of my father Donovon Abraham Coffin, stained glass artisan, is fitted as a cap atop an ancient well in the basement floor of the house I inherited from him.

The Dream Lens also serves as a hatchway, leading down into the tunnels below Charter Street, which communicate with the labyrinth hidden beneath Copp's Hill Burying Ground, but I have never dared venture into them and never will. For, among other fears, as much as I miss my mother I would not wish to encounter her again down there.

I removed the blue plastic tarp I had taken to covering the convex Dream Lens with, in so doing being careful not to bump and disturb any of the odd instruments fitted around its rim, though they were held in their positions by tightened thumbscrews. Then, I turned on one of several lamps my father had also fitted about his device, to illuminate its variously colored, variously shaped panes so that he might view what lay beyond them. Though *physically* what lay beyond them was that stone-lined shaft into the earth, what one might *see* through them was an entirely different matter. My father was a remarkable artist indeed, and his muse was love. How much greater might my own artwork have been, had I ever known a love like that he held for his strange albino wife?

I turned on more lights about my work area, and lit some candles with sigils etched into their wax by my own hand, so as to shine upon the canvas I had placed horizontally onto the spare easel I kept down here. On a paint-spattered table where my half-rolled tubes and jars of brushes awaited me, my gaze fell upon a bottle of Japanese whiskey, candlelight fluttering through its honey-hued depths so that it glowed like one of the Dream Lens panes. I reached for the bottle's neck, but instead of unscrewing its cap I hid it away in a cabinet where I hoped it wouldn't call to me. For some reason, my visitor today had left me in more of a self-reflective mood than usual.

But not so self-reflective as to abstain from the job at hand. No ... I must not see this as merely a *job*. This work, though commissioned by another, even down to its precise subject matter, felt much more personal and ambitious than that.

Now, if only the Dream Lens would perform to its fullest potential today, to lend me fresh inspiration. I couldn't predict its effectiveness, the not infrequent inconsistencies that might have to do with the alignment of planets, or more likely the alignment or other conditions of overlapping planes of existence. I hoped for clarity, so that I might view that which Jacob Orne expected me to transfer to my canvas.

As an artist, I have always been first and foremost a realist. I might even say I am singularly unimaginative in regard to my subject matter, though the admission would doubtless shock anyone who has viewed my work.

The first of the five paintings I'd created for my patron—all of them upon canvases set the long way, 24x36 inches—portrayed a bleak, rocky landscape, but not of this Earth. No ... Earth is present only as that distant orb in a sky so black it all but drowns the pinpricks of stars, an orb streaked white upon blue, bisected into a hemisphere by dense shadow. But this is not some moonscape as experienced by arrogantly puny human astronauts. Rather, it is the moon of dreams. More specifically, the *other* moon of the Dreamlands.

As seen, when conditions are favorable, through one violet-tinted, pentagonal pane of the Dream Lens, the satellite we know from our night sky is translated into that parallel heavenly body ... just as in the Dreamlands, the planetoid Pluto finds its alternate self in the sphere those who are aware of it call Yuggoth. Ah, if only the Dream Lens permitted me to reach that far in my sight, so as to view and paint Yuggoth's city of green pyramids, its colony of winged, crustaceous Mi-Go!

Yet, our nearby Luna as it appears in the Dreamlands is inhabited, too! In my first moonscape, I portray its denizens as they appear from a distance, flitting in and out of their windowless buildings built from rock mined by the slaves they've acquired from the Earth of the Dreamlands, these slaves brought to the moon on the weird black galleys the lunar beings sail through cosmic gulfs. In the distance in this first painting, one can see the masts of several of these galleys rising between the stone buildings. The denizens themselves, the Moon-Beasts, are as yet but dimly-seen, naked white forms.

In the second painting, now we see a full view of a few of those black galleys, where they are docked in a pool of milky white fluid that fills a lunar crater. The Moon-Beasts are driving their slaves to load one of the galleys with crates. Though the viewer cannot see within, these crates contain rubies that the slaves also mine from the moon's subterranean tunnels. As yet the slaves, too, are only seen at a distance, but they are more human than their masters—for the most part, though the artist knows that the turbans they wear hide small horns on the heads of these folk captured from Leng. The cargo of rubies will be traded by the Moon-Beasts upon the Dreamlands version of Earth, in return for more Leng slaves and for gold, though why the Moon-Beasts care so much for that metal is unknown.

The third oil painting is a close view of the Moon-Beasts driving the enslaved beings of Leng up the ramp onto one of the black galleys. On that alternate Earth, it will be these turbaned slaves who interact with humans, while their inhuman masters hide belowdecks. Now we finally see that these lunar creatures are generally frog-like in form, their grayish-white flesh translucent and gelatinous. Their only pigment lies in the pinkish tendrils they have in place of a face, which resemble the tentacles of a sea anemone. This still image can not portray how, in life, those pink feelers vibrate weirdly so as to sense their surroundings in ways a human could not imagine. The Moon-Beasts are cruel masters, and while we may not ascertain this from their facelessness we can detect it from the broken misery in the faces of the captured men—and women— from Leng. Envisioning my painting now, against my will I recalled the horrible story Maeve Cawley had told me about those imprisoned, tormented primates. How monstrous, when one race considers itself that superior to another.

In the fourth painting, the galley lifts from its milky moon pool, its prow pointed toward that half-shadowed, white-and-blue ball suspended in the inky firmament. Beneath the craft's deck, powerful Moon-Beasts pull at the oars which—like the raised, membranous sails—somehow propel this galley constructed from the black wood of titanic lunar mushrooms, which grow in underground caverns.

And here ... here before me ... now beckoned the fifth painting, propped upon its easel. At this point I had only sketched in the composition with a pencil, and then covered the canvas in a thin wash of sepia to enhance depth. It waited for the layers of paint that would build it up, flesh it out, bring the scene to life. Again, as with the others, there would be no secret ingredients mixed in. No moon dust, no blood from me or another, no conjured insects, no flakes of skin from a mummified hand in a bottle. The only special ingredient would be *fervor*.

This last painting, per the direction of Jacob Orne, would portray the Earth of the Dreamlands grown large in space as the galley approaches its darkened face, sleeping unaware in its blanket of night. On the deck, gazing toward that globe, a Moon-Beast stands beside a slave woman from Leng, her wrists lashed behind her naked back. She wears no turban, but with her back turned we can't see the nubs of her horns, only her flowing black hair, and we notice that her legs start out shapely before tapering oddly into hooved feet. The Moon-Beast has gripped her long hair roughly, as if to force her to look toward the Dreamlands Earth ... their destination. What nefarious fate awaits this woman there, when she is a bound prisoner and not part of the crew like the other slaves?

While I had the privilege of viewing such creatures through my father's Dream Lens, Jacob Orne surely had no means of his own. He could only imagine these beings, these scenes, from having read the most obscure tomes of esoteric knowledge, such as could be found in my own library. Even if he did possess such books, which he had never admitted to me, he was certainly in possession of a lively imagination to have dreamed up the scenes he had asked me to produce.

Before taking up my palette and squeezing onto it the colors I would be working from, I first would bend my eye to the brass telescope I'd shifted on its armature so as to be directed toward that pentagonal window of glass. Like all the others composing the Dream Lens, its tint was subtle, so its distortion of the natural hues of the scene beyond would be minimal. In his brilliance, my father had even crafted the lenses of this telescope.

I pressed my cheek to the eyepiece, wondering if I would have to make adjustments to the focus, or the distance of the viewing instrument in relation to the violet pane. Right away, however, I saw a glittering starfield spread before me. Viewed closeup this way, through the lens, it was as though I were not perceiving this cosmic expanse from a remove, but whilst floating within it, drifting in that airless and infinite abyss. But alas, the black galley was distant from me, almost swallowed by the shadowed face of Dreamlands Earth, which loomed against the starry background. I would have to attempt some adjustments after all, if I hoped to catch another close look at the craft and its crew.

As I peered through the telescope, however, I finally became aware of a tiny white shape that seemed to have been cast overboard from the receding black galley, on its way no doubt to the many-towered Dreamlands city of Dylath-Leen, to trade its cargo of rubies and other lunar resources. This white, cast-off object tumbled through space, and as it grew steadily larger I realized it was swiftly coming in my direction. As it approached I finally realized that it was no discarded object, but rather one of the pallid Moon-Beasts themselves, which had leaped toad-like off the deck and into space so as to hurtle toward me.

Closer and closer it came, and I watched with fascination and horror, until suddenly the thing seemed to slam against the inside of the domed Dream Lens, though of course this was impossible. But one of its hands, with splayed and padded fingers like those of a gecko, did slap against the other side of the violet pane as if to purposely obscure my view. This action was so startling that it caused me to jerk backwards, away from the telescope's eyepiece.

My heart thudded, and yet I felt a grin carve my features. "You cheeky fiend," I said aloud.

However, when I again brought my gaze to the telescope's lens, through the pentagonal window I saw only a void of blackness, with not even a single star gleaming, only vague nebulous mists rolling across my view. I knew I hadn't bumped or otherwise disturbed my viewing instrument ... but whether the Moon-Beast had done something to thwart my spying upon it, or if the Dream Lens itself had simply stopped cooperating, as it was often wont to do, I did not know.

VI

On All Hallows' Eve, I considered the fifth painting for Jacob Orne completed.

Yes, I could have continued tinkering with it; forever, in fact. A painting is never finished ... one simply stops working on it. I might have obsessed over every tiny detail, the grain of wood in the black boards of the galley's deck, every strand of the Leng woman's lush black mane, so as to crystalize it with realism. The problem with that is, once you crystalize one object or area, for consistency you must do so throughout. The process can be tedious and the overall result mechanical, drained of its raw energy and spontaneity. I preferred to allow my brushstrokes to remain somewhat rough up close, but when the viewer stepped back from the canvas to take it all in ... oh yes, then would these slashes and dabs of pigment coalesce and focus into a sense of tangibility. I have seen many a blotchy Impressionist painting, such as those by Monet, that far more effectively capture the quality of light than the work of a Hyperrealist, however impressive their impersonal technique.

I called the number of the Orne home, and a woman's voice answered as it usually did; doubtless this was Mrs. Orne, Maeve's mother. If I wasn't mistaken, I detected a slurred quality to her speech.

"May I speak with Mr. Orne?" I said.

"Who's calling?"

"Enoch Coffin, madam."

"*Who?*"

"Enoch Coffin ... the artist."

"Oh yeah, yeah. The artist. Hold on, please."

After a minute the man's voice came on. "Mr. Coffin! I'm delighted to hear from you."

"Hello, Mr. Orne. You may be further delighted to know that I have today finished work on the last of your paintings."

"Oh yes, yes, and what an auspicious day for that! If only you could bring it to me tonight as well—that would be too perfect—but I imagine you will want to let it dry before moving it, as with the others."

"Yes; I wanted only to let you know where things stood. As I mentioned when you sent the young fellow for the first painting, even when the surface is dry to the touch, the paint might not be fully dried and stable for as long as a year, so it must be handled delicately. Later, in a few months, I could add a protective layer of varnish to all five paintings, if you wish."

"Ah, but those I already possess are so beautiful, I am quite satisfied with them as they are! My impatience, I fear, prevented me from waiting for those additional measures."

"Well, you can always reconsider down the road, if you desire that extra measure of protection. At the current stage, again, even framing the painting must be handled carefully."

"Which I trust you will take care of yourself, once again?"

"Of course." I had been framing the series in black wood, to complement the fungal timbers of which the galleys of the Moon-Beasts were constructed. "So, I could have the painting framed and in your hands, say, a week from today? Feel free to send your stepson Aidan on the seventh."

There was a pause, as I had anticipated. For one thing, Orne had never told me that the boy who picked up the first four paintings was his stepson, nor his name, only that he would be "sending someone" for them. I had told Maeve Cawley that I would ask around about her brother Aidan, but I confess that I hadn't. But then, I seldom went out these days except for groceries and such. In the past I'd enjoyed attending readings at bookstores and bars by poets and fiction authors—which was how I came to illustrate some of their books or paint an author's image for their back cover—along with gallery exhibits of other artists, but I had fallen away from venturing forth for such events, and hence from hobnobbing and meeting new people. Thus, who was I to ask about the missing young man ... if he was, indeed, still missing? Whatever Orne said next might enlighten me to the situation.

"Ah, but my stepson has gone off on some adventure or other, Mr. Coffin, and remains incommunicado, the young rascal, much to the agitation of his poor mother. I would come to collect the painting myself, but you see, I have a physical condition that makes it difficult for me to leave the house these days."

"Oh, I didn't know; I'm sorry to hear that." I almost said that Maeve hadn't told me, but I didn't want him to know that his stepdaughter had come to see me.

"Yes, such a frustrating state of affairs for someone who used to travel the world!"

"I would be happy to deliver the painting to you in person, then."

"Oh ... my goodness, that is too, too generous of you, Mr. Coffin! Are you sure you don't mind?"

"I don't mind at all, and in fact I would love to see the other paintings as you have exhibited them in your home."

Again there was an odd pause, before Orne replied, "Of course. Of course ... you must. We could drink a toast to your accomplishment."

"If the toast is coffee, then I surely accept."

"You don't drink, Mr. Coffin?"

"Trying to quit, sir."

"For the best, and I should myself. One can easily come to overindulge in one's pleasures, eh?"

"Indeed, Mr. Orne. Indeed. To one's own detriment ... or the detriment of others."

VII

I took a cab to a friend's garage, where I stored my battered old pickup truck, which I had inherited from another chum—an artist who had sadly ended his own life. I paid my living friend a small rental fee, and allowed him to make use of the pickup for his own needs when he required it to transport something or other, his own vehicle being quite small. Since I seldom used the thing, it was in no worse shape than the last time I'd seen it ... whenever that had been. I felt the truck better complemented my own fleshly vehicle more and more with each passing year.

Once I got out of the frustratingly twisted and traffic-clogged "cow paths" of Boston, it took me about forty-five minutes to drive to Eastborough. Actually, I could have taken a train from North Station to the station at the periphery of Eastborough, but then I would have had to walk or call a taxi to get to Orne's residence. Remember, I had the oil painting with me, carefully wrapped in bubble plastic. I'd made sure not to set forth during rush hour, which would have caused a considerable delay. Your humble diarist is no autophile.

Once upon the highway I was much more at ease, coasting right along in my rattling conveyance, though when I entered Eastborough I drove around in confusion for a bit before I found the right street, as I didn't have one of those GPS thingies in my sad old jalopy, nor a mobile phone equipped with such a feature. Orne's house was on Mill Road, set back from the street a bit, the neighboring houses not too near and screened off by trees. To the right was a sizable barn, while behind the house was a woodsy area, cut through by train tracks. Perhaps I could have bribed the train to let me off right at Orne's back door!

I pulled into the drive and disembarked, taking in the property for a moment. An unremarkably handsome house, painted a deep rustic red, with two floors and an attic above that. Perhaps I had expected more from Orne, considering his supposed wealth, but then again Maeve had said he came from money so he might have inherited this domicile, as I had mine, and it held sentimental value. It did have the look of an old house that had been modernized, and I knew Eastborough to be a generally affluent town. I wondered where, in relation to this property, was located Lake Pometacomet, which had something of a reputation for being haunted, as did Eastborough Swamp.

There were three vehicles already parked here, but off to the side in front of the barn, as if to make room for my arrival. I didn't feel they all belonged to Orne, as one of them had Connecticut plates.

After I had taken only a few steps up the walk to the front door, I halted and held my sensitive hands in the air before me, because I had detected *something* radiating from behind that door; some anomalous vibration or pulse of energy. As I struggled to understand what I was sensing, a voice called out to me from the direction of the barn. I'd been taken by surprise, so absorbed was I in feeling at the atmosphere of the place, and as I turned toward the voice I dropped my hands as if I'd been caught at some questionable activity.

"You must be Mr. Coffin," said a tall, powerfully-built Black man with a bald head. He was sharply dressed.

"I am," said I. "And yourself, sir?"

Having reached me, the man extended a hand and crushed my own within it. He watched my eyes intensely, as if he were trying to gauge my own energies through the contact. "An honor to meet such a brilliant painter. As you may have guessed, I'm not Jake Orne ... I'm Abraham Koroma."

"Ah, Abraham ... my father's middle name."

"Oh really? Well, you can call me Abe."

"And apparently, one calls Mr. Orne Jake?"

"That's right. He's a down-to-earth guy." Koroma released my hand and turned toward another man who had followed him from inside the barn. In profile, I saw that Koroma had a strange symbol branded on the side of his head, like a raised keloid. It wasn't a sigil I was immediately familiar with, but one cannot memorize every such character one encounters in arcane tomes. Anyway, it even suggested being two symbols combined. "Here comes Gavin," he said. When Koroma faced me again, I saw he had another glyph or merged pair of glyphs branded on the other side of his prodigious head.

The second man was also large in build, a White man with close-cropped red hair and a great fiery beard. Under his collar showed the tops of cryptic-looking and likely extensive tattoos. "Hey, Mr. Coffin," this ginger giant said to me, also squeezing my hand. "I'm Gavin Ross."

"Charmed. And you youngsters are … ?" I wanted to ask if they were professional wrestlers but bit my tongue.

"We're friends of Jake," Koroma explained. "When he told us you'd be coming to deliver his painting, he asked if we'd want to meet you."

"Of course we wanted," Ross put in. He nodded at my bubble-wrapped package, which I had temporarily leaned against my leg while I felt at the house's subtle but peculiar emanations.

"I am flattered, gentlemen."

"In fact," Koroma said, "we would have been happy to come out to Boston to collect it for Jake, what with little Aidan having run off to wherever, and save you the trip … had you not already offered to bring it yourself."

"As I told Mr. Orne—*Jake*—I am truly intrigued to see how he has hung its predecessors."

"Well, on that note," said Koroma, gesturing toward the front door.

Upon entering we faced a staircase to the second floor, where Maeve had told me my paintings were displayed, but I was directed to the left into a living room. Immediately upon stepping within I found the Orne residence was far less prosaic on the inside than the outside. Perhaps Orne preferred that outwardly his home did not call attention to itself … did not give away the bizarre and varied treasures it had accumulated behind its façade.

"What fascinating decor," I said, glancing around.

"I've told Jake he should charge admission," joked the bushy-bearded

Scotsman. "It's a cross between the Smithsonian and the Addams Family's place."

"Jake's a collector, for sure," said Koroma, taking a seat in a leather chair. "He's been all over the world."

"So I've been told."

"I'll go let him know you're here," said Ross. "Make yourself at home."

"It does remind me, rather, of my home."

I was tempted to gravitate right away to the overstuffed bookcases, one of which ran the length of an entire wall, but I was distracted by all the outré art pieces, artifacts, and scientific specimens that abounded upon the fireplace's mantelpiece, shelves, and a variety of tables. I stepped toward a taxidermied monkey, wondering if it was of the same type abused by the torture group that Orne's late wife had been involved with. Curiously, this snarling creature had apparently been born without eyes, its face above the snout a furry blank.

There were odd fossils, one of them a spiral mollusk as large as a platter, or was that a coiled monstrous millipede? Quite striking was a display of the blood vessels of a human head with brain included, as preserved through plasticization, all vividly red in color and suspended within a block of acrylic. The subject with his mouth hanging open appeared less than pleased with the fate of his corporeal vehicle. Less successfully preserved was a yellowed, flattened jellyfish in another block of Lucite. It seemed an unremarkable specimen upon first glance, but bending to it I was intrigued by two odd crumpled areas on the bell that suggested the folded lids of human-like eyes.

"Is this Mr. Collins?' asked a familiar female voice behind me. I turned to see that Jacob Orne and his wife had entered the living room. I was instantly struck by Orne's appearance; he was suddenly the most shocking specimen in the room. Maeve's mother was less notable, though I could tell that once she might have been as beautiful as her daughter.

"Coffin, dear," her husband corrected her, approaching me with a frightful grin.

Mrs. Orne seemed to flinch at the word. "Oh! Coffin."

"Love, why don't you go fetch our guest some coffee?" Orne said. "In lieu of the demon rum."

"Coffee," Mrs. Orne muttered to herself, turning away blearily in search of her kitchen. "Coffin ... "

"You must forgive my wife," Orne confided in a lowered voice. "She's been in quite a state with that selfish son of hers having left us unexpectedly. I gave the boy a roof over his head, and tried to give his life some structure besides, but ... " He threw up his hands. "In any case, Mr. Coffin, please excuse me for not shaking your hand, but as you can see ... "

"No worries, sir."

As you may gather, I am not squeamish or faint of heart, but even I would have been disgusted at shaking the man's hand, looking as he did.

VIII

The man's hands were a mass of red, open ulcers, with several digits deformed and a few missing their final joint, ending only in nubs. His head was even more shocking: a raw red ball with patchy black hair, that contrasted with his neat and expensive clothing. His nose had eroded, leaving bare slits, as had his upper lip, revealing yellowed teeth that had become startlingly pointed. Black hair had grown upon his chin and both cheeks right up to his eyes, which were hidden by a pair of sunglasses such as a blind man would wear. My first impression was that he had been recently burned in a fire, but my second thought was confirmed by his words.

"Acute porphyria," Orne explained. "It sneaked up on me only about a year ago, else I never would have been able to travel as I did, especially in the sunny climes of Southeast Asia. Believe me, it's even more painful than it looks."

"I'm sorry to hear that," I said inadequately. That condition would explain his werewolf-like hypertrichosis. It is sometimes called "the vampire disease." Still, I found it hard to believe he could have suffered such severe effects in only a year.

"My poor wife, having lost the handsome man she fell in love with," Orne joked. "Perhaps it was from my ghastliness that young Aidan fled. Please, take a seat while we wait for your coffee, Mr. Coffin. Can I call you Enoch?"

"Yes, and I understand you're best known as Jake?" I seated myself.

"To friends old and new, Jake it is." Orne tossed up his hands. "So now you can see why I don't venture outside myself, at least by day. Even artificial light, if too bright, can affect me. I'm having one of my flareups, but even the intervals between them don't reverse the most significant damage. Pah! But enough about me. Here you are, the man himself— Enoch fucking Coffin!"

"Er ... the same." I didn't correct him that my middle name was Donovon, after my father. "You have quite the collection of books and artifacts here, I'm not surprised to see ... given your commission from me. I must say, you have a most vivid imagination, Jake, to have requested such specific images. Your imagination would seem more pronounced than my own. How did you come by those concepts?"

"Through my reading, of course ... through reading. For a man who can no longer travel, I suppose I was attracted to images that conveyed not only the freedom of passage from one sphere to another, but beyond this prison of the waking world."

"I see."

Mrs. Orne reappeared carrying a tray bearing coffee pot and cups, but her steadiness was questionable and Ross stepped forward swiftly to take the tray from her hands. He set it down on a table between me and Orne.

"I'm going to go lie down," the woman announced.

"Good idea, my love," said Orne. "You do that."

"Nice to meet you, Mr. Collins," said his wife, departing from our company.

"Sad about her boy," I said nonchalantly, spooning heaps of sugar into my black brew. "I hope he returns, to end her worries. Does she have any other children?"

"A daughter, who lives in Worcester," was all that Orne would enlighten me.

"Ah, good old Wormtown."

"It is quite wormy," said Orne, raising his own cup. I noticed that neither Koroma nor Ross came to claim coffee for themselves, both giants now seated and watching us in silence as if they were taxidermied specimens themselves. Orne must have noticed my glance at them, from behind his shades. "I hope you don't mind that I invited my dear chums Abe Koroma and Gavin Ross to meet you in the flesh, Enoch."

"Not at all; they've been most cordial."

"Two lovely choirboys, are we," said Ross.

"I can hardly wait for the big reveal," Orne said, nodding at the package leaning beside me.

"Nor can I," I said, referring to the four others in the set. "Well, I suppose I shouldn't keep you in suspense any longer." I twisted away from the table, lest I accidentally knock over my coffee, and took up the bubble-wrapped parcel so as to open it. Tantalized, Orne sat forward in his seat as I produced my switchblade from within my jacket and flicked open its blade.

"Huh," commented Ross. "Cool toy."

I used the knife to slit through the tape holding the wrap's edges together. Replacing my knife, I removed the painting delicately from its cocoon and held it aloft in both hands, by carefully gripping the upper and lower parts of its frame of black wood, then tilting the work toward its new owner.

To my additional horror, Orne removed and folded away his dark glasses, revealing eyes that were entirely bloodshot, the wet flesh they rested in even more vividly crimson. "Oh my!" he gushed. "*Oh my!*"

"Whoa," said Gavin Ross, and Koroma only grunted and nodded in approval.

"You have outdone yourself, Enoch!" Orne raved. "Oh, it's *perfect!* Particularly that fetching inhuman slave girl!"

I wasn't surprised he would say this, as I had made the captured female the focal point of the composition. And, though the being had generally been patterned after actual creatures I had spied through the Dream Lens, I had taken the inspiration for her long, raven hair and sensuous figure directly from the gorgeous Maeve Cawley.

IX

As I mounted the steps I had seen when I'd first come in, following Orne and with Koroma and Ross trudging heavily behind me, I knew that the vague oscillations of energy I had detected outside the house emanated from the room wherein my host had hung my artwork.

I was almost as convinced that he had asked Koroma and Ross here not only because they were bosom buddies, but to act as bodyguards. However Orne had heard about me, he had no doubt also heard rumors that I was adept in the *arts*, not just at art. That, apparently like himself, I held a fascination with the Other. How adept he was himself in the arts I could not as yet ascertain, but the fact that he had wanted muscle here meant that he feared me. Which was not a bad thing; surely better than the other way around.

We reached a landing, and Orne unlocked an innocuous-looking door by means of a keypad. I noted that none of the other closed doors up here were equipped with such a keypad. Orne's body almost blocked my view, but not quite, and I innocently took note of the numbers he entered: 050351. The door unbolted, and as Orne turned to me I looked up, pretending to have been shifting in my hands the painting I carried.

A smile cracked his ulcerated visage, like a fresh wound opening. "And here we are," he announced.

He stepped across the threshold first, reaching just inside to activate a series of track lights on the ceiling. They were positioned in such a way as to illuminate my paintings tastefully, as in a gallery, without shining distractingly off the gloss of their paint or bleaching their carefully modulated hues. Of this I approved, and I have to say I found it attractive the way they stood out against walls that had been painted in matte black. It was also flattering, whatever his intent, that this room seemed dedicated solely to the exhibition of my work. The four paintings hung centered upon four of the odd-shaped room's uneven walls, just as Maeve had described it to me, with a fifth wall being bare. The ceiling, too, was painted black, but the wooden floorboards were golden and lustrous. There was only one thing missing, from what Maeve had told me.

I moved to the center of the room, where stood a narrow base of polished black stone. Maeve had said a globe of Earth's moon should be resting here ... and yet there was nothing. I laid my hand upon the empty spot, and seemed to feel a throbbing through its surface, like the idling of a vehicle that waited to be driven to some important destination. And yet my paintings, too, were the source of the emanations I was sensing, and I knew I hadn't consciously imbued them with any properties that should account for that. Rather, it had to be this room—and what Orne got up to in it—that had instilled my work with this anomalous power. Of course, simply using actual scenes of the Dreamlands for their inspiration had to have automatically imparted *some* kind of uncanny quality to the paintings. Sometimes I don't know my own strength.

"Everything looks lovely!" I said. "I am honored indeed, Jake. Is something missing here, though?"

"Oh yes, unfortunately," said Orne. "I had a lunar globe there, to complement the paintings. The thing even lit up from within! Sadly, when my stepdaughter Maeve visited recently her mother unwisely let her into this room, at Maeve's request, and she swept the globe to the floor and shattered it. I don't know what got into the girl. A moody child, like her brother. I suppose they both resent me to some degree, for replacing their daddy. At least my wife was able to pull Maeve from the room, and lock the door again before she could create further havoc … such as attacking your gorgeous artwork."

"Heaven forbid," I said, with sincerity.

"I'm having the globe repaired, however," Orne added.

"Ah! Well, perhaps I could return some time, to enjoy this room's full effect … with the globe restored and this final painting hung. Or would you like me to do that for you myself, right now?"

Orne narrowed his bloodshot eyes at me strangely, and said, "I appreciate the offer, Enoch, but I think I'd like to hang the last painting myself when I'm alone. As I mentioned, this series of images has personal meaning for me, and I'd like to make the moment a private one."

"Sort of like a little ritual, eh?" I said.

He held my gaze, still looking wary. Was I being too obvious in my probing of him? "Something like that," he replied.

"Well, I can understand. In that case." I stepped over to the bare wall and carefully leaned the painting against it. When I turned toward him again, I saw Orne had pressed a hand to his side—perhaps over his liver, which I knew could be affected by porphyria due to accumulated toxins—with a wincing expression. "Oh dear, Jake; you look to be in discomfort."

"Nothing out of the ordinary, I'm afraid," he said, trying to regain that awful grin of his. "Pain—what an invention! Physical pain is a flawed concept as a warning system that danger is at hand … that damage has been done. What good did suffering excruciating toothaches for years on end do for generations of people before proper dentists existed? If I have a stinging cold sore on my lip that takes days and days to go away … okay, I get it, I have a cold sore … thanks for the info! Why can't I turn that alarm buzzer off, now? I used to think that pain is a punishment from God; that it was *designed* as such. A punishment for the sin of being alive.

For the presumptuousness of *existing.*"

"It seems a prerequisite for gods to be sadistic," I said. "So, do you believe in one, Jake, if I might ask? That is, in the Judeo-Christian sense?"

"Oh, no, no … not for a long time, Enoch." Orne seemed to become a bit fired up about this topic, which made me wonder about his upbringing. "If only the religious knew the true nature of the beings they sense and call angels, or devils. As if such extradimensional entities align themselves to human notions of 'good' and 'evil.' When angels occasionally seem to intercede to benefit any human being, their own motives are actually so alien to us that they are all but unknowable, even to someone like me who doesn't view reality from behind the opaque pages of this or that holy book. The motives of angels, if they could truly be glimpsed, might be terrifying beyond what we imagine as the plotting of demons."

"Hm!" I said. "I would have to concur with you on these sentiments, Jake, for the most part. I might be as wary of meeting a being we humans would consider an angel as one interpreted as a demon."

"Not to say," Orne added, "one might not gain something from such an encounter."

"Such as?"

"Knowledge of the beyond. Of the *Other.*"

"Ah, yes. The elusive and beguiling Other."

"I think we're rather alike, Enoch," Orne said, looking toward my new painting where it leaned against the fifth wall. It was thus perhaps a good thing that he didn't see the expression I felt flicker across my face. "We are very much in tune with our imaginations … and it would seem, in our taste for esoteric reading. But my God, as I say, this last piece is perfection! It's like you plucked that slave girl straight from my mind!"

So had Jacob Orne, then, also used Maeve Cawley to spark his imagination? Thinking of her made me wonder when she had attacked this ritual space, so as to disrupt the power she too sensed. Surely it had been after her visit to me, or she would have mentioned it. When I hadn't agreed to abandon my commission, she must have lashed out in frustration.

Orne winced again, again clutched his side. "Uh! I'm sorry to be a rude host, Enoch, but I fear I must take some painkillers and go lie down for a bit. They exhaust me as much as the pain."

"Not rude at all, sir."

"Abe, if you would."

I looked behind me to the man with his doubly branded skull and saw him hold out to me a thick, folded wad of bills. "Four thousand dollars, Enoch."

"Oh?" I said.

Orne explained, "Three thousand plus a bit of a bonus, as we conclude our little collaborative project. Again, Enoch, I would shake your hand but I'll spare you that. Perhaps we will indeed have the pleasure of meeting again, but if you'll excuse me I'll have Abe and Gavin see you out."

X

That evening I made the mistake of giving in to temptation, and digging out a bottle of merlot I had stashed away as if hidden from myself. Not for celebration of my payday, but in an attempt to soothe my unease after my visit to the home of Jacob Orne. My body still seemed to hum like a tuning fork after my exposure to my own displayed artwork, and I was coming to be less flattered by its exhibition and more resentful that it was being used for purposes I could not quite fathom. Though I had my suspicions, given the series' subject matter and what Orne had claimed it meant to him in his physically tormented state.

After one glass of wine had become another, and another, until the bottle seemed to magically empty itself, I finally retired to bed. If I had felt unease whilst awake, however, my anxiety was only magnified once I fell into dreaming.

I saw a woman standing before me, turned to a pillar of flame. Her arms were upraised and head thrown back, as if calling unto the sky. She appeared to be posed at the edge of a plateau, while beyond her rolled vast, white-glowing clouds. As they churned, sometimes through their billows I caught broken glimpses of a shockingly immense mountain that my dream self seemed to understand was none other than legendary Kadath.

In my hands I realized I was holding two objects, and I looked down to see that I gripped the tails of a pair of dead, limp monkeys. Their heads had been severed, and I had used their dripping blood to form a circle around the woman who stood enveloped in flames at its center.

Looking up again, I found that the woman had in fact vanished, like a sacrifice accepted. In her place stood another form, very much larger, the hem of its black cloak barely contained within the summoning circle.

This looming entity was apparently human-like in form overall, though I could not be certain what lay beneath its flowing garment. Yet while the towering figure possessed a human-shaped head, devoid of hair and obsidian in coloration, the thing lacked ears or even a face. Instead, a black orb circled the head slowly, like a moon orbiting a world, and eyes of varying sizes with variously-colored irises continuously opened and closed across this rotating sphere's surface. Each of them gazed down upon me, with what I felt was icy contempt.

I took this eidolon to be one of the thousand forms of the Strange Dark One, that Faceless God worshipped by human cultists and beings from far-flung worlds alike. And then suddenly, for lack of a face, it spoke its words directly from its mind into my own, though they seemed to thunder deafeningly.

"You think to summon me, as you would call a servant unto you?"

At which point, I was not so much awakened from my dream as *ejected* from it, as if rejected and cast away by the Faceless God my dream self had so arrogantly sought to conjure. I scrambled out of bed and rushed to my bathroom, where I emptied my sorry guts of the vessel of wine I had unwisely consumed. While so doing, I found I was holding one hand clamped against my side, about where my liver sulked.

It was then that I thought: *Ah yes, Mr. Orne. We* have *become rather attuned to each other, haven't we?*

‡

Over my morning coffee, the cramp in my abdomen thankfully gone but replaced by a formidable headache, I called the number of Maeve Cawley. I hoped to catch her before she departed for whatever job she'd said she had in Worcester, but was met with her answering machine. That is, voicemail as the kids call it.

"It's Enoch Coffin. The painter, not the one who expired in 1761. You may call me back at your convenience."

I was about to hang up when a hurried voice came on. "I'm here, I'm here … I just had to pull over to the shoulder."

"I wouldn't want you getting into an accident on my account."

"So what do you want, Mr. Coffin? If you're going to tell me you delivered my stepfather his fifth painting yesterday, I already know. I spoke to my mom on the phone last night. So unless you've learned anything about the whereabouts of my brother … "

"Sorry; I haven't. I take that to mean you and your mother haven't, either?"

"We have not. So, what did you think of my stepfather? Personally I find him as charming as he is attractive."

"You neglected to tell me about his … condition."

"I have the feeling it's the least ugly part of him. Though, I have to admit, he was a hell of a lot better-looking when I first met him."

"So this state came on pretty rapidly."

"It did. I'm sure my mother wouldn't have become involved with him looking like this, wealth or no."

"He told me it's porphyria, but I suspect it's something else that

159

simply gives the appearance."

"What do you mean?"

"I think perhaps that your stepfather has made a number of attempts, without proper knowledge and safeguards, to make contact with the realms of beyond ... and certain denizens therein."

There was a brief silence, except for the humming sounds of highway traffic in the background. "Are you trying to say he's conjured demons?"

"I said nothing of demons, but I do think he's suffered a corruption of his body and spirit—and no doubt his mind, though I imagine it was already corrupted enough—through his careless experiments."

"I'm still not getting it. It sounds to me as if whatever crazy stuff he believes in, you believe in it, too."

"Miss Cawley ... when we met you said you sensed a *wrongness* to the room in which he's displayed my art."

"I do sense that, but it's an intuition about the things I think he might be getting up to ... occult rituals or whatever, yes. But that doesn't mean I believe in the stuff that the two of you do."

"Your senses are correct; you should trust them. I feel he means to perform a ritual involving my paintings ... to bring about a means of transporting himself to another realm, a plane known as the Dreamlands, where his failing body can be reconstituted and he can live a better existence."

Another long pause, followed at last by: "Are you fucking kidding me, Mr. Coffin?"

I sighed. "I thought you would be more receptive to what I had to tell you."

"How *can* I be? It's insane! Just tell me this, okay? Is my mother safe there with him? Do you think it was him who actually set his first wife on fire in their backyard?"

I did not illuminate her about the dream I had suffered last night, which now felt more to me like a vision. If not a shared memory. "That may still be the case, so as to prevent her from implicating him in her crimes. However, I'm leaning toward the idea that she did indeed willingly sacrifice herself, knowing that she would soon likely be incarcerated. Judging from what you told me about her perverse and dark nature, it would seem she was of a similar character to her husband. As for your mother, I imagine his attraction to her was largely just physical."

"Sacrifice, you said? Do you mean literally? Sacrifice to *what?*"

"You asked me if your mother is safe there. She may be, as your stepfather now appears to consider her a mere afterthought. Surely they are no longer intimate. But, she may also be in grave danger."

"Thanks for being so clear about things."

"I just can't say at this point. My time with the man was thankfully brief. I did find him more than a little intriguing, where he has similar interests to my own in some ways, as you've pointed out. However, his presence is highly toxic, as is that of his two beefy henchmen."

"Abe and Gavin? Yeah, they give me a very creepy vibe, to say the least. The way they look at me when I'm there … like tigers eyeing some meat."

"And does your stepfather look at you in that way? That is, in a lustful manner?" I didn't tell her how she had inspired my interpretation of the slave girl, as seen from behind, in the fifth painting … and how excited Orne had been about that nude figure.

"I get that sense," Maeve admitted. "After all, I look a lot like my mom. Why, did he say anything suggestive about me?"

"No … he only told me that you recently shattered that lunar globe you had mentioned to me."

"I wanted to do more than that, but I couldn't bring myself to."

"So you couldn't destroy my magnificent paintings, after all."

Maeve gave a bitter snort. "That wasn't it! It was just that I was afraid of what he might do to me, if I'd done so."

"I do believe you shouldn't anger him. And if you can help it, you should stay away from your mother's home. If you must visit with her, I suggest doing so outside somewhere."

"I'll keep that in mind. Better yet, as you said so yourself before, I wish I could convince her to divorce him. One last thing, before I have to be on my way to work. You feel my stepfather is toxic, you say. Corrupted, and dangerous. So … do you feel he might have done something to my brother Aidan?"

"Your sibling may simply have fled from him, no longer able to stand his presence and be ordered around by him," I told her. "However, I do feel there is also the possibility that yes, he may be directly responsible for your brother's disappearance."

XI

With the Dream Lens covered again by the blue tarp, like a far-seeing eye sleeping under its closed lid, I started my next painting in my attic studio instead of the basement. This was no commission, but purely for myself. Without first penciling in a sketch to paint over, I launched right into pushing pigment around … and soon realized, as if my unconscious had been plotting it all along, that I was going to try capturing that imposing black figure I had seen in my nightmare. The Strange Dark One, with a thousand faceless faces. That mysterious pharaoh, that Messenger of the Outer Gods; he whom the Moon-Beasts serve. *Nyarlathotep*, if I dare write that name here.

By evening, after a long session of pure inspiration, I had fleshed out the image nicely. The towering figure was quite as I recalled it: the obsidian-black head without a countenance, around which orbited a black globe covered in variegated eyes. The body draped with a flowing black cloak. Except, in my dream-vision no limbs had shown outside that garment, but in my painting I had the compulsion to portray one arm reaching out from its folds, the fingers spread, as if grasping toward the painting's viewer. After roughing in this limb I stepped back from the canvas and studied it, questioning myself about having added this feature. It was not only an inaccurate detail, but I feared it was excessively dramatic. And yet, in the end I decided to trust my instincts and leave it.

I would work further on the painting later, to bring it more to life, but I was very much satisfied with the results thus far. Despite being commissions, the paintings for Jacob Orne had seemed a breakthrough for me, and I felt I had found my way back to myself. And I hadn't drank a drop throughout the entire hours-long session. Ah yes, my perhaps future readers: it was the return of Enoch Coffin.

As I had worked, though, my mind had wandered back to Orne and the quintet of pieces I had created for him. I was now convinced that he meant to use them, as I had suggested to Maeve Cawley, as part of a ritual that would transport himself into the Dreamlands to begin a new life in new flesh.

There were said to be a number of different ways to reach that plane, besides the brief visits we make astrally when we sleep. One method was supposedly to locate and descend, whilst in light slumber, seventy steps to the so-called cavern of flame ... and from there, to descend seven hundred further steps to the Gate of Deeper Slumber. Some used lucid dreaming or hallucinogenic drugs in their efforts. A few years back, a young freak from the Sesqua Valley had come to seek my assistance in crossing over to the Dreamlands, specifically the Plateau of Leng, along with some friends. At his request, I had given him some small fragments from a mummified hand in my collection of oddities and wonders ... and had never heard from him again.

One thing I couldn't understand: if Orne wanted to project himself into the Dreamlands, and sought a collection of paintings that portrayed a journey to the alternate version of our world, then why hadn't he asked me to paint him into those images, riding on that black galley of the horrid Moon-Beasts? Well, partly I supposed it was because I had never seen him in the flesh during my work on those paintings. A stronger consideration, though, was that Orne wouldn't want me to portray him in those images in his corrupted state, afraid that when he was translated into that other realm he would find himself in the same hideous body.

I, who had never attempted to enter the Dreamlands bodily, couldn't quite understand Orne's method. It might well not even work, of course, though there was the possibility he had attained certain knowledge beyond my own. In the end, so what if he was successful in his endeavor? Wouldn't that satisfy Maeve, after all—if her despised stepfather disappeared forever, and her mother was left with his fortune?

As I left my studio to go downstairs and start some dinner for myself, I glanced back at the painting and decided on the morrow I would add a troupe of Moon-Beasts cavorting in dance around the hem of the Faceless God's robe, playing on flutes inserted between the tendrils of which their faces were composed.

XII

It was now toward the end of November, and late in the afternoon when I returned home from a day spent in Providence, where I'd met my friend Candice for lunch at a favorite sandwich shop. Their Thanksgiving sandwich was the closest I would come to celebrating that imminent holiday. We had then walked about that city, visiting several book stores, and it had felt good to be visiting another person after my increasing isolation of the past few years.

Because darkness came so early now, I almost didn't spot the figure sitting on the sidewalk opposite my door, curled almost into a ball with her arms hugging her legs and her back to the ancient graveyard's brick wall.

I crossed little Charter Street to stand before Maeve Cawley. "What are you doing here … attempting to freeze yourself into a statue that might be added to the burial ground? What a delightful idea; then I might admire your beauty there every day."

The young woman turned up her face to me, and I saw her eyes were filmed in tears. "I've been trying to call you for hours."

"I was out. The only phone I possess is in there." I motioned behind me. "What has happened?"

"They found my brother Aidan," she sobbed.

"I see. Let's get you inside."

Within my house, I sat her down on a sofa, found a quilt to drape about her shoulders, and put on a pot of coffee. She accepted the cup I handed her and I seated myself opposite her. My visitor's hands trembled as she took a careful sip of the scalding brew.

"He's dead," she croaked. "I guess you gathered that much."

"How?" I asked.

"Murdered." The tears and sobbing were renewed. "I had to identify his body. It was terrible ... so terrible." She set down her cup, lest in her trembling she spill its contents on herself.

"Where was he found?"

"In a tree! As if a leopard had left him up there, or something! A tree near Lake Pometacomet, in Eastborough. Who knows how long he might have been there, rotting away, if two people walking their dog hadn't spotted him. He was naked ... and ... and ... "

"If I might ask, do they know how he was killed yet?"

"They're going to do an autopsy, but it's clear he was murdered. Those horrible ... mutilations ... "

"Sorry, Maeve, but tell me about the mutilations."

"I can show you," she said, reaching into a pocket of her jeans for her cell phone. "I insisted they let me take pictures of his body."

Another person might have discouraged her from taking that action, and asked if such images were really something she wanted lodged in her head whenever she thought of her brother, but for my part I admired her strength for having done so. I moved from my chair to seat myself on the sofa beside her as she handed me the phone, that I might examine the series of images for myself.

As Maeve had said, the young man was nude, except for a thin gold chain bearing a small medallion or pendant. In macabre contrast to his body's sorry state, Aidan Cawley still retained the beauty that I remembered from his visits to my home to collect the first four paintings, though his half-lidded eyes looked gray rather than green in death, and his formerly lovely pink lips were colorless, slightly parted as if his final exhalation would be drawn out through eternity. There were scratches upon his face and body, as if he had been dropped into the trees from an airplane and crashed through the branches until coming to rest upon stronger boughs. Indeed, one leg was unnaturally twisted, with a jagged end of tibia protruding from the wound.

Most striking, however, was a series of odd wounds dispersed across the body, though all of them were shallow. These had not been made by any fall. Each was of equal size and shape: a long, elliptical portion of skin, pointed at both ends, had been neatly excised from various areas. Maeve had asked the attendant to move the body upon the steel table to allow her to take pictures even of its back. In all, I counted twelve of these identical wounds across the chest, the back, the thighs, the outside of the arms.

"So precise," I said. "But these are not lethal injuries."

"Like I said, they still need to do the autopsy."

"He couldn't have inflicted these wounds on himself. Certainly not the ones on his back."

"Of course not—and why would he?"

"And these flayed panels of flesh ... none were discovered at the scene?"

"No. At least, not that they told me."

I didn't want to say to the poor bereaved woman that I wouldn't rule out the missing flesh having been consumed, as part of the ritual I'd been speculating about. Instead, I noted, "He doesn't seem to have been dead long. There's no decomposition. So where has he been all this time?"

"I told the police to go interrogate my stepfather," Maeve blurted. "I know he had something to do with this ... I know he did! Sure, he's not so strong himself, but I'll bet he had those goons of his, Abe and Gavin, hold him captive somewhere all this time. Who knows, maybe even out in the barn. My mother never goes out there."

"Anything is possible," I said. "If your stepfather is responsible, though, I doubt he would be so unwise as to have left any evidence at home."

"It isn't so easy to get away with murder these days, Mr. Coffin. Plus, as you've seen yourself, my stepfather is insane. He slipped up somewhere, and they'll find out where!"

I handed her back the phone. "Is your mother still at the house with him?"

"Yes! She doesn't believe what I tell her! She pities that awful man. She thinks Aidan ran into the wrong crowd somewhere … met a lover who turned out to be a killer. But I know better, and so do you."

"Hm," I muttered, as I lifted my own cup of coffee for a pensive sip. "Those curious markings. And his body found up in a tree … "

"All part of that psycho's black magic! A few days ago, before the police called me, my mother met me for lunch in Worcester and told me my stepfather had been acting weird lately … extra weird, I mean. He'd been locking himself in that room with your paintings, and when he'd come out he'd be all grouchy and not want to talk to her."

"His attempts at whatever ritual he seeks to perform have been unsuccessful," I theorized.

"Of course they're unsuccessful … it's all just madness!"

"The madness part I won't dispute." I sighed. "Let me know how it goes, with the police questioning him."

"I don't dare go to the house myself," Maeve said, her lovely eyes turning fiery. "My mother told me he wants me to join them for Thanksgiving dinner—he's been very insistent about it. Ha! As if! I don't trust myself; I'd stab him to death with the carving knife!"

"I think it's a good idea to stay away," I agreed. "But as for myself … I believe I'd like to make another trip to Eastborough."

‡

When Maeve left, she thanked me for having said I planned to go visit Jacob Orne again, to see what I might glean from that meeting. When I was once again alone, however, I asked myself why I even intended to. Of course I pitied the poor child, but I was surely no righteous hand of the law. And yet, though I would hate to admit such to her, I did feel some degree of guilt for having contributed in any way to Orne's obsession. And then there was my pure sense of curiosity about this strange, corrupted individual with his similar interests in the Other. Why not probe him a bit? After all, I had my money already and didn't need to be concerned with alienating him.

That night, with these matters on my mind, I had another ominous and vivid dream.

In this one, I stood at the attic window that looked out from the back of my house. Here, the view would normally be of the baseball field of Langone Park, from which came such obnoxious noise during the warmer months, but it was obscured from view by a thick and churning fog. Despite this fog, however, a full moon shone huge and clear in the sky, and it glowed a crimson red. So much so, that its radiance caused my studio to resemble a photographer's darkroom.

In gazing upon that bloody orb, I felt the attention of a cult of Moon-Beasts who similarly contemplated me from afar, as if they possessed a Dream Lens of their own. Unnerved by this intense sensation, in my dream I pulled the shade and drew the curtains to shut out my sight of that horrid globe.

And then, with the sun not yet risen, I awoke to an epiphany.

At first I had suspected that Jacob Orne had consumed those twelve slabs of flesh flensed from his stepson's nude body. But now, I realized what they had reminded me of on some subconscious level.

The paper panels, called gores, that manufacturers glue in place to form the surface of globes of the Earth.

XIII

I made my second trip to the house on Mill Road without calling ahead to forewarn its owner. I didn't know who would answer the door when I rang—Orne or one of his flunkies—but it turned out to be Maeve's mother. The woman didn't appear drunk yet, which surprised me given the news about her son, but the day was young. "Oh," she said, in a voice drained of all life, "Mr. Collins."

"Yes, Mrs. Orne, as you wish. Have I come at a bad time?" I asked innocently.

"Oh ... you haven't heard?" Now her voice fractured, and tears came forth. Her face with its echo of past glory resembled her daughter's when in anguish. "My son ... my son, Aidan ... they've found his murdered body."

"*What?* Oh dear! Oh, Mrs. Cawley, I am so very sorry to hear this. I feel horrible for having barged in at such a time. Should I go?" I half turned away from the door she held open.

"Did you come to see my husband?"

"Yes, I did ... oh, but at such a time. He must be grieving for his beloved stepson."

"I could tell him you're here," she assured me, bravely fighting to hold back the dam from bursting entirely, though in agitation she fingered a thin gold chain she wore. Whatever pendant the necklace might bear was hidden inside her blouse. "You've come so far, haven't you?"

"Well ... if you think it would be all right. I have something for him, you see." As I stepped over the threshold I raised the bubble-wrapped package I had brought along with me. "A little gift."

"Jake's soaking in the tub right now," the woman informed me. "It brings him comfort. His pain, you know. I'll tell him you're here ... " She began to step away, but I lifted a hand to halt her.

"Oh no, no, I wouldn't dream of disturbing him. Let him emerge from his comforting soak when he's ready. I'll just wait quietly for him."

"If you're sure you don't mind."

"Mrs. Orne … you say your poor boy Aidan was *murdered?* Do the police know by whom?"

"No, they've only just begun investigating. They were here a few hours ago to talk to Jake and me. It's too terrible … my beautiful boy … oh, I can't bear it … "

I reached to put my free hand on her arm. My compassion, I assure you, was not feigned in this. I too was the only son of my mother. "Did he have any enemies? Do they have a suspect?"

"Not that I know of, but I think it must be someone in Boston, where he was staying with some friends before he disappeared. The police are talking to them, too."

"Well, I dearly hope they find the culprit soon, before the fiend harms someone else."

"Yes … oh yes," she said, still unconsciously plucking at her necklace.

I wagged my head sympathetically, and as I withdrew my hand I said, "In the meantime, Mrs. Cawley, while I wait … I presume you have two bathrooms, in a home as lovely as this? Is Jake upstairs or downstairs?"

"Downstairs. Upstairs we only have a shower."

"Ah, perfect," I said. "Then if you'll excuse me, may I make use of your upstairs bathroom? As you say, it has been a bit of a longish drive, if you catch my meaning."

"Of course, of course," Orne's wife said. "Be my guest. I was just about to make a gin and tonic for myself. Would you care for one, too?"

"No, madam, but thank you. You should surely go sit down now and rest. Oh, if I'd known about your tragic loss I would have delayed this visit."

"You're very kind, Mr. Collins," she sniffled.

And so I turned and started up the stairs opposite the front entrance, while the piteous wraith drifted off toward the kitchen. I could hardly blame her for seeking her liquid oblivion.

Once I'd ascended to the second floor, I was confronted once more with that innocuous-looking white door from behind which radiated strange waves of energy, like the throbbing of some great living heart. This emanation was much stronger than the last time I had been here; I would go so far as to say oppressive. I almost winced against its power. Whatever his failings heretofore, it was unquestionable that Jacob Orne possessed abilities.

My eyes fell, of course, to the keypad set into the door above its metal knob. As I raised my free hand to enter the number I had had the foresight to memorize—050351—I detected a presence behind me and whirled about, startled.

There, having mounted the stairs barefoot and stealthy, stood none other than Jacob Orne himself, wrapped in a thick, white bathrobe. What few black strands remained on his sore-encrusted head were plastered wetly to his skull. His eyes with their fully pink sclera stared with a fearsome intensity, and his pointed teeth showed in a nauseating smile.

"What a surprise, Enoch," the man said. "You should have told me you were coming."

"But then it wouldn't be a surprise, Jake, would it?" said I. I'm sure my own smile was not much more convincing.

The man nodded at the package I carried. "What do you have there?"

"The nature of my surprise. I had hoped to leave it in your private gallery, for greater impact, but just now I remembered that one requires a passcode to enter."

"Is it a painting, Enoch?"

"It is!" I declared brightly.

"Ah. But I only requested five from you. Not at all to sound ungrateful, but I wouldn't want to disturb the series … "

"Of course, of course. But after you gave me an extra thousand dollars as a bonus, I was inspired to answer your kindness with a kindness of my own. May I enter?" I nodded at the locked door. "In any case, I've been dying to see your gallery with my fifth painting in place."

I could see that Orne was hesitating, his smile quivering as if it were on the verge of collapse. He glanced behind him, perhaps to see where his wife had got off to. Or might those two other men, Abraham Koroma and Gavin Ross, be here? I remembered one of them had a car with Connecticut plates, so they obviously didn't dwell on the premises.

"Why not?" Orne said at last, and I stepped aside as he moved forward to punch in the code I'd taken note of. The door was opened, and he waved me inside with an affectation of graciousness.

Right away, my gaze fell not on my final painting in the commissioned series, where it now hung in place on the fifth of the oddly-shaped room's walls, but on the globe seated upon a stand atop that black stone base which had formerly stood empty.

"I almost expected a magic circle to have been painted on the floor since the last time I was here," I told him, approaching the room's center.

"Do you take me for a satanist, Enoch?"

"Oh, but I'm offended, sir! I myself have been known to utilize magic circles."

"Then no offense was intended."

The globe atop its pedestal was not a moon, as Maeve had reported to me. Perhaps it once had been. Now, that sphere was covered in discolored, leathery petals that appeared to have been glued in place. I didn't need to count them to know they were twelve in number. Surely, if the police had already been here to talk to Orne and his wife about the discovery of Aidan Cawley's body, Orne had hidden away this object before they could see it.

"This is unusual," I said, reaching to touch the thing.

"Ah!" Orne cried. "Please don't! It's rather delicate. My stepdaughter Maeve shattered it, as I mentioned, and I have only just had it repaired. I needed to use this method to hold it together."

"It must be of great importance to you, to have made the effort. Is it still meant to represent our moon Luna?"

"Perhaps *that* version of our moon Luna," Orne said, pointing to one of my mounted paintings, in which was represented the moon of the Dreamlands.

"I see. 'The sacred moon overhead, Has taken a new phase,'" I recited.

"Hm?" said Orne.

"Oh, sorry. It's from Yeats. I'm a fan. It ends: 'And lifts to the changing moon, His changing eyes.'"

"Oh! That's perfect. We are indeed attuned, you and I. And so." He pointed at the package concealed in bubble wrap. "Your gift?"

"Yes, of course." From a jacket pocket I removed my switchblade, clicking its blade into place. As I moved to cut the tape holding the package closed, however, I suddenly looked up to Orne's face. "But oh!" I exclaimed. "When your poor wife let me in she told me the shocking news about your stepson!"

"Oh yes, of course ... dear Aidan," Orne said, his horrid features attempting to express sorrow. I could swear I heard a scab on his face crackle.

"What a fool I am for not calling!"

"But here you are, Enoch. With an unexpected gift, no less."

Still my blade was poised unmoving. "She said the police came here to interview the both of you?"

"Yes, only a couple of hours ago."

"Do they have any leads?"

"Not that they've yet disclosed to us. Who knows what kind of people that troubled boy hung out with. His mother and I tried our best to set him on a straight path, but ... " Orne leaned toward me and confided in a hushed croak, "I suspect it had something to do with drugs."

"Hm! Drugs. Could be, couldn't it?"

For a long moment we held each other's gaze, neither of us speaking, until Orne gestured at the package I had brought. "But your *gift*, Enoch?"

"Of course, of course!" I finally began slicing through the tape. "I'll leave this for you and be on my way quickly. I'm sure you two would rather be alone at such a distressing time." As I cut the last piece of tape, I asked nonchalantly, "And what of your stepdaughter? Has she been told the news?"

"Yes, my wife has called Maeve, as did the police. Sorry to say she and I are no longer on speaking terms, apparently. Through no desire of mine. A troubled child, like her brother. I truly hope she never comes to such an end as he did."

These words caused me to look back up at Orne for a moment. "I truly hope not, too." And then, I pulled back the wrapping from the painting that stood leaning against my legs.

XIV

Aghast, Jacob Orne took a step back from my revealed painting, as if from a rearing cobra. "What is this?" he cried out. "Why have you brought it to me?"

"It's an image that came to me in a dream," I explained.

It was, of course, my most recent painting, which I had meant to be solely for myself. Against a background of heaped clouds soared the dramatically steep mountain that I took to be Kadath of the dream realm, and the mountain in turn formed a backdrop for that ebon titan wrapped in its long cloak. Before its blank face hovered that sphere covered in eyes, but I had added other, translucent versions of the same satellite to indicate how it circled the figure's head. One arm had emerged from the cloak to reach toward the viewer—as if to pass beyond the limits of the canvas—while about the concealed feet of the Faceless God gamboled a sect of Moon-Beasts, made puny in contrast, flutes in their webbed hands.

"How could you have seen this thing, just as I saw it?" Orne all but choked.

"You've said we are in tune with each other, Jake, so that's why I thought you might appreciate it."

Orne clapped his hands over his eyes. "Why did I let you bring that thing into this room, to corrupt what I've created here?"

174

That *he* had created? Harumph! I had done most of the work for him. "So you're saying you're familiar with this specific image, Jake? Did you see the Strange Dark One in a dream, yourself? Or did you perhaps even summon it at one time? Might that even be the true cause of your physical degeneration?"

"What do you think you know?" Orne dropped his hands from his eyes, and I saw that tears of blood had begun running from their ducts. Other thin streams trickled from the slits that were all he had left for a nose.

"You seem to deride the notion of using a magic circle in one's summoning," I said, "and yet didn't you yourself make use of one, when you sought to communicate with the great Messenger of the Outer Gods? In my dream, I saw a circle drawn with the blood of headless primates ..."

"Leave me!" Orne cried out in a phlegmy voice, or was that blood in his throat now? "Take that abomination with you!"

I held out my hands in innocence. "As I say, I meant it only as a humble gift!"

"Give me that blade of yours and I'll slash the thing to ribbons!"

I lifted the painting by the edges of its frame and held it protectively. "I think not, sirrah!" Why did everyone seem to want to destroy my paintings of late?

"What game are you playing with me, Coffin? Why would you torment me, after how generous I've been to you ... how cordial, when you first came here?" He gestured at my painting with one ghastly claw. "Take it away, I told you!"

"But I thought perhaps we might make a trade! I give you this fine painting, and in return I take that interesting globe of Luna you have padded in such an interesting covering of leather ... "

"Out, out, get out!"

I backed toward the black room's doorway, carrying my exposed painting and leaving the bubble wrap behind like a snake's shed skin. "Where did you have the boy hidden while he still lived, Jake? In a cage out in that barn on your property? At what point did you take the flesh from him for that globe … and was he still alive when you did?"

"You will regret this, Coffin!" Orne shrieked, stalking toward me to urge me out of the room, but still keeping his gaze averted from the painting. Though I would not have him tear it with his gnarled, outstretched fingers, I still held it in front of me like a shield to keep him at bay.

"I suspect the forthcoming autopsy will find that the poor youth was drugged, so you could do as you would with him. But you've prepared for that, haven't you, by suggesting he was into drugs? After you took his flesh from him, to serve as offering and impart potency to your rite, did you then use him as a guinea pig to see if a portal would open—even before the fifth painting was in place to complete the machine, as it were? Or was he simply a living sacrifice? If so, you failed, and the sacrifice was rejected … spat back out into our world over at Lake Pometacomet, said to be a haunted spot. You really are a fumbling novice, aren't you, Jacob Orne? But a dangerous novice indeed."

"Out of my home! *Now!*"

I had backed out of the room into the hallway, and in following me Orne slammed the little gallery's door shut. Once again the lock was engaged. I smiled at him. "What are you going to do, Jake … call the police on me? I imagine they'd be as intrigued by your globe of Luna as am I."

"Call them back here!" he barked. "That globe won't be in there when they come! What are you going to tell them, Coffin; that I sent my stepson through a portal into another plane of existence?"

"Perhaps if they search your barn they'll find some trace of his blood, his DNA … "

"They might very well, since he lived here, didn't he?" Orne stood trembling violently, blood flowing more copiously from his ruined nose and streaming down his cheeks. The sclera of his eyes had gone from pink to scarlet. "I thought we were alike … that you possessed an authentic zeal for discovery; that you were an explorer of the Other! Little did I realize your interest lies only in imbuing your art with cheap effects, for the sake of self aggrandizement! Where does this moral superiority come from? You've only revealed how sadly timid you are!"

"I resent that you've sullied my art, Orne, by involving me in a murder." I turned from him and started down the stairs, where I saw Maeve's mother stood looking up at us with a glass in hand and a worried expression on her once radiant face.

"What's going on up there?" she asked, once again plucking at her gold chain in what I now took to be a common nervous mannerism.

"I am truly sorry to have made a scene here, at this time of bereavement, dear lady," I said, moving past her to the door. As I put my hand to the knob, I looked back at Orne one last time, where he stood poised halfway down the stairs. "I do hope, sir, that bringing my painting into your ritual room hasn't tainted its power, as you fear. After all, it would be best for everyone if you were successful ... and left this terrestrial plane for another."

"If you feel that way, then why did you come if not to thwart me?"

"To let you know that I know, Jacob Orne," said I. "And as I say ... to express my displeasure about the misuse of my talents." I nodded toward his wife. "How do you think she would respond if she were to understand everything?"

Orne's voice then could not have been more ominous in tone. "Do not put her at risk, Coffin. That would be on you."

"Jake?" the woman said, looking back and forth between us with glassy eyes. Though she hadn't been gone long to the kitchen, this was likely not her first gin and tonic.

"Don't be concerned, my love," Orne said. "Mr. Coffin and I just had a slight disagreement, over the price he demanded for his latest painting. He was just leaving ... aren't you, Mr. Coffin?"

"For now," I told him. I tipped the brim of my hat to Mrs. Orne. "Again, madam, my deepest condolences for your son having been taken from you so cruelly." And then, leaving their poisoned abode, I welcomed the lessening of those vile emanations as I walked toward my parked truck.

XV

An artist does not live on paint thinner fumes alone, so in Eastborough center I parked within walking distance of a diner I recalled having lunched at a good number of years ago. I soon found that sometime in the interim it had been transformed into a Korean restaurant, of all things, but that was fine by me and I ordered beef bulgogi and glass noodles. While my meal was being prepared and I snacked on the various delightful side dishes, I contemplated what my next action should be. How had I gotten myself into this odd situation? By inviting fetching strangers into my home, I supposed. Or by accepting art commissions from madmen. Both of which weaknesses were not alien to me.

I was hesitant to enlighten Maeve about the use to which her brother's missing flesh had been put, which confirmed her stepfather's role in his demise. If she in turn notified the police, as Orne had told me himself he could swiftly hide away that ghoulish globe, and hadn't lawmen already been to his home today? Nor might they find anything untoward in the barn, since it was possible Aidan Cawley had never been imprisoned there, so near to his mother. It was more likely Koroma and Ross had held him captive at another location. What did those two men have to gain from aiding Orne? Well, besides the fact that he was probably paying them handsomely—after all, Orne wouldn't need money where he intended to go, and he likely didn't care all that much about providing for his wife when he was gone—it seemed clear to me from the brands on Koroma's head and the tattoos partly glimpsed on Ross's person that they were also committed "explorers of the Other." There might even be others in their little cult.

Maeve had made it clear that she herself didn't much believe in matters pertaining to the Other; that she thought of Orne and me, alike, as sorely deluded. Also, there was the possibility that informing her about the globe would only send her raging to that residence to confront Orne … whereafter she would likely find herself in dire jeopardy. No, at this point it seemed more prudent to merely insist to Maeve that she call her mother and beg her to come stay at her place, or somewhere else so long as it wasn't under the same roof as Jacob Orne. Especially after the threat he had made to me, in his wife's uncomprehending presence. And yet, I feared the woman was devoted to him even in his hideously transformed state, and wouldn't abandon him. At least, not without having her husband's crimes unequivocally revealed to her. Again, this might only put both women in an even more dangerous position.

I kept coming back to the thought that the best course of action was simply be to leave Orne to his devices, so that he might complete his rite of transportation and flee this world for another, after which he would no longer pose a danger to anyone here.

Still, I was haunted by how enthusiastically he had responded to that image I had centered the fifth painting around: the sensuous nude slave girl of Leng, who in a fevered inspiration I had based upon his stepdaughter Maeve. This reminded me of what the young woman had told me: that he had tried to convince her, through her mother, to come to the house to join them for Thanksgiving dinner.

Knowing now about the fate of her brother—the flesh taken from him for the gallery's centerpiece, and the odd teleportation of his corpse—caused me to fear that Orne would try bringing a second offering through the portal with him when he was ready. This time a beautiful, unmarred offering … that would buy his passage aboard the black galley of the Moon-Beasts, as they ferried him to his new life within the Dreamlands.

Yes, as I sat there munching delicious food and digesting my own thoughts, I became absolutely convinced of it. Orne hoped to make his stepdaughter Maeve Cawley his true offering to those beasts of the

Dreamlands, who serve the Faceless God.

‡

I drove back toward Boston and the telephone in my apartment, thinking that perhaps it wasn't such a bad idea to give in to modernity and acquire one of those blasted little mobile phones, after all.

At the very least, I needed to reinforce to the young woman that she must under no circumstances go to her mother's house ... and again, that she must try her hardest to impress upon Orne's wife that it was in her best interest to leave him.

When I unlocked my door and entered my house at last, I realized I'd made a serious mistake in lingering in Eastborough to dine, rumbling tummy or no. Already there ahead of me and seated inside my living room were Abraham Koroma and Gavin Ross, who I assumed had picked the aged lock rather than used any supernatural skills to open my door. Ross had a pistol in one hand, resting casually in his lap like a dozing cat. I am not a gun person and couldn't tell you the model. It was, to the best of my recollection, the first time such a vulgar device had been inside these rooms, even during my parents' time.

"Well, well," said Ross. "Come in, Enoch, and make yourself at home."

"I see you blokes have done so," I noted, setting down the painting I carried, then removing my hat and setting it aside. I next half turned from them to remove my jacket.

Koroma made a scolding noise and bolted up from the sofa to stop me. He reached into one of my jacket pockets, removed my switchblade, and transferred it to a pocket of his own. "Just in case you decide to be stupid. Though, judging from how you spoke to Jake today, in our absence, it seems you're already plenty stupid, Enoch."

"I've been accused of worse," I said. "So, then ... what is the purpose of this visit, gentlemen, if I might be so stupid as to ask?"

"God, that painting!" Koroma exclaimed, shifting to look behind me. "It's exactly like Jake described! He didn't tell you about the summoning that went so wrong?"

"No, but he unknowingly shared it with me in dream."

"Don't look at it, Abe," Ross advised. "We don't want to end up like Jake."

"So faint-hearted," I commented, "for men who profess to be explorers of the Other. I stared at the thing for hours as I painted it and it did me no harm." I then mocked a twitch at one corner of my mouth.

"Stupid *and* a comedian."

"What an incredible collection of stuff you have here, man," Koroma said, glancing around him. "Even an original *Pickman?* Gavin and I are going to have to come back here another day and gather things up. What would you say are your most valuable items?" He smirked at me.

"Well," I replied, gesturing at the weapon in Ross's lap, "since I'm being asked at gunpoint, I have to confess it's probably a construction of stained glass my father created, in the basement. It has unheard-of properties. I'd be happy to show you, if you promise not to harm me."

"If we want to see it," Ross said menacingly, "we'll see it without your permission."

Koroma held up a staying hand. "I suggest we don't, Gavin. Anything he's *willing* to lead us to is probably something we should keep far away from."

"True ... true."

These Neanderthals were not as dumb as they looked. I had hoped to coax them into entering into the tunnels secreted beneath the Dreams Lens, which I normally kept locked for my own safety. They wouldn't have been the first unwelcome houseguests to venture into the labyrinth that extended beneath Copp's Hill ... never to return.

"Like I say," Koroma resumed, "we'll do some antiques shopping another day. Right now, the only thing Gavin and I are stealing from this place is you."

"I've already been to see your master once today," I said. "We mustn't tire him."

"We're not going to take you to his place," Koroma said. "You're coming to mine."

"And why is that?"

"To hold you until Jake is ready for you. He needs to perform a purifying ritual in his special room, thanks to you." Koroma looked over to his friend. "I'll go bring the car out front. Keep that gun on him."

When Koroma left us alone together, I spoke to his ginger-bearded brother of another mother, as the youngsters say. "Until Jake is ready for me, eh? So he no longer means to use his remaining stepchild as an offering to bring along with him?"

"You're less delectable than that little bitch," Ross said, "but a much rarer specimen. I think Jake will be warmly received if he has a prize like you to turn over."

"He assumes the creatures he'll meet there will bargain with a mere human of this world? Look how things went when he summoned the Faceless God."

"He bit off more than he could chew that time, admittedly. Think of it this way, Enoch: now you too can start a brand new life in a brand new world!"

"Thank you for the opportunity, but I'd rather not. Not as a slave to the Moon-Beasts."

Ross took on that menacing look again, and lifted his handgun to point it straight at my midsection. "It's either you go with him, or he's forced to use his wife ... since Maeve is keeping a safe distance. Jake would rather not go with that option, because for some reason he has genuine feelings for that poor boozy whore." Ross then rose from his chair, motioning with the gun. "Put your hat and coat back on, dearie ... night is falling and it's chilly out there."

"And if I simply refuse to go with you?"

Ross extended his arm to its full length and leveled his cannon with my face. "You can either start a new phase of your life, or end it completely."

XVI

At one point early on, the car Koroma drove—while Ross sat beside me in the back—became mired in Boston's infamous rush hour traffic, and in the dark I put my hand on my door's latch. I thought to slip out quickly, in the hope that Ross wouldn't dare fire his gun here, wedged in traffic without speedy escape, and I would then wind my way through the jammed rows of vehicles on foot. However, I found that Koroma had engaged the back door locks from the driver's controls, and Ross jabbed me rudely in the ribs with the muzzle of his gun.

"We told you," he snarled through gritted teeth and his beard in need of grooming, "don't be stupid!"

"What's he doing back there?" Koroma asked.

"Trying the door. And my patience."

I sighed heavily. "Do put your roscoe away, will you, Mr. Ross?"

I had no weapon of my own, since Koroma had confiscated my switchblade, which I much resented as it held sentimental value. All I had in my pockets now was the charcoal pencil I carried for impromptu sketching, and even thinking about pulling it out, stabbing it into Ross's eye, and seizing his pistol was far too exhausting. In any case, I imagined Koroma had a handgun of his own on his person.

Thereafter I made no further attempts to free myself from Koroma's car, and we drove for quite some time. In gazing out the window, after we had finally reached a highway where the car could pick up speed, I realized we were on our way to Connecticut. "Isn't kidnapping across state lines a matter for the FBI?" I inquired casually. When no answer was forthcoming I asked, "Are we going to the casino?"

"Don't try your luck with me, Enoch," Ross quipped, and he snorted at his own little joke. We were all of us getting along splendidly.

At last, the car exited the highway and shortly thereafter we came to an address in a little town that signs had seemed to indicate was named Dayville. The house was the first on its little back road, with no others in its vicinity that encroached too closely, and appeared fairly old and in less than stellar upkeep. Koroma parked in front of a dilapidated outer building that functioned as a garage, with its wooden door closed, a few paces from the residence's rear entrance. He got out first and opened the door for me, while Ross slipped out the other side. At first I thought they would take me into the garage, where they might have a dog crate or such, for this was how I pictured the unfortunate Aidan Cawley had been confined. Instead, I was directed to the house's back door, which Koroma unlocked. Within it was little less chilly than outside, and I heard no sounds to indicate there were other inhabitants. The place looked fairly barren; certainly free of the many interesting books and artifacts that filled Orne's residence.

"May I use your facilities?" I asked.

"But of course," Koroma said, and he nodded at Ross, who stood in the bathroom's doorway openly watching me as I relieved myself. Meanwhile, I heard the muffled voice of Koroma in the kitchen, in conversation with someone on his cell phone; no doubt Orne himself.

"Am I to be robbed of all dignity, sirrah?" I asked as I finished.

"Zip your lip and zip your fly, Enoch."

I turned to him. "And now I suppose it's to the basement with me?"

"Oh no, not for our esteemed artist guest. Let's go ... upstairs with you."

With Ross leading the way and Koroma behind me, we ascended a narrow creaking staircase to the second floor. Here three bedrooms branched off from a tiny landing, and I was conducted into one with a slanted wall that corresponded to the roof close above. There was but one window, and it had been firmly boarded over. A twin bed was pushed up against one wall, and a flatscreen television stood upon an old bureau with all its drawers removed. The door had also been removed from the one small closet.

"You see, Enoch?" Ross proclaimed. "You'll be comfortable here for the time being, and you can even watch Bob Ross on TV. No relation, by the way. You might pick up some tips from him! We'll bring you some grub later."

I tossed my hat onto the bureau. "Is this where Aidan slept while you had him? And was this where you peeled those strips of flesh from him, or was that at Orne's place while the boy's mother was so close by and unaware?"

"You should have been a gumshoe, Enoch," Koroma said. "Why do you care so much about that surly little punk? Were you fucking him? Is that it?"

I didn't dignify his crudity with an answer, and as they left and closed the door after them, for the second time that day Gavin Ross said to me, "Make yourself at home, Enoch."

I heard them fit a padlock in place outside, and close it.

XVII

"Well, well, well," I said to myself, removing the charcoal pencil from my jacket pocket and turning to survey the bare little room again. I tapped the pencil against my lips. Ross had told me to make myself at home ... and what I did at home was draw.

That easily reached, slanted section of wall—without wallpaper, and painted white—was tempting, and interesting things can be done with angles when it comes to conjurations and manipulating the cosmic grid, but I decided to work within that little closet. Its back wall would not be visible to someone looking into the bedroom from the doorway; not unless they came further into the room.

No hangers hung from the wooden bar within it, of course, but I found the bar easily lifted out of its slots. It was about two feet long and not heavy, but at least it was something. I hid it under the ratty quilt kindly provided for the bed, then returned to the closet and got down on my knees to begin drawing. Again, the wall here was white and made for a good surface, unlike the floor of dirty dark boards where I might otherwise have chalked or painted my design.

With my handy pencil, upon that back wall of painted plaster I drew a circle, then various lines and curves cutting into this circle, and finally symbols at the meeting places of these pathways like the nodes of a circuit. All well remembered from another such circle I had chalked on the floor of my attic studio only a matter of weeks ago. Beneath my breath, more internally than through my lips, I muttered words to complement these strokes of my conjuring instrument.

Upon drawing the last symbol I jerked back sharply, when outward from this vertical circle beamed a cylinder of light, looking like sunlight though outside it had become dark. Like dust motes floating through a shaft of said sunlight, whitish-translucent insects swam in the air, wriggling their legs, reminding me of the sea monkeys, or brine shrimp, an aunt had gifted me with as a child—one of the dear sister aunts who had raised me after the disappearance of my tormented artist father. Of course, these animals were not brine shrimp nor any other animal known to earthly biologists. Yes, it was all very much as before.

This time, however, instead of capturing some of these extradimensional creatures on a paintbrush, I jumped to my feet and rushed to the bedroom's door, pounding upon it forcefully. "Help! Help!" I cried. "There's something in here with me!" I then hurried to the bed, and got up onto it on my knees like one terrified of an intruding mouse.

Only moments later, a voice outside the padlocked door called through the wood roughly, "What are you up to now, Enoch?"

"There are creatures in the room with me! Insects! What are you trying to do—torture me with your witchcraft?"

"What are you on about?" I recognized the voice as belonging to

Gavin Ross. "You really want some trouble, don't you? You know, I'm sure the Moon-Beasts will still accept you even with a bullet in one kneecap." I then heard him fumbling with the padlock.

"Hurry! Dear gods, hurry! More of them are coming ... they'll spread throughout the room!"

The door was flung open, and there stood Ross with his handgun thrust out before him. His blazing eyes fell first upon me ... but then he switched his attention to that beam of alien light radiating vertically from the back wall of the closet. "What in hell?" he cried, stepping closer for a look. Oh, what a foolish thing to do, but then he had clearly never encountered something like this before.

"What are they?" I babbled, trying to sound hysterical.

"You mean you didn't do this?" Ross cried, hunching down nearer to the beam, to try to work out what these tiny animals were. I saw his features twist in confusion, and then in revulsion as the wrongness of the beam of light registered in his mind. He had drawn so close that the uncanny light now illuminated his brutish countenance.

"You should get Abe up here!" I sobbed. "Where is he?"

"He went out for pizza," Ross said.

Ah, these two poor fools. They were the best Orne had managed to recruit to his miniature cult? "Oh, goody!" I exclaimed. "I do enjoy a good pizza!" And with that, I leapt off the bed and struck the man in the back of his skull with one end of the wooden rod I had hidden, whereupon he overbalanced and fell face first into the closet.

I loathed having to use crude violence—it simply wasn't my way, children—preferring to let these visitors from the void of transdimensional space do all the work for me, but I needed to properly agitate them. One must do what one must do, in an emergency scenario.

The creatures were indeed agitated by Ross tumbling into their beam of radiance, and responded immediately. And just as immediately, Gavin Ross began screaming. In his panic, the pistol still gripped in one fist, he actually fired off a single shot before he let go of the thing to frantically paw at his head and body with both hands. Fortunately the bullet had gone through the back wall without disturbing my summoning circle.

The more Ross struggled, rolling back and forth on the floorboards with his upper body inside the closet, the more ravenous the swarming creatures became in their attack on him. At one point Ross rolled from his belly onto his back, his legs kicking madly, and at last I could see how the animals were feasting on his face. Through their clustering bodies I saw that they had eaten away the tip of his nose and both lips, so that he was coming to resemble his master. His hands, too, were bloody ruins coated in more and more of the creatures. Those that crawled or dropped out of the column of light soon melted away in our atmosphere, but as long as they remained within their own environment they seethed with vitality. Ross was howling in agony, and more of the animals took this opportunity to pour down his throat. I might have fled from the room then and made my escape, but I couldn't help but linger to avidly watch. Perhaps this macabre scene would one day inspire a painting.

For their part, the things did not buzz or chitter, working silently apart from the rustling of their chitinous bodies and the cumulative sound of their wet munching. Finally, Ross's thumping legs went still and his hands fell away from his face. Ah, except he had no face, his head being one solid mass of those translucent insect-things.

Keeping clear of the uncanny cone of light, I pulled off one of Ross's boots and then his sock. Having knotted the sock to one end of the closet rod, I swabbed the sock in the pool of blood growing under the man's corpse, soaking it sufficiently. Then, acting quickly so as not to give the creatures time to collect upon my arm, I leaned in and smeared away one of the nodal symbols at the charcoal circle's periphery. Instantly, the tube of light was extinguished. Those extradimensional arthropods left behind dissolved rapidly. In the end, every last one of them was gone, leaving Ross's skeletonized face gaping up at me.

"No pizza for you, Gavin," I said. I bent down and like a common thief claimed the money from his wallet, as I was stranded here and might need more than I had on me. I also took his pistol, but this I buried in the trashcan in the kitchen. Then I was crossing to the back door, pulling my slouch hat onto my head, and stepping out into the frosty November night.

XVIII

I suspected Koroma had called in his food order in advance to allow time for preparation, and thus would return very soon, but as I stepped outside I was struck by something I hadn't been aware of when I'd first been led from his car to the house. At that time, I had been too overwhelmed by my situation. But here I was a free man again, emerging into the concealment of darkness, and along with the cold air that swept over me I felt a kind of unhealthy energy radiating from that nearby garage structure, which looked to have been shoddily constructed generations ago. It was not as potent as the energy that emanated from the chamber in Orne's home wherein he had arranged my paintings, but it was something of that character.

I held out my hands with fingers spread, so as to better intercept the unpleasant waves, and stepped to the garage door. I found it padlocked, however, as was a side entrance. I then debated whether to go back into the house to check Ross's pockets for a set of keys. Surely, though, that would be tempting fate. I might reward my curiosity at the expense of my life. It was best to put as much distance between myself and this property as I could, before Koroma returned and discovered his friend's body, especially since I was stranded in another state without a vehicle. I had no idea which direction along this road might lead one to whatever passed for civilization in little Dayville, Connecticut. I certainly wouldn't be trying to find my way back to the highway to hitchhike.

I tore myself from that ugly old building's poison spell, turned and started walking further along the road. Actually, I had a hunch or intuition that this would lead me away from any commercial district, but I had reminded myself that Koroma's pizza joint would doubtless lie that way and it wasn't him I wanted to catch a ride with. The direction I chose appeared darker, lonelier, more rural, its houses with ample breathing room between them.

There was no sidewalk so I tramped at the edge of the road, and hadn't traveled far when I heard a car approaching in the distance behind me, and glanced back to see its headlights. I ducked off the road and hunkered down behind some large plastic trash receptacles a homeowner had left at the end of their driveway for collection, but the vehicle whooshed past and I saw it hadn't been Koroma's. I continued walking, and while I did so pondered what might have been concealed within that garage. Had I been able to get inside, might I even have found a series of empty cages for monkeys? Had those torture films that satisfied some perverse hunger for cruelty in the late Heidi Orne been filmed in this country after all, and not in Thailand? Or would the noise of such an enterprise have only drawn too much attention? On further thought it seemed improbable, but that was how poisonous that stain of dark energy had felt to me. I was glad to have passed out of its range.

I wondered if it had been in there, and not at Orne's place, that the panels of flesh had been removed from Aidan's body. Or had Koroma and Ross gotten up to untold atrocities of their own invention, that Orne wasn't even a part of? One could only speculate. Why did so many people with a desire for esoteric exploration and knowledge, who obtained special gifts and abilities along their journey, turn toward such abominable pursuits? Power and perversity appeared to walk hand in hand, but I was well aware that there were those who even viewed me in such a light.

Another car appeared, and though it came from the other direction I crunched my way into some brush to slip behind a tree trunk that wouldn't have been adequate cover were it not night. Again, the vehicle passed right on by. This was becoming tiresome, and certainly couldn't go on for long, and yet I had no plan. There was now no doubt: this old paint-dauber *must* acquire a mobile phone.

For the next car, I stepped over an old stone wall and crouched partly behind it. Perhaps I could make a game of finding a new form of cover each time a vehicle came along! Soon I came to an auto repair shop, on the right side of the road, and I crossed to it but was not surprised to find it closed. Onward I trekked, picking up my pace and constantly throwing looks over my shoulder. Ah, but fate soon smiled upon me. After quickly hiding from only two more passing cars, ahead I spotted a humble-looking family-style restaurant, again on the right side of the road. I wove my way through the cars that filled its lot and slipped inside this oasis in a hostile wilderness.

Inside was a comforting chatter, as the establishment was doing a healthy dinner business. When it was my turn at the hostess's station, I doffed my hat for a woman older than myself and buffed up the old Coffin charm. "Madam," I said, "I hate to trouble you at such a busy time, but my car broke down near here and I'm not in possession of a cell phone. Might I make use of a company phone, or at least ask you to summon a cab for me?"

"You mean an Uber?" the woman asked, her eyes twinkling as if she were feeling the call to supper, herself. *Ah, Enoch, you handsome rogue,* thought I. *You still have it.*

"Yes, one of those would be wonderful!"

A hand clapped me heavily on the back, and I turned with a start to see Abraham Koroma there, his grin bright as if we were long-lost compadres. "Hey, Enoch, not so fast! Let's have us a bite to eat, then I'll call an Uber for you myself if you want. That's going to be a pricey ride, though, from here to the North End."

The hostess watched this exchange, thrown off and maybe a little perturbed at having our intimate moment interrupted. I said to Koroma, "But I wouldn't dream of keeping you and Gavin from your pizza, Abe."

Koroma's grin faltered for a moment, but he caught himself. "You know Gavin doesn't have much of an appetite now, Enoch. Don't worry ... nothing like cold pizza for breakfast. Come on—my treat!"

"So," asked the hostess, "a table for two, then?" She was growing irritable now as more customers began to queue up behind us.

"Apparently so, my dear," I told her.

XIX

When we'd been seated and handed our sticky menus, Koroma leaned toward me and said, "I saw that formula you drew inside the closet, Enoch. Very clever."

"You might want to keep that—it's a Coffin original."

"Huh ... indeed. But what exactly did you do to my friend?"

"I did nothing but watch, Abe," I assured him.

"You're scaring me, Enoch. And I don't scare easily."

"It takes a real man to admit such a thing," I said. "Hm ... they have quite the extensive menu. Even pizza, though you didn't order yours here, I take it?"

"No, but I saw you walking into the parking lot and followed you in."

"I see. Hey, look at these cocktails for fall. 'The Headless Horseman'? Oh my."

"Have one. Again, I got this."

"I'm trying to swear off the spirits, but thank you."

Koroma sat back in his chair to appraise me with narrowed eyes. "I'll confess another thing. I don't know what to do now. I haven't even called this in to Jake yet. I'm thinking, though, he'll probably have to resort to using his wife, after all. Though I don't expect you to gallantly volunteer yourself in her place."

"Are you trying to put a guilt trip on me, Abe?"

"I just thought someone like you, obsessed as you are with peeking behind the veils, might find Jake's project to be the culmination of all your explorations. Think of it: actually entering into the realm of the unknown! Look at how much effort Jake has put into doing that very thing, *willingly*."

"And I might even be tempted to take that journey, Abe, were it not—as I've said—for the little matter of being brought along merely as a gift to the denizens of that realm. Though, for all we silly humans know, the Moon-Beasts could reject both myself *and* Jake, as gift and gift-giver, and find some more horrible use for us than as slaves. Jake is willing to risk that because his mortal shell is failing and he doesn't have much to lose. Whereas I, as you can see, am rumpled but still fairly robust, with an appetite for ... " I consulted the menu again " ... Fra Diavlo, I think, since you're being generous. Do you know what Fra Diavlo is, Abe?"

He indulged me by consulting the menu. "Assorted seafood with pasta," he summed it up, in a more concise way than it was described.

"In Italian it means 'Brother Devil.' And I apologize, by the way, for *your* brother devil."

Koroma held my gaze without speaking for a few moments, until our waitress appeared so as to take our orders. Koroma requested only a cognac, without ice. When the pretty young maiden had left, in a lowered voice my dining partner said, "I guess I can't kidnap you at gunpoint right here in front of all these fine people. Who knows what will happen when we leave, though. Even if you have an Uber take you away, will you feel safe returning to Charter Street, Enoch?"

"How safe can anyone really feel, in this world or the next? How safe will *you* feel henceforth, Abe?"

"Sure I can't give you a lift?"

"No thank you. If you're feeling generous, however—beyond paying for my meal, that is—might you return my switchblade? I'm rather fond of it."

Koroma hesitated, but finally said, "Whatever." He slipped my knife from out a jacket pocket, covered it with his cloth napkin, and pushed it across the table to me. I pocketed it myself.

"I do believe you and I are getting along much better now, Abe."

‡

While I waited for my food to arrive, I excused myself to use the bathroom, not really caring if Koroma believed me or not. I again approached the hostess, again asked to use a phone, all but batting my eyes at her. She handed over her own cell phone, and I stepped away from her to call Maeve Cawley, whose number I still had on that receipt I had now transferred to my wallet. I feared getting only her voicemail, but she picked right up.

"Your mother is in serious danger," I told her without any preamble. "You are as well, but your mother perhaps more so at this time. However you achieve it, you need to get her out of there. If you have a lover or male friend, take him with you."

"How do you know this?"

"I'll get into it later; just trust me."

"Should I call the police?"

"We can't convince them of the reality of this situation. I can't even convince you, at least not rationally, but you recognize it in your gut. Don't take her to your home in Worcester ... I was at my home and they were waiting for me there. Go to a motel."

"Okay, I will, but I want to understand more about why you're saying this—the specifics!" she demanded.

"I'll call you again soonish. I may even be joining you wherever you end up, since my own home is unsafe, as I say."

"I really don't think I can convince my mother ... "

"Then lie to her! Whatever it takes."

"All right, Mr. Coffin. Thanks ... I'm on it."

I handed the phone back to my new inamorata, then returned to the table just as my food was arriving. Thank goodness it hadn't already come in my absence, or I wouldn't have trusted Koroma not to tamper with it in some way. As I seated myself, I saw the man was putting away his own cell phone.

"I think I'll be going, Enoch." Koroma shot back the last dregs of his drink. "Things to do. Do you want me to call that Uber for you before I leave?"

"I'll ask the hostess," I assured him. I liked it better this way, in any case. How was I to know that the driver he called for me wouldn't be another member of Orne's circle, resulting in my second kidnapping of the day? "I wouldn't want to make the driver wait while I enjoy my meal."

"And about that … I promise to take care of the bill on my way out."

"You are quite the gentleman, Abe." I dropped my voice and leaned forward. "One thing, though, before you go. If Orne absolutely *must* take some offering with him, why does it have to be an innocent person? Why not bring a murderer? A rapist? A fentanyl dealer?"

Koroma smiled as he got up from his chair. "You just answered your own question, Enoch. Who would want any of them?" He then nodded goodnight to me, and turned away to seek out our little waitress.

I took my time eating my meal, which was of good quality considering the modest environs, and thereafter went over to the hostess a third time to ask for another favor, pressing a twenty into her hands. She blushed and told me it wasn't necessary, but accepted the tip anyway. She used an app on her own phone to summon a driver. "We have to call them sometimes," she explained, "when customers drink too much at the bar." I didn't enlighten her to the fact that I was sadly acquainted with the consequences of imbibing in excess.

I waited near her station for the driver to alert the woman to his arrival, wary of Koroma lurking outside, waiting for me to emerge. When the Uber person arrived, however, I didn't spot Koroma's car amongst the dwindling number that remained in the parking lot.

"This is a bit of an expensive ride," the driver, a young Black man, forewarned me as he pulled his vehicle out of the lot.

"No worries," I reassured him. Where Abraham Koroma had paid for my meal, my ride home was courtesy of Gavin Ross.

I hadn't given the man my own address of Charter Street, but that of my friend who stored my truck for me. I didn't think Koroma would immediately return to my home, out of fear that I might alert the police to the earlier break in, but it was wise to be prudent. I would then ask to use my friend's telephone to see what was going on with Maeve.

As we approached the offshoot road that would cut us to the highway, a fluttering glow spread before us in the night. "Oh wow, what's this?" said the young driver, craning his neck past his steering wheel for a better look. But from its direction I had already guessed, as soon as I spotted the orange glow above the trees, which illuminated from beneath columns of smoke that billowed into the night sky.

The driver slowed his car as we drove past the old house and the ramshackle, work shed-like garage. Both were fully engulfed in flames. Not only smoke poured from those structures in waves, but crazed pulsations of virulent energy, as if some malignant sentience thrashed in its death throes.

"Please keep going," I said to the driver. "No one has responded yet, and if someone sees us lurking here they might think we're responsible."

In a way, I was.

XX

My friend who stored my pickup truck for me asked where I was headed to in the middle of the night, as he knew I wouldn't be driving that stalwart jalopy to my place without a dedicated spot to park it in, but I was vague in my reply since I didn't want to concoct any lies. He left me alone to go brew some coffee for me, so that I might use his telephone in privacy. However, when I called Maeve's mobile I was answered only by her voicemail, after several attempts. I recorded a message indicating that I was at a friend's house, and that she should call me back at this number ... if she were indeed able to call anyone at all. My concern for her was mounting, and I imagined any number of grim scenarios, all of which ended with Maeve becoming Jacob Orne's unwilling companion in the Dreamlands. And I hadn't even had the chance to have the beauty model for me yet! At least, remembering my fifth painting for Orne, not in the proper sense.

This was frustrating indeed, since I couldn't go to her apartment in Worcester to check on her welfare without knowing its address. I asked my friend for a physical telephone directory, and though he didn't possess one (what had gone wrong with this world?), he did look her up on his home computer. I wrote down the address he'd uncovered, and was about to embark with a travel mug of fresh coffee to fortify me when the phone rang and my friend picked it up.

"It's for you," he said, handing me the receiver.

"Sorry," Maeve Cawley said. "I was in the shower."

"Where are you?" I asked.

She told me the name of a motel in Shrewsbury, adjacent to a shopping plaza at a spot roughly centered between Eastborough and Worcester. "I was able to convince my mother to come with me, but I had to tell her I have a friend who has secret information about Aidan's murder. It isn't a lie, is it?"

"No, though I'll have to figure out how much to actually tell her. How was it when you got there; did your stepfather attempt to stop you from taking her?"

"No ... it looked like he was upstairs, locked inside his little black room. He might still not realize she's gone."

"I don't suppose you brought a male friend with you, in case things had got dicey?"

"I didn't," she admitted. "For one thing, I'm between boyfriends."

"Well, I was keeping Messieurs Koroma and Ross occupied, fortunately for you ... not that Orne might not have other dangerous cohorts. In any case, I'll be there as soon as I can. Give me about an hour."

"Take your time. My mom has already passed out on her bed. Her nerves are absolutely fried."

"I believe I know how she feels," I said.

‡

I opened my eyes to find myself in Jacob's Orne's "little black room," as Maeve had called it. I couldn't recall how I had got inside, but I did remember that I'd memorized the code for its keypad lock.

I spun around, but didn't find Orne in the chamber with me, nor anyone else. And yet, this was not what so surprised me. No ... what sent a thrill of shock through me was that my five paintings had disappeared from the room's black-painted walls, though the pedestal bearing the globe sheathed in Aidan Cawley's skin remained at the room's center.

In place of those paintings of mine were five windows of the same dimensions as my canvases, and they were even outlined in the same black wooden frames. And behind the glass of every one of those windows crowded an uncountable horde of Moon-Beasts.

All around me, the repulsive entities pressed their webbed hands with padded, gecko-like fingertips flat against these windows. Did they mean to push the panes forward, popping them out of their frames, or adhere their fingers to them like suction cups and pull them out?

The tendrils at the fronts of the things' pale, hairless heads seemed to deepen in their pink coloring as they visibly vibrated, either in communication or with fevered emotion. In some individuals, perhaps frustrated that they couldn't get closer to the glass, the tentacles practically blurred with vibration. Those that had managed to get right up to the windows pressed their tendrils against the glass along with their hands, flattening the worm-like, boneless appendages, the vibrations of which subtly rattled the panes in their frames.

As I whirled around, observing how the masses of bodies climbed over each other in their frenzy to get at the windows—to the extent that they blocked out entirely whatever scene lay behind them—it finally dawned on me that the room's door was missing from one of the five walls. How, then, had I entered this chamber ... and how was I to escape it?

A loud thump startled me, and I whipped around to see that one of the grotesque beings had pounded the flat of its hand against the glass with extra force. As I watched, it struck the pane again, so hard that I saw it shiver in its frame. With a third blow, a thin white crack appeared.

Now, imitating this individual, all the other creatures that could get in close to the windows began to pound their hands against the glass in a similarly violent fashion. I saw, and heard, more cracks forming.

In desperation, I clawed at my jacket's pockets, hoping to find my sketching pencil, so as to draw a protective circle around me on the room's lustrous floorboards. However, somewhere along the way I had lost it, though I thought I'd replaced it after drawing the summoning circle in the closet of that other room in which I'd been held prisoner. Even my switchblade was gone, though I *knew* Koroma had returned it to me, so there was not even a chance of etching a crude circle into the floor with its sharp tip.

A louder crack. Another ... and that drumming of hands kept growing louder, as if to crack my very mind. With nothing else to use as a weapon, I looked again to that orb resting on its base only a few steps from me. Was this what they wanted, this sacrificial flesh? Perhaps not, since the Dreamlands had vomited out Aidan Cawley's body as if in contempt, but I had nothing else to offer the monstrous congregation, except myself. I reached to the vile thing, with the thought of tossing it to the first creature that broke through the glass, as a child might throw a ball to another.

Before I could touch the globe, however, I saw that beads of blood were welling up along the seams between the twelve panels of human leather that so gruesomely upholstered it. I hesitated, watching transfixed as more blood bubbled up, little trickles beginning to run down the object's curved sides. An especially loud thud against a window over to my left snapped me out of my reverie, however. Somehow I now knew that dislodging this object from its base, like removing a battery from some technological device, would disrupt what was occurring.

So, overcoming my revulsion, I put both my hands out to the sphere, and the instant I made contact with its bloody flesh the thing blazed like a sun. A fraction of a second later, without a sound, the blazing orb seemed to explode, like a star going supernova, the effect so dazzling that my vision went entirely white. I was blinded.

‡

I opened my eyes and turned my head blearily to the left, where a pale hand thumped against my driver's side window. A head lowered into view and I flinched, but I saw that this head possessed two eyes, a nose, a mouth. A human man of middle age, glaring through the glass at me.

"Hey," came his muffled voice, in a particularly pronounced Massachusetts accent, "are you okay in there?"

I sat up quickly, having at some point slumped low in my seat, and rolled the window down to let in night's biting chill. "Sorry," I mumbled.

The man pointed up toward the traffic lights that dangled over the intersection in front of me. "The light turned green but you didn't go. You apparently didn't hear me honking my horn, either. Now, as you can see, it's red again."

"I'm sorry," I repeated. "I seem to have dozed off while I waited for the light to change."

"Have you been drinking?" he asked in an accusatory way. Was he an off-duty police officer, or only a concerned citizen? He'd brought his face in closer as if to sniff at my breath.

"No, I assure you."

"Then you're okay? You sure you haven't been drinking?"

"I've quit," I told him. "As I say, I simply dozed off. It's been a long and … unusual day."

"If you say so," he grumbled, turning to head back to his car, which idled behind me puffing out clouds of exhaust.

I sat up further in my seat and clenched the steering wheel tightly, as if in so doing I might get a better grip on the reality of the waking world. Because, you see, I didn't feel that what I'd experienced had entirely been a dream. At least, not of the prosaic sort.

XXI

As I drove the rest of the way toward the motel in which Maeve had secured a room for herself and her mater, I thought that I would likely want to take some sleep there myself, as I was thoroughly exhausted by the day's events, and my strange little doze at the intersection had hardly satisfied me. If the room was a twin, as I suspected, the two women could take one bed and I the other. In any case, it was just a matter now of locating the place … but as it turned out, that unfortunately proved easy. It was that motel ahead of me now, just off the highway, with the blue and red flashing lights of emergency vehicles in its lot. As I pulled into the parking lot myself, I saw these lights were being cast by a firetruck, an ambulance, and two police cars. I had the distinct feeling that my day was only going to grow longer.

I parked a discreet distance from the chaotic scene, but nevertheless as I approached on foot I was quickly detained by a policeman who stepped in my path. "Please keep back, sir," he advised me sternly.

"I'm looking for my friend Maeve Cawley, officer. Is this about her?" I asked, gesturing toward the first responders clustered around the open door to one of the motel's rooms.

"Cawley, you say? Are you a relative?"

"He's with me!" cried a familiar voice.

I looked past the man to see Maeve Cawley slipping between those solemn figures washed in strobing colored lights, and she walked briskly toward me. To my surprise, she fell into my arms wracked with sobs, burying her face into my chest, and I held her awkwardly so as to comfort the poor creature.

"What happened, Maeve?" I asked her.

"It's my mother," she wept, her voice muffled against my jacket. "It's my mother … "

‡

"I can't stay here. I can't," Maeve said, glancing about the motel room she had rented, after all the grave men and women in their respective uniforms had left—including the coroner, whose van had joined the collection of emergency vehicles to claim the deceased body of Maeve's mother.

"Of course not. We'll go talk to the desk person about switching rooms for you," I said. "Under the circumstances I'm certain they'll accommodate you. I would offer to take you to my place, but when I tell you what happened to me earlier this day I think you'll understand why I'm wary about that."

Maeve stood facing the bed from which her mother's corpse had been removed. I hadn't seen it, myself; only the body bag that was rolled out on a collapsible stretcher. With her back to me, I saw the bereaved young woman fiddling with something in both hands. In a faraway voice, she related, "When you told me you were on your way, I thought I'd wake my mom up so she'd be ready to hear whatever you decided to tell her. I figured it would give her a chance to sober up a little. But when I touched her, she was … cold." She sucked in a long, shuddery breath. "I rolled her over, and that was when I saw her eyes were staring open."

"Were there any marks of violence on her?"

Maeve swung toward me, her features contorted as if she thought me mad. "Violence? I was with her the whole time, not even sleeping! I just took a shower … that's all! The police asked if she was taking any medication that she might have overdosed on, either accidentally or not. I told them what I think—that she had a heart attack! All this stress over Aidan's killing, her damn husband's declining health … me getting her overexcited and insisting she come with me tonight … "

"You mustn't blame yourself at all for this."

"They're both gone … my brother and my mother. I just can't accept this! I *can't!*"

Feeling inadequate, I crossed the room toward her, wondering if I should embrace her again to offer some small measure of comfort, but I stopped a few paces from her when I saw what it was she'd been toying with in her hands: a thin gold chain, onto which was threaded a small medallion or bauble of some kind. "What is that you have there?" I asked.

Maeve looked down at the necklace, as if she'd forgotten she held it. "It was my mom's. When I turned her over, she was holding this charm or whatever it is in her mouth. Don't people do that sometimes with crucifixes, when they're executed? At first I thought she'd swallowed it, and it had choked her to death, but it was only resting on her tongue. I don't know if she did that on purpose, or gasped and ingested it accidentally."

"May I see it?" I asked, extending my hand.

"When I saw it was in her mouth, I got so freaked out I tore it off her," Maeve explained as she poured the chain into my palm like a trickle of liquid gold. I saw the chain's fastener had been broken.

As I examined the tiny pendant the chain supported, I recognized its design. It was identical to one of the pair of sigils, or combination of fused sigils, that were branded on the sides of Koroma's hairless head. The flesh of my sensitive hands all but tingled from handling the piece of jewelry. "Did your stepfather give her this?"

"Yes, and he gave the same thing to me and Aidan. I can't remember what he said it was supposed to represent. I never wore mine ... I still have it at home. Aidan wore his, though; my mother insisted on it, to show his gratitude. *Fuck* gratitude!"

"I remember seeing the necklace now, in those photos of your brother in the morgue," I told her. "At the time I was too focused on his horrible wounds."

"Does it mean something?"

"It surely does, but I don't know exactly what. It's outside my own knowledge. At the very least, though, I might suggest it was given as a kind of tracking device, as it were. Not literally ... that is, not in a technological sense. But still, a means by which Orne might know where the three of you were at any given time ... and thereby reach out to you."

"Reach out to us?" In an involuntary way, Maeve turned her head to look back toward the bed, as if she expected to see her mother's cooling remains still lying there upon that stripped mattress. "Are you saying you think my stepfather did this to my mother somehow? Through magic?"

"Again, I am afraid to expound on such theories with you, Maeve, since you have expressed to me your disbelief in these matters."

"No ... no, come on, look ... it had to have been a heart attack!"

"As you wish, then."

She whirled at me with her gorgeous eyes gone crazed. "This isn't as I wish! None of this is as I wish!"

"Of course not," I said in a calming tone. "Come now ... before we both pass out from exhaustion, let's go see to having another room assigned."

Maeve drew in a long breath, nodding. "Anyway," she said in a quaking voice, "we'll know more after they do an autopsy on her. Now it's the results of *two* autopsies I'm waiting for."

"May I keep this for now?" I asked, cupping her mother's necklace.

"You can keep it forever," Maeve said. "It's from *him*."

"You were wise not to wear your own."

"As if!"

"You have good intuition, Maeve, though you find it hard to accept certain truths." I slipped the necklace into a pocket, glad to break the diseased thing's contact with my skin.

XXII

Maeve insisted she wanted to hear whatever I had learned that had caused me to call her with my warning to remove her mother from Orne's house, but I urged her to lie down for the time being until she was less distraught. She was too overwhelmed to argue, as the reality of her loss grew upon her and the initial, protective shield of shock gave way. She ended up lying on one of the two beds sobbing incoherently, while I sat on the mattress beside her and held her hand. After a time, she mercifully cried herself to sleep, though even then her tear-wetted face was tense with suffering.

I eased my hand out of hers and stood from the bed, gazing down at her. She had removed only her shoes, and since she had fallen asleep atop her covers I draped a blanket from the other bed over her, gently so as not to rouse her. She muttered for only a moment.

Envying her slumber, however tormented it was, I went to the other bed and stretched out upon it, having only removed my hat first. Even if Maeve had had the strength then to listen to what I had to tell her, about the use to which her brother's flesh had been used and about my kidnapping and escape, I myself wouldn't have had the strength left to relate it.

Within moments of laying down my head, I too passed into sleep.

‡

I awoke to find myself seated on a hard, uneven pavement with my back propped against a wall, my knees drawn up to my chest and my forehead resting upon them. I lifted my head in confusion, only to be greeted by a dense mist that wasn't helpful in orienting myself. It was night, I knew that much, and I appeared to be seated in a narrow back alley paved with cobblestones. Achingly, I pulled myself to my feet, wondering for how long I had been asleep. How had I got here, wherever here was? The last I remembered I had stretched out on my bed in the motel, with Maeve passed out on the other close by. At some point had I risen and left the building to go sleepwalking? Or was I still dozing at that intersection, while the traffic lights changed from red to green and back to red again? Had I not yet arrived at the motel, and thus might Maeve's mother still be alive? The line between the waking and dreaming worlds had become blurred.

I stumbled along a few paces as if drunk, though I had surely not imbibed, supporting myself with one hand on the wall I had been propped against. Its surface was rough under my palm, oddly porous, as if the building that rose darkly above me—and the similar buildings that lined this crooked alley—had been chiseled out of one massive block of basalt.

The fog that choked the alley had an ashy character, like smoke, but also a scent that hinted of the sea, though I knew Shrewsbury was nowhere near the coast. Nor would one find cobblestoned lanes in Shrewsbury, despite its quaint name, similar to Acorn Street in Boston's Beacon Hill.

Still guiding myself along with my right hand, I realized my left was clenched in a fist. When I paused to open my hand and look down, in my upturned palm I saw a thin coiled chain onto which was threaded a strange little pendant. Gazing upon the symbol that formed the pendant caused me to shudder involuntarily, repulsed. I slipped the thing into one of my pockets and brushed my hand across my pants leg as if to wipe away a psychic slime.

"Enoch Coffin!" a voice at my back called to me, in a whisper that nonetheless penetrated the fog.

I whirled toward the sound, and through the mist spied an arched doorway in the black wall of the opposite building. Framed therein I barely made out a robed figure, its face hidden within the dark garment's hood. A pale hand emerged from a wide sleeve to beckon to me.

"Who are you?" I demanded.

"Shh." The hand raised a finger to the black void where lips might be. "There is said to be much crime in the streets of Dylath-Leen. You had best come with me straightaway."

"Dylath-Leen!" I hissed, glancing around me though little could I see. Dylath-Leen ... one of the great cities of the Dreamlands, said to lie near that world's Southern Sea. Here, at the city's Bay of Wharves, were docked the black galleys of the Moon-Beasts—from which their slaves were sent forth to conduct trade on their behalf, while they themselves remained hidden. The shock of this revelation lifted the haze from my mind, if not from my surroundings, and I faced toward the cloaked stranger again. "I asked who are you!"

"You do not recognize my voice, coming from a healthy body," the robed figure said with something of a chuckle. "Nor would you, I think, recognize my restored face."

"Jacob Orne!" I cried.

"Yes, Enoch. As you can see, I was successful in my ritual. The Lunar Gate opened for me."

"And you brought me here, too? So I'm to be your offering to the Moon-Beasts, after all?"

"I didn't bring you here, Enoch ... you brought yourself. You are not beholden to me ... though once more I note how you and I have become connected. Why, I even sensed your arrival out here! Come with me now inside, where we can speak more comfortably." The shrouded figure of Jacob Orne waved one arm toward the darkness of the passage at his back. "This is my new abode."

I hesitated for a moment or two, but I was determined not to let this fiend frighten me. Thus, I strode across the cobblestones toward the archway. "Lead on, then, Orne."

"Ah, my brave friend Enoch ... now a fellow oneironaut, as was your destiny!"

Orne stepped back into the arched passage to permit my entrance, but I hesitated at the portal. Thumping a hand to my chest, I asked, "Am I here in body?"

"You have a body here, which is not the same thing as having traveled here bodily. The difference between you and I is that sooner or later, as long as your life essence is not destroyed here, you will arouse and return to the waking world. Whereas I will never reawaken there. Your vessel awaits the return of your astral self. My body there is gone, never to be discovered. I will never be summoned back to life in that wretched shell. I am free! But come, Enoch ... come."

XXIII

Once I had crossed the threshold, Orne closed and bolted a sturdy wooden door. Then, taking up a hurricane lamp he had obviously set onto a little side table earlier, he led me toward a staircase with worn wooden treads. I remained where I was, however, to point toward another closed door at the end of the hallway. From behind that door emanated a foul smell, reminding me both of rotting flesh and the musk of some animal. More disturbing than that, however: there also seeped a disturbing energy, not unlike that which I'd experienced in Orne's black-painted gallery. "Where's that go? The back way out?"

"That way lies the cellar. I've been given the rest of this building for my use, but not down there. Those who do make use of it prefer another means of access, through a rear bulkhead. I suspect there are also interconnected tunnels below us."

"Who is it that gave you this place in which to live?"

Though Orne faced me, and now held his oil lamp, his cowl still shadowed his features so that I couldn't yet take in his transfigured appearance. In answer to my question, he said, "The Moon-Beasts arranged it, of course. That is, through their Lengian slaves, who act as their agents here. The locals are, shall we say, rather put off by the Beasts themselves, so they remain on their galleys whilst in town. For the most part, that is. Sometimes they sneak forth, and venture further into the city ... and when they do, they need safehouses in which to hide, or store certain wares. So you see, we have an arrangement. Do be a good friend, Enoch, and don't report me to the authorities." Orne chuckled. "Though it's my understanding the law is pretty lax around here, as I say. But come ... come ... upstairs I have a fire."

I followed Orne up to the second floor, slipping one hand into the pocket where I kept my switchblade to assure myself of its presence. Indeed, my fingers closed around it. Yes, I could have taken it out then and buried its blade in my host's back, since surely he was mortal in this world, but I am no common murderer. In any case, much as I loathed the man, I was consumed with curiosity bordering on awe. It is said that all of us briefly visit the Dreamlands, at one point or other in our lives—perhaps even on numerous occasions—without being aware of the difference between those visits and our common dreams. But this experience was different. I was profoundly *here*, so very present and aware.

"They're behind technologically here, Enoch, so I apologize on that account," Orne said as he reached a hallway at the top of the stairs. Here, several wall-mounted gaslight sconces offered a murky illumination.

"I have no great love of technology," I assured him. In the hallway we faced each other. "Why risk inviting me into your new home, Jake? Aren't you afraid of me?"

"Afraid? I don't think you'd want to start a scene here, Enoch. Not with my ... benefactors presently doing whatever it is they get up to in the basement."

"Hm," I grunted. I tried not to show any unease about this statement.

"Anyway, think about it ... what animosity do the two of us truly have against each other?"

"Aside from you having your goons kidnap me to use as an offering to your ... benefactors?"

Orne waved a dismissive hand. "Forgive me! Forgive me! All in the past, now. And didn't you have your revenge on poor Gavin for that?"

"Koroma told you about it? Is he here?"

"Of course not. He is free now to follow his own terrestrial pursuits. Though who knows; one day he might endeavor to join me here. That's up to him, isn't it?"

At last, still holding his lantern, Orne reached up with his free hand to cast off the cowl of his dark brown robe. The head revealed was quite unextraordinary. When we meet people, often it is our impulse to compare them to celebrities such as film stars, but Jacob Orne reminded me of no one at all because he was just that unremarkable a person, though certainly a vast improvement over his appearance the last time we'd met. He was now devoid of his festering sores and rashes, with the end of his nose and upper lip restored, and the unusual facial hair gone. When he smiled, his teeth were no longer rotted down to sharp stubs. He might have been some business executive of about my own age, with a full head of dark hair.

"What do you think?" he said. "Of course, I'd prefer to be twenty-five again, but I mustn't be ungrateful."

"Did the Moon-Beasts transform you thus, as another favor?"

"Oh no, this is simply due to my having successfully passed through the Lunar Gate. My infection has been filtered out and I am restored, as it were, to factory settings! Ha!"

"I see. The Lunar Gate. So that was how you thought of that room with my paintings, and its globe. To sneak into Dreamlands Earth through the back door, so to speak, and bypass other obstacles, you first ported yourself to the moon of the Dreamlands. Then, bribed the Moon-Beasts to bring you here."

"I'm sure you already had all that figured out."

"Yes, but what of your dear wife? She's dead, as I'm sure you know ...

I happened to have seen her body."

Orne gave an exaggerated pout, tossing up his free hand. "What other recourse did I have, with Maeve being so slippery and you escaping so cleverly from my associates? It was my last resort, and not done without regret."

"I'm sure you regretted it as you would regret dropping a favorite coffee mug."

"Oh, Enoch, Enoch. Do come into the other room before you continue your interrogation! As I say, I have a fire in there and you must have been chilled by that damp fog in the street. It's a gas heater, actually, not a fireplace, but it has the same cozy mood ... plus I don't have to fret about obtaining wood for it." With that, Orne led me to the end of the short hallway, and to another arched door of heavy, ancient wood. It opened with a creak, and the chamber beyond was indeed much warmer.

"You'll forgive the spartan nature of my flat. I only just got here myself, you see. Empty as it is, I felt like a college kid again, stepping into my first dorm room! Please, take the leather chair."

The walls of the chamber—a smallish living room or study—were of the same porous black rock as the building's exterior, devoid of any bookcases, shelves, or paintings. As Orne had said, a cast iron gas heater stood against one wall, giving off a bluish flame, with a leather armchair that had seen better days turned toward it, while a faded rug covered much of the wooden floor, the boards of which had long lost their sheen. Other than these things, there was but a plain wooden table with one chair for it, and atop the table rested a ledger to write in, an ink well in the shape of a nautilus, and a few dip pens in a cup used for a holder. Though, one of these pens was thicker, shorter, seemingly made of ivory or bone; perhaps not a pen at all.

Watching me take in my surroundings, Orne said, "I know, it isn't a patch on my place in Eastborough, but I'd rather have a rundown home than a rundown body. In any case, this is just the starting point for me here! From now on it's up, and up ... though of course, I need not stress myself with ambition, either. After all my health struggles and my efforts to get here, I deserve a rest, don't you think?"

Per his invitation, I took the chair he'd offered and he turned the chair that accompanied the table toward me, lowering himself onto it. He smoothed the robe over his knees with a grin.

"Ah! So here we are, Enoch! It's like a fresh start for us, isn't it?"

"Next you'll be inviting me to be your roommate," I said.

"Oh no, no … sadly, I don't think our relationship could ever be *that* amicable. But as I say, it need not consist of enmity, am I right?" He wagged his head. "Gods, Enoch, look at you here with me, only a short time after my own arrival! And you accomplished it so much more easily than I. Of course, again, you are only here temporarily, while your living body waits for you to inhabit it again. Did you come here consciously, so as to chase me?"

"I thought at first you had pulled me here, but you say that wasn't the case." I then remembered the necklace I had found gripped in one fist when I came to awareness here; waking into my dream, as it were. While I was dozing off in that motel, had I pulled the chain out of my pocket, perhaps only meaning to examine its sigil again before I slept? Or perhaps meaning to place it on the table between the beds, so as not to have the thing touching my body even through fabric? Could it even have been intentional that I'd clutched the object in sleep, in an attempt to probe the realm of dreams … intentional if only in an unconscious sense?

"No, Enoch, I repeat: your presence here is not of my doing."

"And I repeat: what of your dear wife?"

"What do you want me to say, Enoch? You said yourself you saw her corpse. Yes, I was able to reach out to her remotely, though I would have preferred to have her beside me when I conducted my ritual. I was afraid it wouldn't work, as a result, but I could wait no longer. With you running free, I feared trouble was about to close in on me. I'm sure you can understand how delighted I was to find myself in the city of the

Moon-Beasts, having successfully activated the Lunar Gate after all, with my dear wife standing by my side."

"And you turned her astral self over to those creatures on the spot, did you?"

"Well, if I hadn't begun haggling immediately something ghastly might have happened to me, you know. But as it turned out, my gift to them was twofold, because little did I know before then that the astral self of my stepson Aidan had been accepted as an offering … before you had even delivered the fifth painting, by which time I'd already been experimenting with the gate. It was only his physical shell that was rejected, to return to our realm. Of course, in the process of said rejection his shell expired, but … "

"So both poor ghosts are now in the custody of those monsters, to serve whatever purpose they might. As slaves … playthings … who knows, perhaps as sustenance."

Orne affected an uncomfortable wincing expression. "Let's not talk of unpleasantries. Look at the bright side: at least my dearest was reunited with her little boy."

"You are a vile creature, Jacob Orne; as ugly now as the last time we met, and always to be so."

Orne seemed to study me, drumming the fingers of one hand upon his table top. "Ah, poor Enoch. So very, very limited. Yet I still find it a bit hard to believe you didn't follow me here by design. Tracking me down, as it were … to start some trouble with me."

"You're the one who brought me into your home," I said, sweeping my arm about me.

"I wanted to take your measure. See what you wanted with me. My wife and her son could mean nothing to you. Unless it's the lovely Maeve who obsesses you … is that it?" He winked. "*That* I could understand."

"It isn't like what you suggest."

"Are you just so bored, then, so empty, that creating difficulties for me is some kind of sport for you?"

"You used my artwork as part of your means of murdering two people. One of them being killed in my stead. And yet you suggest your actions don't involve me, *Jake?*"

Orne drummed his fingers some more, still gazing at me with narrowed, thought-filled eyes whose sclera were no longer red, but were no less malignant for that. At last he heaved a sigh. "I do wish it didn't have to be this way, Enoch. I truly feel we might have been friends. But ... c'est la vie." Having said this, Orne twisted in his chair, reached to that cup holding dip pens, and pulled forth the stubby little implement of bone. Before I could ask him what he was doing, he brought the thing to his lips and blew into it.

Then, a horrible scream like that of a woman in the process of being murdered filled the room, stabbing icepick-like through my ears and causing gooseflesh to wash over me. The bone instrument made a sound like recordings I had heard of so-called Aztec death whistles.

After one blast on the thing, Orne lowered it to his lap and grinned. "They'll be coming now, Enoch."

"Who is that?" I said, my ears still ringing from the assault.

"Why, my benefactors, of course."

XXIV

I stood from my chair by the gas heater.

"Going somewhere, Enoch?"

From my jacket pocket, I removed my switchblade and flicked it open. "I suggest you toot that thing again to call them off."

"Ooh!" Orne pretended to recoil from me. "Look at that pigsticker. Are you going to start singing now about what it's like to belong to the Jets?"

I cocked my head, sensing them before I heard them. But soon enough I heard them, too. Somewhere outside this room's closed door, a thumping of heavy bodies moving below us. I remembered that door at the end of the ground floor hallway. And now, the thumping was proceeding up the stairs … bringing with it an increasingly potent aura of psychic pollution.

"Call them off, Orne!" I shouted.

"Our means of communication is limited, I'm afraid. Mostly I have to go through their Lengian slaves, who act as go-betweens. Sorry, Enoch … it's now out of my hands."

Keeping my eyes on the door, and noting that it had no means of being locked from this side, I thrust my knife toward Orne's face and snarled, "I swear, I will bury this in your throat if that door opens!"

Orne got up from his wooden chair and backed away from me. "I wonder what else they might grant me," he said, "now that I'll have given them a third offering … and one so much more unique! You escaped Abe and Gavin, but out of the frying pan and into the fire, as they say!"

I could tell the rumbling bodies had reached the head of the stairs and now proceeded down the short hallway out there, toward this very door. The excited vibrations of the Moon-Beasts' face tendrils vibrated in my own brain jelly.

Then—just when that heavy wooden door shook as the first body crashed into it—I reversed the knife in my hand, swung it down, and stabbed its blade into the top of my own right thigh.

‡

I let out a cry, my exclamation awakening me from my dream just as much as the pain in my leg did. I sat up on the mattress upon which I'd passed out, clamping a hand over the wound in the top of my thigh. Blood began to soak the fabric of my pants and ooze between my fingers. On the carpeted floor, near my shoes, I saw where my switchblade had fallen, a smear of blood on its open, gleaming blade.

"What is it?" Maeve cried out, startled awake also and scrambling out from under the blanket I'd covered her with. "What's going on? Oh my God ... did someone attack you?" She looked wildly about for some intruder.

"I did it to myself," I reassured her. "I was ... dreaming."

"Jesus!"

"No, not of him; another sorcerer who cheated death."

From the glow that shone around the room's closed drapes, I saw that morning had come. That seemingly interminable day of nightmares had finally come to an end, not that I felt all that rested from my slumber. I reached down to gather and close up my knife, then began limping toward the bathroom with one hand still clamped over my wound. Watching me go, Maeve said, "We should get you to an ER."

"I have no health insurance, my dear. I don't believe this is very deep or serious."

"Look, there's a pharmacy walk-in clinic not very far from here ... I think it's on Boylston Street, in Worcester. I'll take you there and pay for it myself if I have to. On the way, you can tell me whatever it was you were going to tell me. We'll take my car, and come back for yours after." She went to where she'd doffed her shoes, sat and slipped them on.

"As you like," I relented. "But I'd rather not reveal that I injured myself, even if it was only in dream, lest they want me held for observation at some hospital."

"We'll tell them you slipped with your knife opening some package or whatever; we'll think of something." She retrieved her pocketbook from another chair and glanced around to confirm she wasn't forgetting anything. "To tell you the truth, I just want any excuse to get out of this motel."

‡

It turned out that I didn't need sutures, the puncture wound being neat and not very deep, as I'd thought. It was cleaned, bandaged, and in no time Maeve and I sat at a table in a little chain doughnut shop over a breakfast of egg sandwiches and coffee. I was relieved to see her eat.

With our conversation ignored by the ongoing traffic of customers lining up at the counter, discounting those men who did a doubletake when they noticed my companion's beauty, I related to Maeve carefully what information I had finally decided to share with her. I censored myself to some extent not only due to her lingering skepticism, but also out of self-preservation.

I told her that I had confronted her stepfather at his house, and been inside his "little black room" (I had almost slipped and called it the Lunar Gate). There, when viewing the repaired globe of Luna at the room's center, I had realized that the leather that formed its covering corresponded to the twelve strips of flesh removed from her brother's body. I knew he'd been alive when it was taken, perishing only when Orne tried to send him bodily through the Lunar Gate, but that detail I omitted. As can be imagined, Maeve was horrified at this revelation and cried out, attracting the attention of customers seated at other tables, if only briefly. Except for a few children, these people had the decency to look away when they saw her start to weep.

I then told her how I'd returned to my home to find Orne's friends Koroma and Ross had broken in ahead of me, to intimidate me for having confronted their master. What I didn't do—my biggest omission, except for withholding the dream journey I'd experienced while sleeping in the motel—was reveal to her that the duo had then kidnapped me, intending for *me* to become Orne's ritual offering. Otherwise, I would have had to detail my escape. I knew that Maeve would want to share the information about the globe in Orne's ritual room with the police, and that as a result they would want to interview me. I couldn't allow them to know I had been to that house in Connecticut, lest they believe it was me who had set it on fire. Especially if the charred remains of a dead body had been uncovered inside ... unless Koroma had removed Ross's corpse first, which I highly doubted. I said only that I had insisted the two men vacate my abode and left it at that.

In the end, I simply told Maeve that in my confrontation with him Orne had hinted that he might do some harm to her mother, as he had her brother, in bringing about the ritual he planned ... and that was the reason for my excited warning to her. As I had suspected, when I was finished Maeve said she meant to contact the police, and have them return to Orne's house to claim for analysis that lunar globe they had missed previously, to tie him to her brother's murder.

"Then they can arrest that sick son of a bitch!" she hissed through clenched teeth.

I didn't want to lie to Maeve, so I kept to myself the fact that her stepfather would not be there when the police arrived. Nor would he be found anywhere else upon *this* Earth.

XXV

Even though Koroma was still unaccounted for out there somewhere, I couldn't be afraid to return home forever, so I did. Before doing so, I warned Maeve to be wary of him, too. (I made no mention of Ross, and wasn't sure if she noticed this.) Knowing what I alone knew, however, I didn't really think Koroma would risk lashing out at either of us now. After all, Orne had succeeded in his goal and so his surviving crony had no further need for either Maeve or myself.

I had only just returned home, though, and was thinking about sitting down at my easel to continue work on a painting I had previously considered finished (*"A painting is never finished ... one simply stops working on it."*—*Enoch Coffin.*), when I received a call. I recognized Maeve's number and picked up. "Are you all right?" I asked straight away.

"I'm okay," she said, "but my stepfather's house in Eastborough has burned down."

"Oh my!" I said. And then, remembering my five masterful paintings therein, I exclaimed with more emotion, "Oh no!" And yet, at the same time I knew this was for the best. I would surely not want those works back; not after they had been contaminated by such cancerous energies.

"I told the police about the globe," my young friend continued, "and what you suspect was done with Aidan's skin, but it might be reduced to ash now. They say the fire probably started in that room."

"Of course it did." Koroma, I thought. He seemed to have a talent for arson. So he was still up to mischief, though I imagined this would be his last act before moving on to more distant pursuits.

"Still," Maeve continued. "they said maybe if they find a trace of the thing they could compare the DNA to samples from me, and even my mom's body. So far, they haven't found my stepfather's body in the house. I'll bet those fuckers Abe and Gavin took him away somewhere. They've probably gone underground together."

"I agree that Jacob Orne has likely flown far, far away."

"Just watch your back, Enoch, and I'll watch mine. Anyway, like I said, I told the police about your theories, and they said they'll probably want to talk to you about your conversations with my stepfather. Also, I took the liberty of telling them how Abe and Gavin broke into your house, trying to scare you. So they'll be looking to find those guys, too. Anyway, I hope you don't mind."

"Of course; it's to be expected."

"In the meantime, I have two funerals to plan. I'll let you know the results of the autopsies as soon as I know, myself."

"Very well, my dear," I told her. "Stay brave. You're doing quite well, given all that has happened."

"Thank you, Enoch. Thank you for being there for me."

I only grunted in response to this, before hanging up. After all, what had I done to benefit the poor child? My paintings had been used to help destroy her brother and mother, and trap their life essence in an alternate world—her mother having been taken as a sacrifice in my place. Considering all this, it was for the best that Maeve did not share my convictions about all that had occurred. Still, I tormented myself that I had delivered that fifth painting to Orne despite her pleading with me not to. Because of this, it vexed me to simply close the book on the whole tragic affair.

‡

I attended the wake for Maeve's mother and younger brother at a funeral home in Worcester, dropping in only briefly to pay my respects. Maeve hugged me and thanked me for coming. As I had requested of her when she'd called to notify me of the time and place, she removed several objects from her jacket pocket and slipped them into my hand as if in some surreptitious transaction. I pocketed these objects myself without looking at them, but I didn't need to. They were identical gold necklaces: the one I had seen in the images she'd shown me of her brother's corpse, and her own —which her stepfather had given her to wear, though she never had. I already had the mother's necklace at my home.

"I'm glad to be rid of them," Maeve said. "But what do you plan to do with them? Not that I care. I mean, go ahead and sell them for their gold if you want."

"No, no. I'll think of some fitting way to destroy them, most likely," I told her.

It had now been almost two weeks since her mother's demise, and the results of the autopsy had come back as "undetermined." There had been no indication of a widowmaker—in this case widowermaker—heart attack, as Maeve had speculated; no ruptured brain aneurysm, no overdose of drugs. More perplexing to those who had examined him was that the cause of death for Aidan Cawley also remained "undetermined." Despite multiple injuries to his body, including the compound fracture of one leg—which I knew to have been caused by his corpse plummeting out of thin air and becoming snagged in a tree—and most notably, despite his odd mutilations, no *fatal* injuries had been found. He hadn't even expired from blood loss. Still, it was obvious that someone had inflicted those wounds on him, and the belief was that this person had for some reason lodged the body up in that tree.

Also, since last I'd seen Maeve I had indeed been called in to be interviewed by detectives from the Massachusetts State Police. I was only too willing to drive to their office in Millbury, which had jurisdiction over the town of Eastborough, as I would scarcely want police officers visiting my home. I had collected far too many questionable items in my years that I wouldn't want to have to explain.

I told the detectives how I had been inside Jacob Orne's house to deliver a painting he had commissioned, and seen therein a globe covered in odd leathery segments that to my mind matched the wounds Maeve had shown me in those photos of her sibling. Maeve had urged them to look for this globe, but the detectives explained it had not been found in the charred ruins of the Orne residence. This led me to wonder if Koroma had removed it, and perhaps certain extra rare valuables from his master's collection, before torching the place.

Because Jacob Orne's body had not been uncovered in the remnants of his home, either, I was assured he was a person of interest in the mysterious fate of his stepson, despite his poor health.

As she had mentioned, Maeve had related to the police how Koroma and Ross had broken into my home to intimidate me, after I had expressed to Orne my belief that he'd had a hand in his stepson's demise. After I described this incident for the detectives—again, leaving out the kidnapping part and my subsequent escape, which I have perhaps unwisely recorded in these pages—they told me they had thus far been unable to find anyone by the name of either Abraham Koroma or Gavin Ross, and suggested these were aliases. In an innocent way, I then claimed that Ross had made some vague threats about bringing me, against my will, to a house in a town in Connecticut. "Was it Dayville?" I asked myself aloud, as if trying to recall. "Yes, I believe he said it was in Dayville."

The detectives hadn't contacted me again after that interview, but at the double wake Maeve revealed that the police had followed the lead I had given them, and discovered a house had burned down recently in Dayville, Connecticut, also clearly due to arson. A badly burned body had been found inside, but so far its identity hadn't been established. "I hope it's my stepfather, or at least one of those two fuckers," Maeve said, "but knowing them it's probably another poor victim like my brother. I don't care what they did or didn't find in the autopsy ... I know my brother Aidan was murdered, and my mother might as well have died of a broken heart, if not a heart attack. I feel like succumbing to that fate, myself."

"But you won't," I said, laying a hand on her arm. "I forbid it."

Before I bid Maeve goodbye—and apologized in advance for not attending the funeral service and reception the next day—I went to the two open coffins placed poignantly side by side, and stood over them gazing in at their pitiful contents: these sad cadavers, just poorly-painted shells that not only looked emptied of their vital essence, but like things that had never even housed such a force. With my back blocking my actions, I reached in and placed my hand atop one of Aidan Cawley's. It was as hard and cold as that of a statue, though a statue would be more lifelike. "Poor boy," I muttered. "Such a waste of beauty."

XXVI

A provocative but actually quite obvious question finally occurred to me. Though I hadn't since heard whether the police in Connecticut had found any other bodies—or anything else of an ominous nature—in the ruins of that house or its outer building in Dayville, I could understand why those structures might have been burned. To destroy any traces of Koroma and Ross having lived there, aside from Ross's unidentified body, that might reveal their true identities ... and their activities.

Perhaps there had been questionable books or other objects therein, in the garage structure or maybe the basement, that fire would obliterate beyond recognition. And yet, what about the house in Eastborough? Yes, perhaps Koroma had done that on his own, not at Orne's behest, to protect himself in case he had left fingerprints or other incriminating evidence on the premises. (Even the barn on the property had been set aflame, the state police had told me.) I suppose I had at first gone on this assumption, since Koroma was obviously the one who had burned the property after Orne had left this sphere … or this *version* of this sphere.

But now, another thought came to me. What if Orne had indeed left orders for his underling to destroy his home, should he be able to successfully cross over? To destroy the Lunar Gate, specifically? And why do that? Because it was a gate, after all … and perhaps might work *both* ways. Orne had wanted that doorway erased because there was a very real possibility, a very real threat, that he could be summoned back through the gate into this world. He would not be so untouchable in that other realm, after all.

Very well, then … if that was true, then he had succeeded in safeguarding himself. The gate was no more.

I did not have a Lunar Gate. But I did have a Dream Lens.

‡

The Dream Lens was not like a television, though, with dedicated channels that your humble journalist could flip through while munching on popcorn. For long, mostly fruitless hours I leaned over the thing while seated on a little plastic step stool, gazing through one pane and then another, in conjunction with this or that of the various optical devices my father had designed to be clamped to the Dream Lens' frame. Yes, certain panes were better than others for viewing particular otherworldly scenes, but I surely couldn't count on them to permit me that view or any view at all. In this regard the Dream Lens was as fickle and unpredictable as Massachusetts weather.

In addition to switching between several of my father's viewing apparatuses on their hinged arms, I also varied my light sources, ultimately settling on a UV LED lamp I had purchased a few years back, clamping this also to the Dream Lens' rim. I had obtained this lamp so as to play around with blacklight effects, having also bought some reactive acrylic paints, though I had never proceeded far with those experiments. In any case, in regard to using this lamp to alter my view through the Dream Lens, I finally felt I was achieving better results.

However, after a session that lasted from afternoon well into the evening, I ended up gaining only two brief glimpses of what I knew to be the city of Dylath-Leen, in the Dreamlands, both views being largely obscured by rolling fog perhaps coming in from the Southern Sea … though this might also be the veil between worlds through which I peeked.

One view was of the city from afar, in which it appeared like a heaped mound built up from tightly-packed pillars of black basalt. The city had been compared by writers of esoteric texts to the Giant's Causeway, in Ireland, and I could understand why.

The second view, through another of the dome's stained glass panes, finally afforded me a street level view. Ah, yes, but which of the city's innumerable narrow lanes was this? Just because I hoped to view the spot I had formerly visited didn't mean the Dream Lens would beneficently grant my request. I *did* try to will the device to cooperate in that way, nonetheless, because who was to say that my will wasn't as helpful in viewing the wonders the Dream Lens revealed as were the various optical apparatuses themselves? Even I didn't know, after all this time, if such were the case.

It very well might have been the same alley, for all I could tell. It was cobblestoned, crooked, crowded by rough black walls of basalt. And then, through the mists a hunched, shadowy figure began to emerge. I saw soon enough that this was not Jacob Orne, venturing forth from the narrow house he had been gifted, nor was it any human figure at all. It was one of the Moon-Beasts, and it must be very late there in Dylath-Leen for the thing to have ventured out into the streets, since those creatures did their best to hide from sight lest they discourage the citizens from trading with the crews of the black galleys. Who could say what furtive errand the Beast was on?

As I watched it begin to turn down the alley away from me, suddenly the Moon-Beast halted in its tracks. It remained motionless for a moment or two, then gradually cranked its body around to face my point of view. As it did so, the pink tentacles at the front of its eyeless head deepened in color and began to vibrate with greater agitation. Then, the thing started coming toward me ... so to speak. Its strange, waddling/hopping movements seemed driven by determination, and I saw its webbed hands come up as if to reach out for me. Nearer and nearer the horror came, as if the creature meant to thrust its arms straight through the glass pane that was my window, shattering it and seizing my head so as to pull it into that other world ...

I flinched back from the pane so abruptly that I actually fell off the plastic stool onto my rump. It might have been comical had I not felt such alarm. Keeping my eyes averted from the pane in question, I flicked off the UV lamp I had trained on that portion of the Dream Lens, then seized the edge of the blue plastic tarp and jerked it across that construction of stained glass.

It seemed I had given the Moon-Beasts my scent, which I was none too pleased about. And in any case, it wasn't as though I was going to reach through that pane myself, to grab Orne by the collar, was I?

No ... I had other methods of interacting with the Other.

XXVII

It was only two nights later, on a snowy evening in December, that I heard a loud crash somewhere downstairs as I sat at the easel in my attic studio. I stood up and moved carefully to the door, mindful of the creaking of floorboards, straining my hearing. And then I heard a raspy voice shout out from below.

"Enoch Coffin!"

I closed the attic door quietly, looked around me in a fresh evaluation of my familiar surroundings, then turned off the lamp I had trained on my easel. Now the only illumination in the attic came from a number of candles. I moved across the room to sit upon a spare chair, away from my propped canvas. Another lamp was here, clamped to the edge of a small table, but I didn't turn it on.

"Where are you, Enoch? I know you're in here!" bellowed that coarse voice, sounding nearer, no doubt approaching the steps to the attic.

Not long after, the door to the attic was flung open, and there framed in the threshold stood a largely unfamiliar figure. I knew, though, that this was a much compromised version of the formerly beefy and imposing Abraham Koroma ... or whatever his real name was.

"So the mountain has come to Muhammad," I said. "You have a talent for bypassing locked doors, Abe."

"You don't sound surprised to see me, Enoch."

"I'm not."

"But are you surprised to see what I *look like?*" he shouted, spittle flying from the ragged remnants of his lips. "No, you aren't, are you?" At this, he drew a handgun from under his coat, the shoulders of which sparkled with melting snow. I couldn't help but flinch back in my chair and raise my hands at the sight of the weapon, though I didn't want to look too ruffled nor sound afraid.

"Now stop that, Abe ... just tell me what's going on with you."

"As if you don't fucking know!"

It was as if Koroma had traded bodies, or at least vitality, with his comrade Jacob Orne. The last time I'd seen the latter, in the Dreamlands, he had been restored to a man of normal, if exceedingly nondescript, appearance. Koroma, however, was at least as afflicted as Orne had been when I'd first met him in Eastborough, if not more so. His head was bald as before, but mossy patches of hair grew upon both gaunt cheeks almost to his eyes, the flesh of his face marred with infected-looking rashes and weeping ulcers. His nose had eroded almost to a skull's open pit, and the sclera of his eyes were fully red. It appeared one of his ears was gone, or had shriveled to a crusted scab, and he was missing at least one finger on the trembling hand that pointed his pistol at me.

"Perhaps your friend's affliction was contagious, Abe, and it's finally bloomed in you."

"Bullshit! *You* did this to me somehow!"

"But did I cause Jake to look that way? No, I didn't, did I? He was already corrupted like this when first I met him. From a conjuration gone wrong, as I understand. Have you attempted something of the same?"

"No, I haven't, but *you* have, haven't you? *Haven't you?*" He jerked that gun at my face as he took several steps further into the room. "You didn't just expect me … you called me here!"

Again I raised up my hands, not feigning my nervousness. "Abe, be careful now. Sorry to say the police are aware of your earlier break in here, and a gunshot would surely summon them. For your own benefit, I suggest you simply leave."

"I won't leave until you reverse whatever it is you've done to me! How did you do this—tell me *now!*" As he growled this in his phlegmy, altered voice he bared teeth at me that had rotted down to pointed fangs like those of a piranha.

"Well," I sighed, "I do have to admit, this might possibly be a consequence of the painting I've been working on recently." Having said this, I nodded at my easel, where it stood at the other end of the room.

"What painting?"

"It's the sixth painting I created for Jake. The one he didn't want, as it turned out. I had considered it finished when I offered it to him, but lately I've been inspired to embellish it. Go see for yourself … right there." I gestured toward the easel behind him.

Koroma hesitated, as if reluctant to take his gun off me, but then turned and approached the canvas on its easel. He bent forward in an attempt to make it out in the attic's gloom, his inflamed eyes perhaps suffering deteriorating vision. Having reached the easel, he leaned in further for a close look. As he did this, I noticed one of the brands on the side of his shaven skull. The raised scar was leaking thin dribbles of blood all along the sigil's outline.

"Here, this might help," I said, reaching to the UV LED lamp clamped to the table beside me. I had already adjusted the head to aim in that direction. As Koroma had said, I had indeed been anticipating a visit from him. Call it my artist's intuition, which had always served me well.

There was no reactive acrylic paint on the canvas that rested upon the easel—this piece was, after all, an oil painting—but where Koroma stood straining for a better view of my work, the ultraviolet light revealed a complex circle I had rendered on the wooden floorboards there. Painted in white, its lines and symbols glowed eerily, as if with an illumination of their own. Both Koroma and the easel stood within this violet-glowing circle.

And yet Koroma hadn't seemed to notice the activated magic circle yet, so fixated was he on the canvas, which now he could see more clearly in the light cast by the UV lamp. "By the way, Abe," I said, "people with eczema benefit from ultraviolet phototherapy. You might consider getting one of these things for yourself."

Ignoring my comment, Koroma screeched, "What is this thing? What have you fucking *done* here?"

"I thought you might be flattered," I said, pouting like a child.

It was my painting of the Faceless God, with that monstrous icy mountain in the background, and a band of Moon-Beasts frolicking about the hem of its cloak as they played at their flutes. Only now, since I had revealed the painting to Orne, I had added another figure to the composition. Previously, one hand of that towering being had reached out as if to pull the viewer into the world the painting portrayed. Now, however, that hand clutched the doll-sized figure of a struggling man. That man was a likeness of Abraham Koroma, painted from memory. The tiny brand I had painted on one side of his bald head, however—seen in profile as he howled in the giant's grasp—I had copied meticulously from the sigil of one of the three gold necklaces I had collected from Maeve. I hadn't wanted to get its proportions wrong.

"Every night I've dreamed this … every night, night after night, for a week now!" Koroma cried, unable to take his horrified gaze from my painting … from his own representation therein. "Every time I sleep! That's when all this started with my body! I've deteriorated this badly in just a week's time … and you planned it that way!"

"Nonsense," I told him. "Well … that is to say, I couldn't be assured that anything of that sort would prove successful. I have, though, been doing some reading along the lines of what your master must have researched in order to open his Lunar Gate, to better understand his methods. I'm certain our libraries coincided to a good degree."

At last, Koroma tore his eyes from the canvas and began to turn back toward me, but finally he noticed the glowing circle in which he stood. "What is this?" he shouted. "What is *this*, now?"

"Alas," I said, rising from my chair and edging toward the attic door, "I might not have it within my knowledge or power to create a Lunar Gate, Abe, but I do know how to cast a spell of containment. I'm going downstairs to grab a fresh coffee. Want anything while I'm there?"

Koroma swung toward my voice, wheeling the handgun around at the end of his arm, but in so doing I saw that blood was running copiously from his tear ducts. Still, I feared he might discharge the weapon blindly, and even if he missed me I dreaded having neighbors summon the police. Should they come into my home, there would be even more for them to find of a concerning nature than under normal circumstances. And yet, either because his trembling hand had weakened too much or because his arm had passed beyond the edge of the confining circle, he dropped the weapon and it clattered heavily to the floor outside the circle's fluorescent border. With that, Koroma sank to his knees with a pitiful strangled cry, blood now streaming freely from his nose and from the brands on both sides of his head. He tried crying out again, but only coughed a bright gout of gore onto his shirtfront.

"I'll take that as a no," I said, slipping out from the attic and gently closing the door after me, as if to leave him to a private experience. Leave him to his communion with my painting … and the terrible being it portrayed.

I did indeed pour myself a coffee from the pot in my kitchen, taking my time, and then mounted the stairs once more to my attic studio.

What I found upon the floorboards there was mostly just a crumpled pile of bloodied clothing, which appeared to be steaming, though there was also a puddle of liquified matter bearing gelatinous chunks. Whatever results I had hoped for with my little trap, this had quite exceeded them. I snicked my tongue in disapproval, knowing I should clean the mess as soon as possible. I decided I would later paint over that section of the floor, so as to cover any stains, not to mention the circle there … but first I would adjust some of the symbols it contained to cancel the circle's binding spell. After all, it might otherwise very well retain some influence, even painted over and with the UV lamp switched off. Which I did then, by the way, turning on a regular lamp instead.

The blood-soaked clothing and whatever foul sludge remained inside it I bundled into an old sheet—along with a pair of shoes, a few pieces of orphaned jewelry, and that handgun—and this package I carried down to the basement. I unbolted the Dream Lens, which acted as a hatchway giving entrance to the tunnels beneath my home and the graveyard across the street, raised it on its hinges, and dropped the bundle into the darkness. Perhaps there was just enough sustenance within to be of interest to the denizens of that darkness. I then quickly bolted the Dream Lens securely back in place, and returned to the attic to see about that cleaning job.

One more thing remained for me to address before I felt I could put this whole regrettable situation behind me. Again, as with the late

Abraham Koroma, I planned to approach it in the spirit of artistic experimentation.

XXVIII

I considered asking Maeve to accompany me to Eastborough, so that if I were noticed poking around in the remnants of Jacob Orne's house and the police were summoned, she could inform them that it was her mother's place and claim she was looking to see if there were any salvageable mementoes in the rubble. However, in the end I decided to go alone, since she wouldn't be receptive to my reasons for wanting to go there, anyway. Not, I'm sure, that she would have forbade me. In any case, if the experiment I had in mind went awry, I didn't want her around, involved, or endangered.

And so it was night when I went, and I brought a flashlight with me as I left my parked truck and crept toward the charred remains. The smoke had long dissipated but the scent of it lingered, even through a light film of snow. The house had burned so thoroughly that all that stood were a number of blackened chimneys, thrust toward the night sky like malignant monoliths, the rest all crumbled away to fill the foundation with scorched debris that was all but reduced to cinders. A barrier of orange plastic safety netting had been erected around the site, and around the remnants of the nearby barn as well, but this was easily bypassed.

Because it was likely that some ghostly traces of the Lunar Gate's influence remained here, I had considered enacting a ritual right on the site—and I was sorry not to—but I felt the risk of discovery was too great if I lingered that long. So, picking my way cautiously, lest the rubble shift beneath me and I twisted an ankle or fell full upon the debris, I searched about for a piece of wood large enough for my needs. There was actually a lot of scrap to choose from, and I settled on a fairly intact rectangular piece that I felt might have been a shelf. Perhaps even a section of bookshelf! Of course, there was no way to be certain that anything in the mix came from the room within which my artwork had hung, and hoping to encounter any remnant of my paintings themselves would have been absurd. Given what use they had been put to and the pollution they must have soaked up, it was best that they were destroyed, sad as it made me. At least as a consolation, most of the money they had earned lived on to sustain me.

Satisfied with my find, I cleared the safety netting again, shut off my flashlight, and carried my scrap of charred wood back to the squatting dark hulk of my trusty vehicle, my sole coconspirator on this frosty night.

‡

In my basement—in the wee hours of the same night—I took one of the three necklaces someone had made for Orne to gift to his wife and her two children, and this I secured to the blackened board with fine metal pins through links in its gold chain. In so doing, I formed the chain of the first necklace into a circular shape. Then, within that circle I pinned another chain, this one arranged into corners to form a triangle. The third chain I secured into a kind of arrowhead shape, overlapping the triangle, so that together they formed a five-pointed star.

When my little mixed media collage was finished I placed the board with its golden pentagram on the basement's cold floor, and knelt over it intoning secret words and weaving signs in the air with my hands. However, before I began this summoning ritual I had first unbolted the cover of the Dream Lens and lifted it back on its hinges. Then, I had taken up the axe I kept down here in case of emergencies and laid it on the floor close at hand.

My fear—more so than a ghoul realizing the Dreams Lens cover was open and thinking to pop up into my cellar for a visit, in which case I would need to get that cover back in place pronto—was that instead of summoning Orne either bodily or in spirit back into our realm, I would instead summon one of the Moon-Beasts in his proximity. If I should accidentally manifest one of *them* bodily, I would grab the axe and attempt to force it backwards past the rim of the open Dream Lens, so as to fall into the tunnel below for the ghouls to deal with. However, I felt the possibility of summoning a Moon-Beast in physical form was unlikely, however frightening a thought.

I wondered, too, if I might inadvertently summon the life essence of either Orne's wife or stepson Aidan, instead, since they were the ones who had worn these necklaces. If that were to occur, would those life energies dissipate peacefully, freed from their slavery, or would they become anguished ghosts trapped in this world instead of that other? Oh, if only I could be sure of rescuing those tormented souls in such a way, but I thought it improbable ... at least with my skills. Whereas Orne's essence was that of a willful traveler, now revitalized and robust, and in theory better suited for making another journey. A *return* journey. I couldn't see him where he was, but I hoped the strange connection we seemed to share would work in my favor. In this way I felt quite like an ice fisherman, my line trailing below an opaque surface as I waited for a nibble.

There were so many unknowns ... but my dears, I *throve* on the unknown. As I say, this was all an intriguing experiment, and once more I was trusting to my artistic instincts. *(An artist is never finished learning ... he just loses the desire to do so.—Enoch Coffin. Or something to that effect.)*

I knelt by that pentagram for quite a while, repeating my incantations and the sigils I drew in the air, while with closed eyes I tried to envision Orne's transfigured but unremarkable face as I recalled it from dream. When my efforts won no results, I tweaked the process and tried other words and signs, but still without conjuring anything or sensing even a rustle of the unseen veil. Nay, not the slightest ripple or sigh from the beyond. I did feel this slab of wood was imbued with some vestige of

233

energy, which was why I had thought to go to the ruin in the first place, but it was perhaps not sufficiently charged with the force of the Lunar Gate to be adapted to my use.

No ... no Orne in body or spirit, no sad ghosts, no Moon-Beast shocked to find its webbed feet planted upon this charred board in the home of a rather obscure New England artist.

After a time I pulled over that little plastic stool of mine to seat my aging rump upon, rather than kneel any longer on the icy floor, and continued in my efforts ... and yet still without results. I considered painting some symbols onto the wood, within and around the outside of the gold circle, to try to amplify its power, especially since I had had such impressive results with the circles I had drawn to thwart Orne's brutish cohorts. I might even do a quick portrait of Orne to add to the mix, though his restored face was hard for me to remember in its blandness. In any case, as for tonight I was feeling exceedingly weary after my trip to Eastborough and back, followed by my efforts here in the basement. Therefore, in the end I heaved a sigh and rose from the stool.

And just in time, as it turned out, because I fancied I heard a furtive scuttling noise coming from that portal to the underground. Hastily, I went to the hatch-like cover of the Dream Lens, lowered it, and once more drove home its bolts.

Was that you, Mother? I wondered.

As I lifted the scorched wood from the floor, thinking to set it aside on my workbench and perhaps paint those symbols on it the next day, a sizable chunk of it broke off in my hand. This portion swung away from the rest of the board, connected only by one of the pinned chains, the pentagram design hence disrupted. Exhausted and frustrated, I tore all three necklaces from the two chunks of wood and stuffed them into a pants pocket before mounting the basement stairs to follow the siren's call of my bed. When I reached it I plopped down heavily without removing any of my clothing save for my shoes. Soon enough, the siren had me in its embrace.

XXIX

Regrettably, the siren was not entirely metaphorical.

I woke as I had the last time, seated with my back propped against a wall, my knees drawn up to my chest and my forehead resting upon them. However, this time I was not outside in the cobblestoned street with my vision obscured by fog, but inside the narrow house I had entered during my last visit to the Dreamlands, the scene before me only too horribly clear. Later, when I was more composed and could reflect upon this change, I felt that it was because I had been granted access to this building on the last occasion that I awoke within it the next.

As before, in this front hallway I was assailed by an effluvium that called to mind both rot and the stench of some animal, but now so overpowering as to inspire nausea. Also as before, a hurricane lamp stood burning on a little side table. The vision its light afforded me as I opened my eyes and lifted my head was of three Moon-Beasts standing over me, the foremost of them leaning so close that its curious, restless tentacles nearly touched my face. When I saw this, I am not ashamed to admit I shrieked and sprang to my feet, my back sliding up the closed front door I realized I had been propped against. However, rather than incite the creature into seizing hold of me, my cry and actions appeared to startle the thing and cause it to back off several steps, with its weird face appendages vibrating nervously. In fact, the other two Beasts behind it backed off a step or two, also. It was then that I realized they were not only wary of me, but afraid. I believed they understood me by this time, and considered me a being of some power.

Still, I hardly wanted to remain here in this enclosed space with them, nor in the Dreamlands at all, and I recalled the means by which I had escaped this realm before. However, when I patted my pockets I realized my switchblade was in the pocket of my winter coat, and my coat hung over the back of a chair in my kitchen. All I had on me, besides my wallet, were the three gold necklaces with their tiny potent glyphs.

As I stood there afraid to spin around and dart out through the front door—lest that prompt the hesitating Beasts into action—and as the trio continued to observe me, I considered my other option: charging past them and up the stairs to where Jacob Orne had his living space, where I might seek him out and threaten him to call these things off. Perhaps I might find some other way out, or at least a room I could barricade myself in until I found another way to wake myself. Unfortunately, I saw that the Moon-Beasts stood between me and the stairs, which I took to be intentional.

I was about to make the Elder Sign in the air with my hand, hoping it might ward the creatures off and cause them to flee down the hallway, to return to the basement through the door there—as worshippers of Nyarlathotep, I figured it might have some effect on them—but just then the foremost of the three extended a hand toward me, with its palm upturned. I looked in uncomprehending horror upon this webbed paw with its padded, gecko-like fingers for some seconds while the thing patiently waited for me to comprehend its meaning. At last it came to my fogged and jolted brain. It was demanding a toll.

From my pocket I extracted the three golden chains, recalling that I had read in arcane literature that the Moon-Beasts inexplicably coveted gold, and through their agents traded for it on their visits to the Earth of the Dreamlands. My guess was proved correct when the reeking, toad-like being took an eager half-step toward me again, that extended limb unwavering.

"Very well then," I managed to say, trying to keep my voice from shaking. "One for each of you, right? Trick or treat." I then poured the chains into the thing's palm, and it closed its fingers around them in a greedy fist.

Immediately the Moon-Beast backed away, as did its two partners behind it, no longer blocking my access to the staircase. They withdrew about halfway down the passage leading to the door to the cellar, but continued to regard me as if curious now what decision I would make.

Would I turn and plunge outside into the maze-like streets of Dylath-Leen, or would I go upstairs to confront Jacob Orne? Well, I knew the latter better than I did the former, and I had no score to settle with this city, either. It was, of course, toward those worn old steps that I moved, taking it upon myself to bring that hurricane lamp with me to light my way.

All the while, the three noxious Beasts turned their corpse-pale heads to follow my progress, their tendrils vibrating anxiously, as I climbed.

‡

The upper hallway being illuminated by those wall-mounted gaslight sconces, I was no longer in need of the hurricane lantern, so I set it down on the floor outside the closed door to the room Orne had formerly ushered me into. Then, without knocking or otherwise announcing myself, I opened that door and crossed over the threshold.

As before, I was greeted by a chamber with walls of black, pumice-like stone, a ratty rug covering much of its worn wooden floor, a cast iron gas heater giving off a bluish flame, and a plain wooden table with but one matching chair. There was also that leather armchair that had seen better days, in which Orne had invited me to sit during my first visit. I could tell that tonight he had been sitting in it himself ... but he did so no longer.

This was because Jacob Orne had levitated into the air above the armchair several feet and hung suspended there halfway to the ceiling, his arms and legs splayed outward from his robed body and his eyes bulging at me in a mixture of fury and terror as I made my entrance. Around the clawed feet of the chair rotated a glowing magic circle containing a pentagram, which gave the insubstantial appearance of a hologram. Its violet luminesce also put me in mind of the circle I had formed with glow-in-the-dark paint, so as to set a trap for Abraham Koroma. But this circle was of a different design than that one, and I recognized it for what it was immediately. Though much larger, it was the exact same design I had created on a slab of charred wood using those three golden necklaces I had just handed over to the Moon-Beasts.

"You!" Orne cried in a strained voice, as if being pinned in the air that way also constricted his lungs. "I knew you had to be behind this, Coffin!"

I took several steps deeper into the room, studying that phantasmal magic circle as it turned slowly in clockwise fashion, and couldn't help but smile in satisfaction. "So," I remarked, "my efforts weren't entirely successful, nor were they entirely a failure. You seem to be caught between worlds now, Jake. But how long can that condition last? What do you think? For eternity? Or ... for not much longer?"

"All right, Enoch ... all right, you've proved your point," Orne babbled, taking on a less accusatory and more desperate tone. "You have shown yourself to be the greater warlock, and I admire and bow to your power. Please, deactivate this spell of yours and release me! I promise, I will give you whatever is in my power to grant, in return!"

"Will you? Then, Jake, can you release from their captivity the stolen souls of Maeve Cawley's mother and brother, so as to give them the rest they deserve?"

"Oh, Enoch!" Orne cried. "It's too late for that! Do you think I control the Moon-Beasts? I merely bartered with them! I'm as afraid of them as you are! Those two entities have been taken away gods know where, and possibly even consumed. It's too late for them now! Please, anything else ... *anything!*"

"Then I'm sure you have nothing of interest to offer me, Jake. That was my one and only wish."

"*No!* Come now ... you must be reasonable! As I say, we are two of a kind, you and me! If we put our heads together—our *powers* together— who knows what we might accomplish both here and in the waking world? Why, we might ... "

"Shh," I hushed him. "I have to return to my ritual."

"What? No, Enoch, no—don't you dare!" Orne screeched.

Ignoring his piteous cries, I closed my eyes and bowed my head, resuming the incantations I had chanted earlier this night in my basement, and repeating those sigils I had drawn in the air with my hands. As I did this, Orne continued to scream himself raw, increasingly incoherent, though finally I heard one long, sustained bellow:

"*Coffin!*"

And then, that bellow was abruptly cut short, and I opened my eyes.

No longer did Jacob Orne hover in the air of this sanctuary of his in the Dreamlands. In fact, he was no longer in the room at all, and the glowing magic circle with its enclosed pentagram had also vanished. I was alone there.

"Goodbye, Jake. Wherever you are," I said. I then crossed to his armchair and settled into it myself. By the gas heater's warmth and the glow of its flame—still exhausted by my long, eventful night—I shut my eyes in this world of dream and waited for sleep within sleep.

‡

I awoke in my own bed, with daylight peeking around my curtains, the only difference from when I'd fallen asleep fully dressed upon my bedcovers being that I no longer had three gold necklaces stuffed into a pants pocket.

A few days later, it was Maeve who called to inform me that police in Eastborough had discovered the corpse of her stepfather Jacob Orne. Some kids playing by the frozen edge of the supposedly haunted Lake Pometacomet had discovered him there. According to what the police had told her, Orne's body looked to have been there for weeks, so horribly decomposed it was, like a half-deliquesced mass of putrescene spilling out of its dark brown robe.

XXX

And so, my perhaps future readers, this entry in the personal journal of Enoch Donovon Coffin brings us up to date, as I relate the events of this very evening ... though I do admit that I've skipped ahead several busy months. Tonight was the opening of the first exhibition of my artwork in some few years, hosted by my friend Marie Lavoria, who owns a little art gallery in the North End's Prince Street, and the Italian restaurant next door as well. I am happy to report that opening night seemed quite the success, and was of course attended by Maeve Cawley, though I pretended to be irritated by her appearance ... accusing her of intentionally drawing the gaze of the gallery's visitors away from my framed series of paintings with the power of her own beauty. Though, to be fair, a number of these visitors recognized Maeve right away from one of the paintings hung on the gallery's walls, remarking on how perfectly I had captured the young woman's likeness.

Maeve came to hug me affectionately, after first crying out, "Uncle Enoch!" I often pretend, also, to be irritated by this nickname she has given me. The reality of the situation is that I credit her in large part with helping to end my self-imposed exile from society of the past decade, the profoundness of which had sadly only increased with my consumption of alcohol. I am happy to report that although I have not given up the habit entirely, it has decreased significantly, to that of my pre-exile years.

In moments of weakness, prompted by my fondness for her, I have almost admitted to Maeve that she is like the child I never had ... though I did become sufficiently weak that I permitted her to drive me to a store to purchase a mobile phone, and help me sign up for a monthly plan. "All the better for you to pester me, I suppose?" I groused on that day.

The past few months have been a mad whirl of activity on my part, as if my muse jolted awake from a long coma with the need to express all its pent-up energy. In fact, several of the nine paintings that hang in my exhibition—which is titled *A Gathering of Ghosts*—are not yet properly dry.

Visitors who recognized Maeve from one of the nine portraits that comprise the series also remarked upon her resemblance to a beautiful if moody-looking young man who is the subject of another of the portraits, and Maeve proudly explained that the youth in question was her late brother Aidan Cawley. For this painting, and the one hanging next to it of her mother as she appeared in life, Maeve allowed me to borrow a number of photographs to use for my models.

Two of the nine portraits are older pieces—including one of the gallery owner, which Marie Lavoria has contributed to the showing from her personal art collection—but among those I've produced of late in a frenzy of inspiration are three so grotesque in appearance they should prevent anyone attending this exhibition from accusing Enoch Coffin of having gone soft in his old age.

One of these three portrays a man seated formally in a chair, just as the other eight subjects are positioned, as if he posed for me in his wretched condition, though of course I painted Gavin Ross entirely from memory. In this painting Ross appears as he did the last time I saw him ... with his skeletonized face staring sightlessly at the viewer, and a horde of strange, whitish insect-things feasting upon its last shreds of flesh, some of their tiny bodies tangled in his bushy red beard.

Next to this are two portraits of men who seem to share a similar horrific skin condition, though clearly they are not related, one being a bald-headed Black man with an odd brand on the side of his head as seen in this three-quarter view of him, and the other being a middle-aged White man. The affliction they share has resulted in the faces of both men—and the hands folded primly in their laps—to be covered in open, oozing sores and painful-looking rashes. Their noses have eroded until they are little more than the nasal opening of a skull, their lips seemingly chewed away. Patchy hair has grown up their cheeks almost to their eyes, and the eyes of both men are so bloodshot that the sclera are entirely red, while tears of blood run from their ducts as they contemplate the viewer. Though their faces are not contorted in fear or agony, nonetheless these two subjects seem to convey a suffering that will last unto eternity.

Pretending to hide behind me in horror while gripping my shoulders, my friend Marie Lavoria commented with a shudder that I felt through her hands, "You haven't lost your touch for the macabre, Enoch."

"So who is this one here, Uncle Enoch?" the lovely Maeve asked, hooking her arm through mine and pulling me toward another of the new paintings on display, momentarily freeing me from well wishers with their glasses of wine and plates of cheese. "He's quite the flamboyant one, isn't he?"

"Don't you dare mock my dear departed friend, brat," I scolded her.

"I'm not mocking him! He's quite striking, is all."

"He was indeed," I told her. "A striking individual in all ways. He was a friend of mine, from Seattle, who passed away a few years ago … sorely missed. A poet and writer of wee fantasies of a gorgeous and singular character, that well expressed his own character. He was an inspiration to me."

Maeve nodded at my words as she gazed upon the subject of the portrait in question, which portrays my friend as he wonderfully presented himself to the world in life. His hair is fashioned in a wispy Mohawk, while his face is heavily made up, with a sequin pasted in the center of his forehead like an Indian's bindi—appropriately, a third eye.

"His name, my dear child," I informed Maeve, "was Wilum Hopfrog Pugmire, Esquire."

Publication History

Matter of Truth and Death, Spectral Evidence, Every Exquisite Thing, Impossible Color, Shadow Puppets, and *Fearless Symmetry* first appeared in the collection *Encounters With Enoch Coffin*, Dark Regions Press (2013).

The Brothel in the North End first appeared in the publication *Forbidden Futures*, Oddness (2018).

The Mummified Hand first appeared as the opening chapter of *The Challenge From Beyond*, a publication for the H. P. Lovecraft Film Festival® & Cthulhucon (2019).

The Lunar Gate is original to this collection.

About the Author

JEFFREY THOMAS is the author of the dark science fiction series Punktown, which was introduced with the collection *Punktown* (Ministry of Whimsy Press, 2000) and includes the novels *Monstrocity* (Prime Books, 2003; Bram Stoker Award finalist), *Deadstock* (Solaris Books, 2007; John W. Campbell Award finalist), and *Blue War* (Solaris Books, 2008). His other books include the short story collection *The Unnamed Country* (Word Horde, 2019), the novel *The American* (JournalStone, 2020), and the Hades Trilogy (Weird House Press, 2023). His stories have been reprinted in *The Year's Best Horror Stories XXII* (editor, Karl Edward Wagner), *The Year's Best Fantasy and Horror #14* (editors, Ellen Datlow and Terri Windling), and *Year's Best Weird Fiction #1* (editors, Laird Barron and Michael Kelly). Thomas lives in Massachusetts.

About the Artist

FRANK WALLS is an American artist best known for his dark surrealism, fantasy illustration, and heavy metal musicianship. He spent the 90s screaming into a microphone for bands like Embalmer and Hateworks, and producing art for others like Incantation and Crypt Kicker. In 2004 he graduated from the Cleveland Institute of Art with a BFA in illustration and went on to work in the gaming industry for companies like Fantasy Flight Games and Wizards of the Coast, as well as creating cover art for authors such as Jeffrey Thomas, Jeff Strand, and Shane McKenzie. He now hails from Hawaii where he pursues his passion for painting, teaches art and design, and works as a freelance illustrator.

www.ingramcontent.com/pod-product-compliance
Lightning Source LLC
Chambersburg PA
CBHW022011010726
47494CB00003B/984